G. N. Darland

# The
# Secrets
# They
# Kept

# The
# Secrets
# They
# Kept

G. N. Darland

*For the readers who survived toxic situations and made it to the light at the end of the tunnel*

*For my husband, who reminds me of my worth every single day, and my son, who never fails to make me smile.*

*To my angel baby, who I can't wait to see in Heaven.*

# Content Warning

The Secrets They Kept is a crime romance book that contains Christian themes as well as religious language. While the main character is a devoted Christian, the story includes dark elements that might not be suitable for some readers. Mentions of parental death, mental illness (anxiety and depression), sex trafficking, sexual assault, rape, torture, homelessness, premarital sex, crimes against humanity, chemical weapons, and trauma are present in this novel. Readers who may be sensitive to these elements, please take note.

# Prologue

In the nineteen hundreds, the Central Intelligence Agency coined the term conspiracy theory to discredit those who spoke out about the corruption of the government. There have always been sinister forces that operate in the highest level of government, hidden by the very people who have vowed to protect the people they serve. Evil likes to hide behind the smiles and handshakes that politicians and officials offer, like masks that conceal their true nature and desire to live a life of wickedness and immorality.

People are aware of the lies and deception that the government operates with, but they enjoy living in ignorance. Instead of calling out the wrongdoings and opening their minds to the truths, they hide from it and chalk it up to conspiracy. The few people who do have the courage to share the truth are called crazy and shunned by society. People can't bring themselves to admit that humanity is evil and that those in power will do all they can to remain in power.

He was aware of these truths when he took the job. He was aware that not everyone in the agency was working for the protection and service of society despite being in the CIA. Still, he had not been prepared for the depravity that transpired in this unit. From all he had seen overseas, it never occurred to him that the true horrors of the world lived here, in the so-called land of the free and the brave.

Once the true nature of what this unit was doing was revealed to him, he knew he had to get out. He could no longer work for people who treated human beings as lab rats. His skin crawled, knowing he had aided this agency in committing horrific crimes. He could no longer sit idly by and watch as the CIA subjected the country's citizens to this evil.

He sat at his desk, staring at the computer screen as he watched the file download onto his flash drive. The green bar was moving slowly due to the size of the file. His knee bounced up and down as his gaze darted back and forth from the screen to the door. He was supposed to encrypt the file for the agents, but instead, he decided to steal it. He didn't know what he would do with it, but that was something to figure out later. They would come for him the moment they realized the file was missing.

As he waited, his heart racing with every second that passed, a warning popped up. Quickly, he clicked the notification, eyes going wide at what he read. The warning indicated that his firewall was under attack. Someone was trying to hack in. He read through the coding of his encryptions, scouring for any source of weakness. Somebody wanted to break into the unit's classified files for whatever reason. The thought of people knowing about this unit made his gut clench in fear. Any hacker with the skill to get into the CIA would likely expose the illegal dealings. If that happened, he couldn't be found here.

He stared at the coding and watched with apprehension until it stopped. The ones and zeros stopped fighting whoever was on the other side fighting their way in. Whoever it was, they seemed to have given up.

His mind played out all the scenarios that could transpire if the secrets of the unit were discovered. Everyone involved, including him, would get in serious trouble and most likely spend time in prison. The color drained from his face as he realized that exposure, while meaning sure incarceration for him, might be the best for the victims. If someone had the guts to hack into the CIA to infiltrate this unit, he was in no position to stop them. He just needed to ensure he was nowhere to be found once the leak happened.

He sucked in a breath, his fingers shaking as they hovered over the keyboard. Without any more hesitation, he broke through his own codes. The green downloading line was almost complete when he added a script that left a gaping hole in the cybersecurity firewall. Any skilled hacker could find it and take anything they wanted. It was wishful thinking, but he hoped that whoever was on the other side would take every piece of information and share it with the world. Expose these animals for what they were doing to innocent people.

He ejected the flash drive from the computer and shut down the software. He gathered all his belongings, placed the flash drive in his backpack, and fled. He didn't know what he would do with the information he had just stolen, but he knew it was better in his hands than anyone else's.

***

Agent Jannis, the head of a secret CIA research unit, noticed the breach almost immediately. He was watching the files disappear and reappear right before his eyes. Each time a document was returned to his files, they came back unredacted and incomplete. His heart rate began to rise, and sweat beaded on his brow, his perspiration worsening with each file. He knew of only one person who could hack into the CIA and break through all the encryptions.

A breach of security in the CIA was next to impossible. At least, that's what the CIA wanted people to believe. All the agency's information was stored on systems that were kept separate from public servers, allowing access to only those with proper credentials. Even if someone were to get into the database, they wouldn't be able to take anything since all the documents are encrypted. The information meant to be highly classified is protected by several levels of security and personnel verifications. It is nearly impossible and doubtful that even the best hackers could see classified documents and information.

The CIA had the reputation of being the agency that held all the country's secrets. The government agency that covered up aliens and hid the cure for cancer. Of course, those are all conspiracy theories, and no evidence has proven those accusations. But with this, Agent Jannis couldn't fathom the ramifications that would come back to bite him if these files were released to the public.

One thing Jannis appreciated about being in the CIA was the level of privacy the agents received. For agents, everything is a secret, and they are granted certain levels of protection that the rest of the country could only wish to have. This made Agent Jannis confident he could conduct his research without fear of being discovered.

Despite knowing what the rest of the world would think about his research, he believed it was for the greater good. The experiments were less than desirable but necessary. Other countries are constantly researching weapons that could be most effective for attacking their enemies. It would only be fair for the United States to be equally prepared. The variety of ethnicities that reside in the United States has made this research easier. Regardless of the nature of these experiments, which would be seen as inhumane, they would make the military more capable of taking out the nation's enemies.

Simply put, the research was necessary. Jannis was working on these experiments secretly; the agency was only aware that he was given his own research team to oversee its operations. Everything that happened within the unit, everyone was ignorant to. This breach of security was not good. If the contents of his experiments were exposed, his superiors in the CIA would end the research and send Jannis to prison.

Agent Jannis adjusted his tie, his face contorting into a grimace, as he called in his colleague, Agent Bennet. Jannis needed Bennet to aid him in circulating the location of the breach. He knew that the good-for-nothing cyber security agent was to blame. He was the only one besides Bennet and Jannis who had access to all the files. Still, the breach seemed to be from an outside source. That could mean one of two things. First, the cyber security agent didn't set up any security measures, leaving all the information open for the world to find. The second explanation was more likely because encryptions and security firewalls were in place regardless of the agent's actions. This meant that any security systems in place were so weak, that anyone in the outside world could easily hack them.

Agent Jannis was the leading researcher in these experiments, but the data was Agent Bennet's responsibility. Bennet knew there would be hell to pay if he couldn't find the location of the breach. Once it was found, they would find the perpetrator.

Jannis stood beside Bennet, his arms crossed, as he worked to pinpoint the hacker's IP address. The computer screen lit up with green circles that surrounded the area where the perpetrator was located. Jannis leaned in to get a better look. His lips pulled up into a sinister smile before heading out of the room. Bennet followed quickly behind him, going to the locker rooms to pack their bags. They gathered all their equipment and prepared for travel. They would find the person who thought it was okay to hack into an intelligence database and take encrypted files. They were on the first flight out to Portland, Oregon.

# Chapter 1

The gunshots rang in Natalie's ears. Her hands ached from the recoil of the gun with every round fired off. The smell of gunpowder filled her senses, acting as a center to her emotions that were on the constant verge of overtaking her.

Natalie had arrived at the shooting range in the early morning hours when the Pacific Northwest air was still crisp and had a lingering smell of freshly cut grass. The weather in the morning had been perfect. Not too cold, not too hot. Now that she had been there for a few hours, the heat was rising, and she was getting uncomfortable as the sweat on her body caused her clothes to cling to her. The heat of the late summer sun caused sweat to bead on her brow, a slight breeze her only relief.

Deciding it was time to end her shooting practice, Natalie pulled her trigger over and over, emptying her cartridge in a rapid fire. Each bullet landed in the same spot, burring a hole in the dummy that sat 25 yards away.

The feel of the gun in her hands and the way he entire body vibrated as she pulled the trigger never failed to ease Natalie of the anxiety that had crippled her for the past six years.

That's how long it's been since she lost her dad, her best friend.

Natalie made sure the chamber of the gun was empty before disassembling it. She stored the pistol in accordance with state law, activating the safety and securing the trigger lock. She placed the gun in its case and started towards the exit of the range.

"It was good to see you, Natalie," said Zeke. His greying mustache touched his cheeks with the wide smile he aimed toward Natalie.

"You too, Zeke," replied Natalie, pushing the gun across the counter to Zeke.

He takes the case and and sets it with the rest of the firearms before returning to the counter across from Natalie.

"Haven't seen you around in a while. How's Nancy doing these days?" He stood behind the counter, folding his arms and leaning down to be at eye level with Natalie.

"You know I've been away at school, Zeke," Natalie said, shaking her head. "And my mom is doing good. She's a lot better recently."

It was no secret that Nancy let her grief consume her after her husband died, falling into a depression that made her almost neglectful toward her daughter. Natalie had to learn to take care of herself at the age of sixteen, contributing to the development of her own mental illness.

"Yeah, I know," Zeke continued. "Ben's little girl is off

at Boston College making a name for herself."

She majored in criminal justice and technological forensics. Her goal was to work as a specialized expert to find missing persons in a human trafficking division. Specifically, she wanted to work with Homeland Security. She had exceptional skills in computer hacking and cyber security. It was a skill she had been developing since high school as a coping mechanism after her father died. She hoped to use her abilities to track down human traffickers and liberate the innocent people sold into this modern day slavery. Once she finished her studies, she would get to work.

Zeke's eyes turned sad as he looked at Natalie. "You look just like him, you know?"

Natalie tried to fight the lump that was swelling in her throat. "You were his best freind, Zeke."

"Anyone with eyes could see you were his best friend. I remember when he used to bring you in here and teach you how to shoot. You were the cutest little thing. I've never seen him happier than when he was with you and Nancy. I still can't believe-" his voice broke.

Six years since he's been gone, and it still affects everyone who knew him. Natalie's dad was a Marine Corps sergeant. He was a sharpshooter, top of his class in basic training. He was in the middle of his fourth tour to Afghanistan when enemy combatants killed him during a shootout. He and his team were on a mission to extract refugees from an active war zone. The Taliban was rounding up Christians and murdering them, setting an example for anyone who thought to practice the religion. When Ben's unit went in to extract a group of Christians who had been gathered up like cattle, they were ambushed. His location was compromised, and he was killed. No one in the unit survived.

Natalie and Ben's relationship was strained during his overseas tours. Their close relationship made it nearly impossible to endure his time away. The idea of never seeing her dad again was always possible, but it never seemed like something that could actually come to pass. Once the unimaginable happened, Natalie's heart shattered into a hundred pieces. Then, her anxiety developed and it took over every aspect of her life.

Natalie didn't go outside or shoot a gun for a long time. Her best friend was gone, and she was left alone to pick up the pieces. Her mom was suffering, too, so Natalie didn't have anyone to lean on most of the time.

She still had occasional anxiety attacks, but she had gotten better at managing them. She had refused therapy for a while, not going until her boyfriend Carter convinced her to go. After they started dating, everything in her life improved. He was the voice of reason in her therapy decisions, convincing her it was the best way to overcome her anxiety. Needless to say, he was right. Therapy taught her different coping mechanisms, and she learned that going to a shooting range helped ease her anxiety a lot.

At times, Natalie felt guilty for not leaning into her faith for healing. She knew she relied too much on Carter to get through the hard times, but it worked for her. She was doing better now.

Natalie placed her hand on Zeke's hand, the softness of his skin revealing his age. They met each other's gaze and shared somber smiles.

"I have to go, but I promise to try and visit more often," Natalie said.

Zeke nodded his head before pulling his hand away.

"Take care, young Natalie."

Natalie left the shooting range and returned to her old pickup truck. As she walked, her stomach clenched. She looked around her, looking for the source of her paranoia. No one was around, but she got the distinct feeling that she was being watched. Quickly, she arrived at the truck and pulled out her keys. Her head snapped around, eyes making sure she was still alone before she was able to unlock her car and get in.

As soon as she shut her door closed, she locked herself in. Her hands gripped the steering wheel, and her head fell forward. She took deep breaths, attempting to steady her heart rate before turning on her car.

The radio screamed at her. A podcast was playing at full volume as it gave gruesome detail about how a young woman was kidnapped, raped, and murdered in the Green River area of Washington state.

Natalie quickly turned down the volume, laughing at herself. There was always a possibility of being kidnapped and murdered by a serial killer. It felt like those possibilities increased after listening to conspiracy theories and true crime podcasts. Natalie didn't know why she felt the need to scare herself before any outing she went on, but she couldn't help herself.

Natalie reached into her back pocket and typed out a quick text to her mom, letting her know she was on her way home. As quickly as she hit send, her phone rang. Her mom's name flashed across the screen as the phone vibrated in Natalie's hand.

"Hey, Mom," Natalie said, answering the call. "I just got to the car. I was shooting at Zeke's. I'm driving home as we speak."

"Where are you? You need to come home now," Nancy

said, clearly ignoring any word Natlaie said.

Her voice was high-pitched and shaky. The hairs on Natalie's arms rose at the tone of her mom's voice.

"Woah," Natalie replied, "Calm down. I am on my way. I just lost track of time. Didn't you get my text?"

Ignoring her daughter, Nancy continued, "You need to get home as soon as possible. It's an emergency."

Natalie's mind was beginning to spiral. Her mom was the calm and collected person in the family. Whenever Nancy spoke, her voice was soft and pleasant. She never allowed herself to panic, not after coming out of her depression from losing Ben.

Every possible negative scenario began to play like an old movie in Natalie's head, knowing something was wrong.

Natalie replied, her voice concerned, "Mom, what's wrong? Is everything okay? Do I need to call the police?"

"No," said Nancy, her voice rising in pitch. "Don't call the police. They're already here."

Natalie's eyebrows furrowed as her eyes scanned her surroundings, hoping to see an explanation walk out of the trees. She scratched her head before resting it on the steering wheel of her car. She tried her best to piece together all the details of her situation. There was a threat that prompted her mother to call the police. They arrived and neutralized the threat. Nancy wanted Natalie home to ensure her safety after whatever had happened.

Thinking of the possibilities only made her panic worse.

Remembering her mom was on the phone, Natalie cleared her throat and responded. "Mom, I'll be home soon. Make sure the police stay there with you to keep you safe until I get there."

"Natalie…" said Nancy, her voice steady and soft, "there is no threat. They are here for you."

Natalie went silent, shaking her head in disbelief. That was the last thing she expected her mother to say.

Her voice was low and trembling as she asked, "What?"

Finding that calm voice that Natalie was so accustomed to, her mom said, "I know, hun. Drive safe, but hurry home. We'll sort this out once you get here. I love you."

"I- I love you too, mom." Natalie hung up the phone, her mouth agape as she set it down on the seat beside her. Her hands found the steering wheel and the gear shift as she started the drive home, her body feeling numb from the unexpected conversation.

# Chapter 2

As Natalie drove, she tapped her thumb on the steering wheel. As far as she knew, her mom was safe. The police were at the house to speak with her for a reason she could only guess. Natalie thought it could have something to do with her studies, but that didn't make much sense since she was still on break. The only police officers she had been in contact with were in Boston. Even then, she never interacted with police officers for anything other than educational purposes.

Everything about this situation was strange. No matter how hard she tried, Natalie couldn't begin to imagine what she could have done to prompt the police to show up asking for her. She played scenarios in her mind like one of those old film kinetoscopes. Nothing she could conjure up in her brain explained why the police wanted to speak with her.

Natalie rushed home, brows furrowing as her truck approached her mom's house. The driveway, where she typically parked, was occupied by vehicles she had never seen before. She parked her car on the curb in front of the house, searching up and down for police cruisers. The vehicles that Natalie noticed in her parking spot were black, unmarked SUVs. She knew some departments authorized unmarked cars for patrol officers, so she figured that was the explanation for the lack of lights and sirens.

Natalie fumbled to find the house key as she approached the door and motioned to unlock it. Sweat began to bead on her forehead, and her hands shook as she entered the house. Her eyes widened, and her footsteps halted when she saw who was waiting for her in the kitchen of her mom's house.

Standing in the room was her mom, eyes wide with noticeably wet cheeks, fiddling with her fingers as she looked between Natalie and the officers. To her left, she was shocked to see Carter also standing there. Standing on the other side of the counter were two men wearing dark suits.

Natalie looked at the officers, her body wanting to recoil at how their eyes scanned her. The taller agent didn't hide that he was looking up and down Natalie's body. Doing her best to ignore their stares, she analyzed the strangers. She took in their outfits and brought back the memory of the vehicles parked outside of the house. The realization struck Natalie almost instantly. These men were not police officers. They were Federal agents.

"What's going on here," Natalie asked, her voice sounding immediately defensive. Carter was the first to move as he approached her and hugged her tightly. Looking past him to stare daggers at the agents, Natalie only accepted his hug momentarily before brushing him off.

"Nat, these officers are here to talk to you. They say it has something to do with research?" Carter said, unfazed by the coldness in her movements. There was an unasked question hidden in his words. What research could possibly be so important that they would show up unannounced?

"First of all," Natalie started, her eyes never leaving the agents, "these are not police officers. They're federal agents." She looked at them, eyes narrowed with cool disdain.

Carter stepped back, his face scrunching in confusion. Nancy placed her hand on her chest and blinked in shock at what Natalie had just revealed. They had no idea, which meant the agents never even identified themselves.

One of the agents, the taller one, stepped forward, "That's not exactly correct," he said. "My name is Agent Jannis. My colleague here is Agent Bennet. We are agents with the Central Intelligence Agency and would like to speak with you, Miss Walsh, about something you have been researching."

As he spoke, Natalie took in their appearances. Agent Jannis was tall. His hair was grey, signifying his age, and he wore it in a buzzcut. He looked to be former military. He had grey-blue eyes that looked devoid of any emotion. Agent Bennet was shorter. He, too, had short hair, but his eyes were a deep brown. They let no secret slip, keeping them narrowed as he stood there and assessed each spoken word.

Natalie finished taking in their appearances before she responded, her voice filled with annoyance and frustration.

"Okay then, Agent Jannis. I'll fully cooperate after you

tell me why you failed to identify yourself when my mom welcomed you into our home."

Silence. The agents just stood there, Jannis' face calm with his mouth tilted up in a subtle smirk. They knew what they did, and they didn't care.

"Fine. If you won't tell me that, then tell me what research you are referring to. I have no recollection of researching anything illegal. All my research is to aid me in Criminal Justice and Forensics, so I don't understand why you're here," she said confidently.

Agent Bennet finally spoke with a hint of arrogance, saying, "We are here regarding the research you are doing on classified government procedures. Research that could make our agency look," he paused, "less than desirable. For this reason, we ask that you turn over your work and stop your research immediately."

Natalie's brows furrowed as her head tilted in confusion. She searched her mind for what felt like hours before it finally hit her. Natalie *had* been looking into the government. However, she wouldn't call it research. It was more of a conspiracy theory that Carter had told her about a few weeks ago.

Ever since the beginning of their relationship, the public park became their safe haven. Carter knew that it helped with her anxiety to be outside, so he prioritized it whenever they hung out. They started dating in high school, and the park was where they could spend time without the annoyance of parents intruding on them. It was also the only place their parents allowed them to be alone since it was in public. Natalie didn't mind the restrictions. Looking back, she saw that she was only a child. She was grateful for the rules her mom placed around her. It showed her that Nancy was still looking out for her, even in her grief.

They were hanging out at a park near her house, enjoying the summer weather and lying on a blanket spread out on the grass. They were having a nice picnic when Carter divulged to her the latest conspiracy theory he had come across. He wasn't too big on conspiracy theories, but he knew Natalie was deeply fascinated with them and always went out of his way to learn about her interests.

Carter was telling her about this theory that the government was illegally manufacturing chemical weapons and testing them on kidnapped homeless people.

"It's insane what people are saying about this. According to the theory, there have been a lot of reported missing homeless people lately, but the police aren't doing anything. I mean, who cares about the homeless, right? That's what makes them perfect for illegal government testing! No one will miss them."

Natalie always found far-fetched conspiracy theories entertaining. They creeped her out while driving her curiosity. After she went home, she took out her laptop, grabbed some snacks, and went down the rabbit hole. She found many redacted files and encrypted documents that she downloaded and saved to her computer. She even had a special conspiracy theory folder on her desktop where she stored all her random theories. They ranged from stories about Big Foot to QAnon. With each conspiracy, she went in-depth and fixated on it for a few days until she got tired of the absurdities.

Agent Jannis cleared his throat, bringing Natalie out of her spiraling thoughts. Natalie looked at the agents, her face contorted in confusion. How had they known? She wasn't doing this research in hopes of bringing down the government, but she still hacked into the CIA. Her research had no malicious intent, only pure interest and curiosity. She had no idea that the government would notice since her entering their servers was pure coincidence. Besides, it was all just a conspiracy theory anyway, right?

"My research is not being shared with anyone." Natalie finally said, her voice low. "It's just something stupid that I was looking into out of boredom."

"Wait," interrupted Carter, "Does this have something to do with that conspiracy theory I was telling you about?" He asked, facing toward Natalie before quickly looking back toward the agents. "That's the whole reason you guys are here? Come on, that's a total joke."

"Classified government files are not a joke." Agent Bennet snapped. "The fact is that you illegally hacked into the CIA database and stole encrypted files. This is a severe crime, and we are not asking but telling you to hand over your computer." Bennet's eyes were filled with rage as he waited for Natalie to respond.

Carter and Nancy looked wide-eyed toward Natalie, but she ignored them.

"No," said Natalie. "I will not be doing that. It's my personal property, and I don't have to give it-"

"Get out of my house!" Nancy shouted, interrupting Natalie.

Natalie jumped at her mom's voice, knowing she was never someone to raise her voice like this. Frozen with fear only moments ago, Nancy was now white with rage.

"You can't just come into my house and demand we give you our personal property," Nancy continued, stepping toward the agents with every word. "If you want my daughter's laptop, get a warrant."

At this, both agents looked at each other and nodded in disappointment at the family. "Mrs. Walsh, rest assured we will have a warrant by the end of the day, and we will be taking more than just the laptop," said Agent Bennet menacingly. "You've just made this harder for yourselves." Agent Jannis followed Bennet out the door and shut it behind them.

Natalie turned to her mom to congratulate her on kicking the agents out. Instead, her mom turned to her with the same anger she had aimed at the men.

"Tell me exactly what you are researching about the government now!"

# Chapter 3

Natalie spent the next hour and a half explaining everything to her mother and Carter. She told them what she found, how she found it, and why the CIA was showing up at their doorstep demanding she turn over her laptop. She summarized the conspiracy theory for her mom; Carter already knew about it. Natalie knew what she did was wrong. She knew she had crossed a line by hacking into the CIA. It was illegal, even if it was all in good fun and curiosity. Still, she had been naive to believe she wouldn't get caught. She still thought that it was an innocent conspiracy theory. Despite it all, she came clean.

Natalie had found herself hacking through websites and servers, hoping to find as much information as possible. She found Reddit posts that highlighted speculative details about the experiments. One of the websites led her to find a black site located in Northern California with tons of cybersecurity encryptions. She looked over the location of Google Earth and saw how guarded it was. It was in the middle of the forest and surrounded by mile-long fencing. Natalie tried hard to hack in, but she was unsuccessful.

It wasn't until she came across the CIA firewall while investigating the server coding that she realized this black site might hold the secrets she sought. It also made her feel like she had taken this theory too far. Still, curiosity was eating away at her, and she needed to find more documents.

Natalie knew there would be no way of hacking into the CIA, but she still attempted to strike the firewall. She tested her codes against it, knowing full well that none of them would break through. She froze, her eyes widening and her blood running cold. Her hacking scripts entered past the firewall and led her into the servers. Natalie didn't know where the backdoor came from, but she knew she couldn't pass up the chance to find more information. She took the leap, went through the back door, and found everything.

Natalie discovered thousands of files and documents highlighting the chemical testing, but with each file heavily redacted, she only told her so much about what was happening. Natalie tried countless times to hack the documents and files but only managed to open up a few that could be used as pretty damning evidence against the government if they were true. But of course, they weren't true. At least, not entirely.

One common thing among all conspiracy theories was that they all contained small truths that theorists took and spun to make something worth wasting your time looking into. Natalie always reminded herself that nothing was ever as it seemed. There was one specific file that she couldn't get into at all. She didn't bother too much with it since she was already breaking too many laws as it was. Deciding to end her sleuthing, she backed out of the database and forgot what she had done.

Once Natalie finished speaking, Nancy burst into tears. The fear that her daughter could end up in prison was overwhelming. Nancy had gone through so much after losing her husband. She became a shell when her other half was killed. She became an absent parent in her grief. After battling through the depression to be a good mom to Natalie, she did all she could to make up that lost time. The thought of losing the only person she had left was unbearable. Natalie stepped forward and wrapped her mom in a hug.

Taking a deep breath to calm her voice, she said, "Please, Nat, just give them the laptop." Her voice was tight. "Give it up and stop with your research. It isn't worth it to derail your whole life." She looked at Natalie with pleading eyes.

Natalie was so close to finishing her undergrad. Getting in trouble with the CIA would undoubtedly prevent all her plans from ever coming to fruition. Still, something was tugging at her to continue down this path of destruction. She unknowingly uncovered government secrets that highlighted crimes against United States citizens. She wouldn't have known this was anything more than a conspiracy theory had the CIA not come to her home to threaten her. Now, she felt she had no choice but to continue her research. She knew where the black site was and how to enter the database.

Natalie knew what she had to do but couldn't bring herself to admit it. She couldn't admit to herself that to help the innocent people in these experiments, she needed to throw away everything she had ever planned for herself. If what she found was true, she had to keep going. She had to uncover the secrets they kept.

Natalie took a step back from her mother and spoke. "Mom, I'm sorry, but I can't do that," she said, her voice soft but firm. "I can't just give everything up. They came into my home and threatened me. They threatened you! I didn't even know that these experiments were real. I would have never known had they not come here. I don't think I have a choice but to uncover the truth about the experiments. I can't let it go on, knowing I can expose them."

Before Nancy could respond, Carter grabbed Natalie's arm and pulled her toward her bedroom. Once there, he shut the door and locked it.

Quickly, he turned to Natalie and said, "You're insane if you think you're going to keep this up." His voice was low and shaky. "Exposing an illegal government operation isn't something they will take lightly. They will come for you and everyone you care about. Will you be able to live with yourself if it comes to that?"

Carter stared deep into her hazel eyes and saw Natalie was on the verge of tears. He noted the mixture of colors in her eyes before pulling her into a tight hug. He knew that she was spiraling and coming up with millions of scenarios in her head. He was the calm in her storm. He knew how to get her to see reason.

Natalie melted into his arms, silent tears trailing along her cheeks. Carter's arms were a place of comfort and strength. She breathed in, smelling the familiarity of him. He smelled of mahogany and fresh rain. His embrace always brought a calmness to her that was unlike anything else she had ever experienced. It was like his touch was a drug that clouded her brain and allowed her only to feel surges of dopamine throughout her system.

Natalie felt a growing sense of desire building, wanting to bring herself nearer to Carter. Slowly, she moved her head up where she knew her lips would find Carter's. His lips were soft and felt like home. In that second, time stopped, and there was only her and Carter. Her eyes were closed as she let her mind get lost in that kiss. Her body buzzed with longing, and she allowed herself to sink deeper into Carter's arms.

It was then that Carter began to pull away. As their lips parted, everything came crashing back in. Natalie wanted nothing more than to stay in his arms if it meant she never had to think of anything negative again.

The two of them stood there for what seemed like an eternity. Natalie looked deep into his blue eyes, her heart shattered by what she was about to tell him.

Her voice cracked as she whispered, "I need to run."

"W-what?" Carter stammered. "What do you mean? What are you talking about?" He stepped back, putting her at an arm's distance away.

Nothing could have prepared him for those words. It was like she was throwing everything away. Him, her mom, and everything she had worked for up until now was like ash in the wind. Carter's face turned white with anger, her body tensing as he started at Natalie with wide eyes. He couldn't let her throw her entire life away.

"They're not going to stop," Natalie explained. "They're going to keep coming back until they have everything."

"They'll stop if you stop your research."

"How can you even say that to me?" Natalie asked, her voice becoming taut. "You really think I would give up on this? They are hurting innocent people, Carter. I can't drop it."

Carter was shaking his head. There was no way Natalie was actually considering this.

"You can't leave," Carter said, reaching out to grip her arm. "This isn't some crime movie where you go on the run and take down the bad guy. You have a life to get back to. One with your mom. One with me." Carter's voice was raised, straining with the volume at which he spoke.

"I won't let you walk out on me because you think you're smart enough to do this," he continued, leaning into her face as he spoke, his hold on her arm growing tighter. "It's insane, Nat. Think about your future. How do you expect to work for the government when you spend the last summer working to take them down before you graduate? You'll ruin our future together. I'm sorry, but I will not let you throw away everything we have worked for. And what about your mom? You're just going to leave her?"

Carter knew he would strike a chord as he released his hold on Natalie and eyed her, waiting for a response. He knew how Nancy handled heartbreak and how vital her mom's emotional stability was to Natalie. He used her weakness to convince her to drop this fantasy and stay.

After Natalie's dad died, Nancy was broken. She didn't eat or talk for weeks. Natalie was worried for her mom day and night. It added fuel to her anxiety seeing her mom like that. She would find her mom in bed when she came home from school. Natalie would climb into bed with her mom and lay there with her. They would hold each other and cry.

After a few months, Natalie came home and found her

mom eating cereal in the living room. Natalie was relieved as she went and sat down next to her mom. The TV was off, so they just sat there sharing the bowl of cereal. Once it was empty, Nancy got up and started doing the dishes. Natalie continued helping her mom around the house; from then on, they cared for each other. Natalie protected her mom from the dark thoughts that threatened to invade. She never let her mom feel alone. Natalie never wanted to see her mom broken like that again.

Carter broke through the thoughts spiraling in Natalie's mind. "Nat, I love you so much, and I just need you to be safe," he said, his voice tender. "Don't let yourself throw your life away for some strangers you didn't even know existed an hour ago. You're needed here. Don't abandon your mom. Don't abandon me." Carter looked at her, his eye communicating the heartbreak he felt. He couldn't let her leave. She was his purpose in life. Everything he did was for her and, by extension, her mom. If she left, he would be lost.

"I love you so much, Carter," Natalie said, stepping closer to him. She stared into his eyes, his words filling her thoughts. "I hear what you're saying, and you're right. I *didn't* know the innocent people being subjected to those experiments actually existed. But that doesn't mean I shouldn't help them."

Carter's brows furrowed, but Natalie continued. "I have to keep digging. I have to do all I can to save these people. You don't have to agree, but you can't keep me here." Her words were final.

Carter stared back at her, his head shaking in disbelief. He had never heard her speak with such conviction. He knew he couldn't convince her otherwise, no matter what he threw at her. He knew that if she was going on the run, she needed to start packing. As much as he would have rather she stayed, he gave in.

Carter inhaled deeply and said, "I love you too, Nat. More than anything. Let's pack a couple of bags to take with us." He turned away towards her closet to find bags.

Natalie froze, her eyebrows furrowing as she stared at Carter."What?" Natalie said sharply.

Carter looked back at her, confused. "What do you mean *what*?"

"You're coming with me?"

"Of course, Nat! You think I'm going to let you go alone? Are you insane?"

Natalie stepped back in disbelief. She shook her head and said, "You are not coming, Carter! I need you here with my mom. I need you here to make sure she's okay. I can take care of myself."

Carter's anger was returning, his face reddening with every word. He responded, his voice like gravel, "I am not letting my girlfriend go off on her own. What kind of a man do you think I am? You must really be crazy if you think you can handle yourself out there."

Natalie flinched at his words. "Carter, I love you," she started, her tone flat. "I want you by my side more than anything. But you can't come with me. I'm the one in trouble with the law, not you. I need you to take care of my mom. Keep her company, and don't let her fall into another depression."

This time, Natalie struck a cord. When he first walked into that relationship, he had promised that Natalie would never have to worry about her mom anymore. He always promised to shoulder any burden she asked. He would take care of everything so she would no longer have to be strong. If that meant staying and letting her go, he had to do it.

"Okay, Nat," Carter said reluctantly. "You win. But remember to send updates and let us know that you're safe. I can't survive without knowing if you're okay." Carter said with a softly

Natalie's heart shattered all over again. "Carter," she said, her voice breaking with each word, "I can't tell you where I'm going or where I'll be. If the CIA even thinks you might know where I am, they could use you to find me. This has to be our goodbye."

Carter was silent, color daring from his face. He didn't respond. He wanted to shake her. He hated this new reality and would do anything to change it. Natalie was leaving, and it wasn't possible to predict when she would be back, if at all.

The silence was growing more and more deafening as they just stared at each other, each holding a piece of clothing waiting to be placed in her bag. Just then, Nancy entered the room. As she entered, she scanned their faces with a look of sadness, confusion slowly starting to blend on her face. She was not aware of the decisions that had just been made. Her look quickly changed to one of comfort as she noticed the worried look on both Carter's and Natalie's faces. She approached them and pulled them into a tight embrace, not paying attention to the clothes in their hands or the bag that lay open on Natalie's bed.

They all stood there hugging each other, wishing this feeling would never cease, but Natalie knew it was only a matter of time before she had to leave. So, she pulled out of the hug before more tears could form and looked at her mom.

"Mom," Natalie started slowly, "I have to go." Natalie's voice was steady despite the tears streaming down her face.

The look of confusion returned to Nancy's face. "What do you mean you have to go?" Her voice was growing concerned. "You aren't going anywhere. What are you talking about?"

"We just decided," said Natalie, "I need to run so they can't find me. I'm going to continue to uncover their secrets. No one can know where I am or where I plan to go. It's the only way to keep you safe."

Nancy was having none of it. "No! You can't just leave! I am your mother. I make the decisions around here, and I decide you are staying here where I can take care of you." Her voice broke.

With every word, Nancy knew she would lose this battle. She knew the stubbornness of her daughter. She replied, her voice breaking, "Natalie, please. Don't do this. Don't throw your life away. Look at everything you have worked for. Just give them your laptop and forget this ever happened. Please." Looking at Natalie's face, Nancy could see her daughter's mind was made up, and nothing she would say would impact her enough to stay.

Natalie held her head high despite the shattering of her heart, "Mom, you know I can't do that. This is too important. Crimes like this are what I have been working to fight against. It might not be in the same realm, but it is still a crime against innocence. It is taking advantage of those who cannot defend themselves. I need to find out all I can and publish these files so the world knows what is happening. I can't do that here, Mom. I need to go."

Nancy stared at her daughter with a deep sense of admiration. It was as though she saw Natalie's eyes for the first time. She inherited her eyes from her father, who shared the same passion when there was something before them that they cared about. Her face only showed her heartache, but on the inside, Nancy could not have been more proud of her daughter. At last, Nancy closed her eyes and nodded in understanding. She then turned and exited the room without another word, her cheeks shiny from the tears that had stopped.

Natalie knew she was responsible for those tears. She was breaking apart her family by choosing to leave. It tore her to pieces to see that she had done this. She made her mom cry and reintroduced the heartache she had worked so hard to put back together.

Carter stepped forward and gently said, "Hey, look at me, baby." He took Natalie's face in his hands and brought her face up so she was looking at him. "I love you, do you hear me? I need you to stay strong. Stay strong, not just for me and your mom, but for yourself. I need you to get this done so you can come home to me."

He pulled her into another hug, but not before Natalie saw a single tear sliding down his cheek. It wasn't something that happened often, him crying. Her guilt was made worse by knowing she had been the cause of pain for not only her mom, but Carter too. He was the one who was supposed to be strong, but she had ruined him.

She welcomed his hug and tightened her arms around him. As they held each other, Natalie couldn't think of a moment where their love for each other was more apparent. The hug ended with Natalie pulling away to look into his eyes. She took in his face and studied every detail like it was the first and last time she would ever see him.

She took her finger and wiped away his tears. Natalie

gave him a quick kiss before speaking. "Please look after my mom." Carter looked as though he was going to interrupt, but Natalie continued. "I know I already told you, but this is important. I can't imagine how hard this will be for her. Knowing that you were here would give me peace of mind. It kills me to leave her alone."

Carter nodded before replying, "Don't worry, babe. I'll protect her." He gave a broken smile before returning to packing.

As he packed her bags, she watched as her life changed before her eyes. As Carter filled her bags, Natalie relived everything they had been through together. They started dating in high school. Carter knew about all the emotional trauma Natalie had gone through. He was there to help her heal from her anxiety and move past her triggers. Carter was also there when she got accepted into college. It was exciting because he got his athletic scholarship to that same school. It wasn't planned that they go to the same university, but that just made it seem like God's plan.

He was there for every up, and down that Natalie experienced. He was her first kiss, her first boyfriend, her first everything. They still haven't had sex, deciding it would be more meaningful to wait until marriage. The decision came with a lot of protest from Carter, but he eventually agreed. Since they planned to get married, they both knew it would happen. Now, she wasn't so sure because she was walking away from this person with whom she had gone through so much life.

Mustering up the little strength she had left, she began to help Carter pack her bags. They packed silently and shared the occasional glance, which Natalie was glad for. She knew she wouldn't be able to contain her feelings if they spoke, and there was no more time for that. She had to get out of there quickly before the agents returned.

# Chapter 4

Natalie packed light, only taking essential items like a flashlight, cash, a toothbrush, and some nonperishables Carter found in the pantry. For clothing, Natalie just packed clothes she would feel comfortable traveling in. She wouldn't need fancy outfits and didn't bother packing extra shoes. She would only have the ones she left with. Once everything was packed, they walked to the living room, and Carter set her duffel bag on the couch. They continued towards the kitchen, where Nancy was waiting for them.

They shared a glance, Natalie and Carter holding each other's hands before Natalie spoke. "I'm all packed, momma. I grabbed everything I feel like I'll need, including some money I saved up in case I need to stop somewhere."

Natalie dropped Carter's hand and stepped toward where her mom was sitting. Nancy stood up from her seat and made her way towards Natalie. Her eyes were red-rimmed and puffy, and her hands trembled as they held something. It was a small wooden box that Natalie recognized instantly. Natalie's eyes widened as she put her hands up in protest.

"No, mom," she said firmly. "You can't give me that! I won't take it."

Nancy ignored the words coming out of Natalie's mouth and placed the box in her hand. Natalie gripped the box as her mom held her shoulders. Both Natalie and her mother were crying as Natalie finally accepted the gift and clutched it in her arms.

Confused at the sentiment, Carter asked, "What is that?"

Natalie tried her best to get the words out without crying, failing as her voice cracked. "It's my dad's. He was saving money for my mom in case something happened. He saved twenty thousand dollars, and it was all for my mom." As Natalie spoke, she looked at her mom, searching her eyes for an explanation.

Nancy never looked away from her daughter as she said, "Natalie, you will take this box and the money in it. It was never for me."

Nancy released Natalie's shoulders and stepped back to get a better look at her daughter before continuing. "Your dad saved this for you. I never felt it was the right time to give it to you. I understand now that I was waiting for this moment. I also put one of your dad's pistols in here. You're going to need it to defend yourself."

Natalie lowered her head, trying to conceal the tears streaming down her face. With a heavy heart, Natalie carried the money box to her duffle bag, and Carter and her mom followed close behind. She packed it in her bag safely, wiping away the tears with her sleeve. She turned to face her mom and boyfriend again, holding her head high in courage.

"I want you to use that for emergencies only," Nancy continued. "Please don't touch it until all your other expenses are gone. I don't know what road lies ahead of you, but I want you to have all the help your father and I can provide you."

Natalie ran into her mother's arms and hugged her tight. "I'm so sorry I did this, Mom. I promise I'll make it up to you when I return." Her mom pulled away from the hug and gave her a saddened smile.

Softly, Nancy said, "Honey, this wasn't a mistake. You uncovered this for a reason. You were meant to do this. Use this information to uncover the whole operation and expose those assholes."

Natalie laughed. Her mom never said bad words, so this was very comical despite the situation.

Nancy pulled her daughter in for a last embrace before letting her and Carter say their final goodbyes. Nancy gave the two of them a somber smile before leaving the room.

Carter wasted no time in pulling her body toward him. He wrapped his arms around her, trying to memorize how she felt when their breathing was in sync. Without allowing a second for any word to be spoken, he reached out his hand, lifting her chin. She looked up, her eyes glossy. Carter brushed his thumb across her cheek before planting a soft kiss on her forehead. Natalie looked up and pulled Carter down for a kiss. It was nice and sweet and everything she hoped to remember after she left. His lips were soft and comforting. It sent a spark through her body that made her crave more.

Their soft, passionate kiss slowly escalated as Carter

pulled her in tighter, and Natalie's hands cupped the back of his neck. They shared a kiss filled with passion and heartbreak. Their lips crashed against each other with raw emotion emanating from both of them.

When Carter's tongue begged entrance, Natalie's lips parted, and he slipped his tongue in her mouth. Their tongues grazed along each other as the heat between them rose. Natalie let out a breathy moan as she continued to kiss him, allowing their tongues to speak a language their voices could not express. Their hands were exploring each other's bodies. Carter's hands ran along her back as he kissed her. His hands found their way down until he was gripping her backside. He gave a quick squeeze before his hands moved to trail up her back again. He allowed his fingers to brush along her spine until his hands were tangled in her hair.

Natalie allowed herself to get lost in the moment. She wanted nothing more than to allow this to escalate all the way since it would be her final moments with the love of her life for what she assumed would be a long time. Her hands moved around his body, feeling his muscles through his shirt.

Their arousal was growing, and Carter began to reach for the hem of her shirt. Natalie was already working his shirt up his back as their breathing grew heavier.

Realty came knocking in the form of Nancy. Natalie pulled away from Carter, taking one last longing look at him before motioning to open the door. Nancy walked into the room with a sense of urgency, and Natalie and Carter quickly turned to see what was the matter, their cheeks red with arousal and embarrassment.

"I'm sorry to cut your goodbye short, but the agents are back," Nancy said, pretending the tension in the room didn't exist. Instead, she focused on her daughter. "Natalie, you need to leave. Now!"

Carter stepped around Natalie, quickly grabbed her bags, and handed them to her. He walked her out of the room and, to Natalie's surprise, towards the back door.

Nancy quickly followed, saying, "You can't leave through the front door. There are more agents this time, and it isn't safe for you. You have to go through the back street and go to the north bus stop."

There was a loud pounding at the door. Time was running out. Carter pulled Natalie in for a final hug and quickly pulled away, looked her in the eyes, and said, "When you finally realize you can't do this, reach out to me. I will find you. I will bring you home."

He turned and walked away towards the front door without another word. His words stung, his lack of confidence in her ever apparent. Natalie knew he said them out of love, but it still broke her heart. She at least expected him to walk her to the gate. Instead, he just left her standing there, reminding her she would be on her own from now on.

Nancy led Natalie outside and gave her a small kiss on her cheek. Nancy turned back towards the house, needing to go back inside to avoid the tears that threatened to burst out of her eyes. In silent understanding, Natalie walked out into the alley.

Nancy had always regretted losing herself after Ben died. Once she recognized how far she had fallen, she was able to pick herself back up. She hated knowing that she let her daughter suffer alone. She was grateful for Carter but felt guilty that she hadn't been the mother she ought to have been. After a while, Nancy dragged herself out of her depression, promising herself that she would do better by Natalie.

Nancy wouldn't allow herself to become a shell again. She would stay strong for Natalie and fight to protect her daughter from these agents. She gave one last glance at her daughter, seeing Natalie close the gate and walk away. Sucking in a breath, Nancy went to answer the door to face the agents.

# Chapter 5

Natalie closed the gate and latched the door before stepping away and heading down the alley toward the main road. She ran, not daring to look over her shoulder at everything she was leaving behind.

Questions flooded her mind with every step she took. What was going to happen to her mom? Would her mom and Carter be arrested for helping her leave? Would she be successful in her escape? Waves of uncertainty crashed through Natalie's mind. It became so overwhelming that she stopped running, unaware of how far she traveled.

Natalie's lungs burned, and her legs ached, coming to a stop. Her vision tunneled, and her hand shot up to grip her chest. Her breathing had stopped even as she attempted to gasp for air. It was as if her lungs had decided to stop working. Natalie's body began to tremble as sweat started to trickle down the side of her face. Her heart was pounding, feeling like it would explode out of her chest if she couldn't get a handle on her breathing.

It had been a long time since her last anxiety attack. They used to come in the night when she was asleep. Nancy had tried her best to be there for her, but she could never offer her the comfort she needed. It had been Carter's methods that finally brought Natalie an ounce of relief.

Natalie did what she could to suppress those feelings, as Carter had taught her. She did her best to recall everything he would do and say to break through her anxiety. She pictured his hands running up and down her arm as he told her to breathe slowly. He'd say things like, "Listen to my breathing. Nice and slow. Breathe with me and let go of your worries." He'd repeat those words, and they would soothe every ounce of anxiety that threatened to cripple her.

As Natalie heard Carter's voice telling her to calm down, she worked to slow her breathing. She breathed in, counting to ten, before slowly breathing out. Being outside in the fresh air helped. She knew she needed to get a hold of herself to keep going. She couldn't risk getting caught now. She pushed back the thoughts of the agents and sent up a prayer asking for strength. Almost instantly, her heart rate slowed as her breathing leveled.

Natalie let out a sigh and opened her eyes. She looked around to remind herself of where she was. She heard cars driving by and the buzzing of people talking. Her eyes scanned the area until she saw the sign for the North bus stop. Wiping away her sweat, she quickly approached the stop and checked the times for the next bus. The bus she needed was the one heading South towards Salem. Luckily, that bus was pulling up to the stop, ready to take her as far as a small town close to California's border. Close to the black site.

Natalie boarded the bus and sat towards the back, where she felt she would be most concealed. The bus was empty for the most part, with a few people who looked like they were on their way to a business meeting. She scanned the bus for any sign of what the time could be when she saw the digital time on the bus announcement screen read 4:35 pm. It dawned on Natalie why people were so dressed up. They were likely on their way home from work at this point. She appreciated the crowded bus. With all these people, she was nobody. She was nothing to the world. She did not exist.

It wasn't even five hours ago when she got the phone call from her mom that would throw her entire life off the rails. She was shocked at how quickly life can change. One moment, she was looking forward to her future. The next, she was on the run from the CIA, dreading what life now had in store.

Natalie sat silently on the bus, looking out the window as the bus drove past all the trees and buildings. She felt as though she was watching her entire life slip away. She was because she decided to chase the liberation of strangers instead of focusing on her own life. She willingly left the stability of her life behind, and now there was no going back. Everything she had ever held dear was gone in a matter of hours.

As Natalie felt the rocking of the bus as it drove on, she began thinking of how lost she felt. She had never truly felt lost as she did now. Back when she had nothing to worry about, her mother would take her for walks around their neighborhood. They would walk around, and her mom would point out the different street names, naming them and saying, "As long as you remember where you came from, you'll always find the way to where you need to be."

Natalie was glad to have the memories of her mom's words. She needed them now more than ever. In a time when she had to regulate her emotions on her own and be the strong one again, she had those words that offered a small ounce of comfort.

The sound of the bus breaking pulled Natalie away from her thoughts. She glanced around the bus as the wheels screeched to a stop. She hadn't kept track of how many stops were made while distracted by her thoughts. From the look of it, the bus was still in Downtown Portland. There was a sudden odor of stale urine as homeless people passed her and exited the bus. Natalie's heart clenched as she thought about the homeless people who had been taken against their will. She thought about their suffering and how it could have easily been one of these people passing her by on the bus. Anger bubbled in her stomach at the level of depravity that someone had to have to have no care for such a vulnerable population. She knew then that leaving was the right choice.

Feeling the need to distract herself from her mind, Natalie rummaged in her bag, hoping to find something to keep her occupied. She had left her phone at her mom's house, not wanting to give the agents any way of tracking her. Leaving her phone also meant no contact with anyone, making her feel even more isolated.

After looking around in her backpack, she found nothing. She had been so preoccupied with gathering only items that would be necessary that she didn't think about the possibility that there would be moments that would feel mundane, like sitting for hours on a bus.

Natalie looked back out the window. She watched the world pass by, disassociating from the reality she found herself in. She watched the people who were out and about, living ordinary lives. They each had their own problems and struggles, but nothing was out of the ordinary for them. The lady sitting at the park could go home and cook dinner for her husband before going to sleep and repeating the same thing the next day. The man riding his bike could meet his friends for drinks later, his biggest issue being who would take him home after going a little too hard at the bar. The point is they were able to go home. They were safe from harm. They were all the things Natalie had to put behind her.

Natalie's throat constricted as she fought the tears that threatened to fall. Her mind was racing. Natalie sent up another prayer. This time, it was one of comfort. She knew she had to get her emotions together before she arrived at the final stop. Still, she needed to feel a sense of comfort, and she knew she would get it from prayer.

Natalie refused to let herself cry. It was easier to pretend like she was okay. Letting the emotions in would be too painful. Carter's voice entered her mind like an answer to her prayer. His voice told her she had to push down her anxiety. She had to suppress it as he had taught her. She needed to keep a level head; feeling these emotions would only distract her. She took comfort in the thought of Carter, pushing down every lousy feeling and ensuring they were locked away. Something told her she should still cry, still feel her brokenness. She ignored that voice, knowing it was a lie.

As the bus continued, her face morphed into an emotionless expression. She rubbed her temples with her fingertips, her head pounding from her earlier crying. There was nothing more for her to do but sit and wait until the bus reached its final destination.

Natalie decided to try to rest despite her headache. She closed her eyes and listened to the shuffling of feet as people got on and off the bus. Sleep never came for her, but she didn't open her eyes until the bus came to its final stop and the driver told her to get off.

***

Natalie gathered her belongings, slinging her bags over her shoulders, and moved towards the bus exit. The last person on the bus, Natalie, stepped out into the world before she noticed that the day had turned to night. She looked around, only a few streetlights provided visibility of her location. She went to the directory and saw that she had made it to Klamath Falls, a small town bordering Oregon and California.

A long way from home, she scanned her surroundings for any sign of a bathroom. She had been on the bus so long without using the restroom that her bladder was about to explode. She noticed a small diner down the street from the bus stop as she looked for a bathroom. It had a little neon sign saying it was open 24 hours. Feeling the sudden hunger pangs, she decided that was the solution to all her problems. She can have her potty break and grab a bite before figuring out the rest of her plans.

Natalie walked into the diner and noticed a sign at the front counter. *Seat yourself. Staff will be with you shortly.* She took this opportunity to find the bathroom before finding a place to sit. She walked into the bathroom, pushing past the metal door. She was met with two tiny stalls next to a grimy sink. She went to relieve herself, covering the toilet seat with a year's worth of toilet paper before washing her hands.

Once in front of the mirror, Natalie finally got a look at her appearance. She hadn't seen herself since before she left. Her hair was disheveled, looking like a bird laid a nest on her head. She tasted her bad breath, and the bags under her eyes would have made headlines at fashion week.

As she stared at herself, she thought about how she looked and could barely recognize the person staring back at her in the mirror. She knew she looked the same as she always had, but she looked like a stranger to herself. Where her once lively eyes and rosy cheeks were now lived a shadow self that radiated sorrow.

Natalie blinked at herself, her hands dripping as she felt her eyes sting as they fought off her tears. She looked towards the ceiling, taking a deep breath and shaking off her hands of any water. After one final glance, she exited the bathroom and returned to the dining area.

Natalie made her way to a small round table towards the back of the diner. Only a few people were there, each one looking tired from long days of travel.

Natalie searched the diner for a clock, finding one that hung above the cash register. 1:45 am. What a bad time to arrive somewhere. She would have to find a place to stay and attempt to get some more sleep. However, that was unlikely since she had her eight-hour depression nap on the bus.

Regardless, she needed to figure out her sleeping arrangements before planning her next move. After she got some food in her system, she would stroll around town and hopefully find a motel with a vacancy.

"Welcome in! What can I get you, hun?" Startled, Natalie looked up to see the waitress standing beside the table with a notepad and a pen with a cute flower on the end of it. The waitress was wearing a pretty checkered blouse with blue skinny jeans. Her makeup was done, which struck Natalie as odd since it was one in the morning.

"Oh, um, hello," Natalie started. "Sorry, I'm a little out of it. Can I get a burger and fries? And a glass of water is fine."

The waitress wrote everything down and gave Natalie a kind smile. "No problem, love. I'll get that right out for you." She walked off, and Natalie watched with jealousy. This waitress seemed like her life was so great. She had a pleasant personality and seemed to light up any room she walked into. Also, her life didn't seem to be falling apart. Natalie mourned the days when she could be carefree like that.

The waitress quickly returned with a glass of water. As she set it down, she asked, "Is there anything I can get you while you wait on that burger? It will just be a few more minutes."

Taking this as the perfect opportunity, Natalie opened up. "Actually, I was wondering if you could point me to any motels with vacancies. I didn't plan this trip, so I don't have a place to stay right now." Natalie didn't know why she felt the need to explain herself or her situation. It wasn't this girl's business, but something about her seemed trustworthy. She gave off the energy of someone who doesn't care about your circumstances. She'd help you no matter who you are or what you've done.

"Of course! I'll get you a brochure that we have for tourists. It has all the information you need about any motels in the area. I'll even highlight the ones with vacancies for you! Be right back."

She walked off before Natalie could even say thank you. She really was as lovely as she looked. Natalie was grateful that there were still kind people like her in the world. As she waited, she looked around the diner, finally noticing the 50s theme it was decorated with. She had always loved diners that looked like they belonged in a different decade.

Her dad used to take her to restaurants like this every year for her birthday. She always looked forward to it. She would get those obnoxiously large milkshakes in the glass jars that were too big for her. Her dad always had to finish hers because she never seemed to be able to. Or maybe she just liked the feeling of having her dad there to help her out, and it just became a habit. She hadn't returned to a diner in a long time, the idea too painful.

Sitting in the diner now made her realize that she felt anything but sad or alone. It actually brought her peace. She felt like her dad was sitting across from her, comforting her and telling her everything would be okay. Feeling a new sense of calm, she took a sip of water, cringing at the taste of tap water. Natalie had always been one of those people who could taste the differences in water. She hated stale tap water but drank it anyway because beggars can't be choosers.

The waitress returned to her moments later, holding a plate in one hand and a pamphlet in the other. "Here is that burger for you, hun," she said, setting it down. "And here is all the information you need on this town." She handed over the pamphlet to Natalie. "There was only one motel with a vacancy. I went ahead and called the concierge to tell him to hold a room for you so you wouldn't be out of luck by the time you got there. Is there anything else I can get you?"

Natalie gaped at the waitress, shocked at her kindness. "Wow," Natalie started. "Thank you so much. I appreciate it. I think I am all good right now, though. Thank you again."

"No problem, hun! Enjoy your meal." The waitress returned behind the counter, and Natalie looked at the pamphlet. It seemed like the motel was just down the street, not too long of a walk. She scanned the rest of the booklet as she popped some fries in her mouth. This little town was adorable, and there were a lot of natural sights around. Natalie wanted to take some time to figure out her next steps and stay for a few days. She also really wanted to explore. It killed her to know that her desires were impossible. She had to keep moving. She wouldn't be able to stay for long, and any exploring ideas were merely wishful thinking.

Natalie finished the rest of the food and went to the counter to pay. The waitress wasn't there, so she rang the small bell next to the register.

As she stood, she felt a presence come up behind her. Her stomach fell. She was scared to turn around, and her mind immediately jumped to the thought that it was a CIA agent. They found her, and it wasn't even 24 hours that she was on the run. That had to be a pathetic world record.

Natalie scratched the back of her head casually and glanced behind her, pretending she was taking a regular scan of the room. Her heart rate immediately slowed as she saw a stranger standing behind her. Not an agent. They made eye contact for a split second, sending chills throughout her body. She quickly looked away and continued her fake scan of the room.

Natalie was taken aback at this man's appearance. He had short dark hair that was ruffled in the front. It seemed as though he hadn't seen a comb in a while. He also had short facial hair that didn't look very well groomed. There were some uneven patches on his neck, and the hair on his cheeks didn't quite connect with his mustache and goatee. He had hooded blue eyes, and he was very tall. Natalie figured he was between 6'2" and 6'4". He wore a dirty white T-shirt with a leather jacket and dirty jeans.

Natalie didn't know what to make of him. She couldn't tell if he was homeless or dressed that way on purpose. Natalie was sure of one thing, though. This man was built. She could see the muscles through his shirt, his body looking very well maintained. Whoever this man was, Natalie was just glad she found no recognition in his crystal eyes.

As she looked back around, her heart rate calmed down. He wasn't with the CIA. Natalie drew in a deep breath and felt her body relax. When she looked back towards the register, the happy waitress was back.

"Sorry, I had to take a quick trip to the ladies' room. You all set to pay?" She was waving around her cute flower pen as she spoke.

Natalie began to pull out her wallet when the pretty homeless man cut her off. "Hi, sorry to interrupt, but I need some coffee. And can you point me to the bathroom? I gotta take a leak."

Natalie looked at him with disgust. This man's attitude starkly contrasted with the waitress she had been interacting with all night. She had hoped everyone in this town would be pleasant. Unfortunately, she was wrong.

Luckily this angel of a woman spoke up, her friendly demeanor switched to one that took no crap from anybody. "Sir, I'm with a customer right now. You're going to have to wait." Her words were clipped, her friendliness from earlier gone. She spoke like someone willing to fight if she needed to.

The man, however, was not backing down. "Listen, lady. I just need the restroom. You can wait on the coffee. Kindly point me to the nearest John, now."

"I don't know who you're calling, lady, but you'll stand there all night with a full bladder if you don't calm down and wait for me to ring this nice girl up. It's called manners ass hat. Learn them." She looked at Natalie and said kindly, "Sorry for this disgusting interruption. Your meal is on the house. I hope to see you back here!"

Natalie was shocked at her words. "Oh no, I can pay. It's no big deal."

"Don't worry about it. I am not taking no for an answer. Now get out before I take you out myself."

This girl didn't play. Natalie cracked a small smile before nodding. "Okay, but at least let me leave you a tip." Natalie dropped $15 in the tip jar and smiled at the waitress. "Before I go, can I get your name?"

The man behind her grunted in annoyance at her question, but she didn't care. The waitress seemed pleased and said, "My name is Evangeline, but you can call me Evie."

Natalie smiled. "It's been a pleasure, Evie. My name is Natalie. You will definitely be seeing me tomorrow morning."

Leaving it at that, Natalie turned around, shot the hot but rude man an icy glare, and walked out into the darkness of the night.

# Chapter 6

The town's streets were empty in the early hours of the morning. The moon's glow was the only light source that prevented the world around Natalie from being pitch black. Natalie walked toward the motel, her steps were quickened as her eyes darted around her surroundings. Like her hikes, she thought of all the different scenarios ending with her being butchered by a sadistic killer. Scaring herself, she walked quickly to avoid becoming the subject of a bad true crime podcast. In an unfamiliar area like this one, you never know who is out and about, and she didn't feel like getting kidnapped and murdered.

She arrived at the motel and walked into the lobby area. A man was sitting at the front desk reading a book. He had earbuds in, but he noticed Natalie as soon as she walked in. His eyes looked her up and down, making Natalie instantly uncomfortable as she approached the desk.

Taking one earbud out and setting his book down, he

spoke. "A bit late for a young woman to be traveling, don't you think?" He asked, his voice sounding slimy with phlegm.

Feeling a twinge of uneasiness in her stomach, she did her best to ignore his comment. "Umm, hi. I was hoping you had a vacancy," she said, her voice shaky. "I was at the diner earlier. The waitress said she called to make sure there was a room available for me here."

The man scanned Natalie and didn't say a word before typing something into his computer and handing her a key card. "You're in room 115. You got a credit card on you, sweetheart?"

His tone made Natalie cringe. She wished she could stay anywhere else. Unfortunately, it was either here or on a bench somewhere. Natalie sighed, accepting her fate. Her only issue was that she hadn't brought any cards, only cash. Credit cards were too traceable. "Sorry, all I have is cash? Would that be okay?"

The man sighed in irritation and said, "Cash is fine, but you have to pay everything upfront. How many nights are you staying?"

Natalie, relieved, thought about how many nights would be the safest to stay. She wanted to explore the town in the morning but gave up on that desire. Now, she only needed to get her bearings and find somewhere more permanent to set up camp. She decided that two nights would be best. It would allow her time to plan her next steps while also not staying in a place so close to where she lived. After finalizing all the details, Natalie handed over the cash, took the key card, and headed to her motel room.

She walked in the dark, her feet dragging with exhaustion. As she approached her room, she pulled the keycard out of the small envelope it was in. The light on the electric lock turned from red to green as she scanned the card. As soon as she opened the door, she was hit with the smell of stale tobacco.

Once in her room, she locked the door using the deadbolt and chain. Maybe it was because she was a woman traveling alone or simply because she wanted to guarantee her privacy, but using every lock felt right. She didn't know how effective each latch would be, but it made her feel safe to put up a barrier between her and the creepy concierge. If the CIA agents showed up, they would have no issue breaking down the door, but she would cross that bridge if she came to it.

Natalie hadn't allowed herself to think much about the agents. Within the safety of the motel room, she thought about why they had come for her. She didn't doubt those agents had something to do with the experiments. From the way Agent Jannis scanned her body as they stood in the kitchen, Natalie felt how his eyes took in every curve of her body as she stood in defiance against him. She couldn't imagine what was going on in his mind, but the slightest thought made her sick to her stomach.

Pulling her mind away from the memories, Natalie scanned the room. She was surprised that it looked nicer than expected. There was a single queen bed with the typical motel bedding. It had a small bathroom, but she didn't mind. She didn't plan on spending too long in this room, let alone the town.

Natalie debated whether she wanted to go straight to bed or to shower. Her body felt devoid of energy, but she could feel the layers of filth that coated her body. She decided to take a quick shower before going to bed. Using the complimentary mini bar of soap, she scrubbed all of her nooks and crannies, finger combed out her loose curls, and then got out of the shower.

After getting in her pajamas, she brushed her teeth, dried her hair with a towel, and got in bed. As soon as her head hit the pillow, she knew it would be a sleepless night. Her mind was restless as she had endless thoughts of the day. She thought about her mom and what happened after the CIA agents realized she was gone. She thought about Carter and wondered if he stayed the night in her room or went home. She thought about what she was going to do from here. There were no clear answers, and she had no idea how this situation would resolve itself.

After sending up a silent prayer, Natalie tossed and turned for what seemed like hours before sleep finally took her.

***

Waking up in a motel room is never fun. It starts with an individual slowly coming into consciousness. The first sense to wake up is smell. Almost immediately, the smell of stale cigarette smoke embedded into the walls and the bedsheets seeps into the senses. That's when the realization hits that this bed and this room belong to a stranger. The reality is much more depressing.

Natalie woke up, not recognizing where she was. As soon as her mind caught up with her senses, it clicked. She wasn't home. A wave of sadness crashed into her as she struggled to sit up. A part of her hoped everything that occurred the day before was a nightmare or a cruel joke. Unfortunately, her suffering was real.

Natalie got out of bed and rubbed her eyes before looking for the clock. It was 7:15 a.m. Her internal alarm couldn't let her sleep in for an extra two hours. Sleep-deprived, she walked to the bathroom to brush her teeth, hating the taste of morning breath. Afterward, she got dressed in the only other outfit she allowed herself to bring. Luckily, motels have laundry rooms that provide her a chance to wash the grime and depression from yesterday's clothes.

While getting dressed, she thought of Carter and how she ached to be with him now. Every item of clothing reminded her of him. She imagined his arms wrapping her in a hug as she slipped her shirt over her head. She imagined his hands on her thighs as she pulled her shorts on and felt the fabric hugging her skin.

Everything would be easier if he were with her. She wouldn't have to worry about when her next anxiety attack would come because he would be there to stop it. She wouldn't have to worry about getting food because he would provide it. She wouldn't have to worry about a creepy motel concierge because Carter would be there to protect her.

It struck Natalie how dependent she had become on Carter. The thought made her feel weak and useless. She wanted to scream at herself for becoming so reliant on someone else's strength. She choked down the tears and suppressed the anxiety that was threatening to form. She needed to remember who she was before Carter when she was forced to be strong to survive.

Hunger pangs interrupted her pity party. She gripped her stomach and glanced around the room for her next course of action. She gathered her dirty laundry, tossed her clothes in a small bag, and left to find food and coffee. She decided to find something to eat and then do laundry when she returned. She gathered some cash, put her laptop in her backpack, and left.

As Natalie stepped outside, she was hit by the morning warmth. California didn't ease you into the heat of the day like Oregon did. Natalie walked through town, noticing the aesthetic of the little town for the first time. It had a vintage look that made her feel like she was in a 50's movie. The diner fit in perfectly.

She walked back to the diner,  breathing in the warm morning air. It was fresh, with the town surrounded by trees and greenery. Natalie imagined the trees brought the temperature down a bit, and she was grateful for it.

Natalie approached the diner entrance and performed the same routine she had done the previous night. The *seat yourself* sign was still up, and lucky for her, the table from last night was unoccupied. She walked straight to it and pulled out the laptop after sitting down. She opened up her computer and powered it on. As it turned on, she realized she had made a mistake. The color in her face drained, and her jaw dropped open as she watched notifications flashing across the screen. Natalie couldn't do anything while she sat there frozen, watching her laptop betray her in the worst way. They would find her.

Once she recovered from the shock, she quickly checked the Wi-Fi connection. It was off. She checked Bluetooth. It was off. She scoured every possible source of connection on her laptop. Everything was off. She quickly went to look at all the notifications and saw they were all dated a while back. She even recognized some, having opened them before. Relief slammed into her chest, and she realized her laptop was catching up. It hadn't been opened for about a week, so everything she did on her phone was catching up on the computer.

Though it was the only explanation, Natalie looked at her laptop skeptically. She understood that the computer would need a Wi-Fi connection to load anything. She got an eerie feeling that something was connecting to her laptop. She thought back to the moments before she left when she was packing her bags. It had been Carter who packed her computer. He must have opened it before putting it in her backpack, causing it to connect to her home Wi-Fi.

Feeling paranoid, Natalie chalked it up to coincidence. Regardless of how the laptop was loading, she wasn't connected to Wi-Fi. She was safe. Natalie took a deep breath just as Evangeline walked up to the table. "Hey, girl! Glad you came back. What can I get started for you?" She spoke with the same enthusiasm she had the night before.

Natalie looked up at her, eyebrows furrowing in confusion. "What are you doing here? Don't you ever get off work," she asked, closing her laptop.

Evangeline roared with laughter before answering with a kind smile, "I clock off in about half an hour. Believe me, I need some sleep. I'm not here out of the kindness of my heart. I need the dough. Anyhoo! What'll it be?"

Natalie ordered her coffee and an omelet, and Evangeline rushed off. Looking back at her laptop, she began doing what she did best.

She opened her files and started sifting through all her accumulated information. There were primarily redacted files, but she had managed to uncover quite a bit when she hacked into the CIA's database.

Most files were journal entries on how the experiments' subjects responded to the tests. There was a document that gave an overarching description of what was going on. That particular document had the most redactions. Natalie couldn't uncover the entire thing but got a good chunk of it.

Experiments were being conducted on an *undesirable* population. A population that the agents deemed disposable. They were interested in seeing how certain chemical weapons affected the different sets of demographics. The different demographics included race, age, height, and weight. The reason they were doing this wasn't apparent, and any time the purpose of these experiments was about to be mentioned, it was blocked out by a bold black line. Had Natalie known the truth when she obtained these files, she would have tried harder to hack through the redactions. Unfortunately, she didn't and was left with files that revealed nothing.

As Natalie continued going through the documents and trying to memorize everything she saw, Evangeline came back with her coffee and food in hand. Natalie looked up and closed the laptop, not wanting Evangeline to see what she was working on.

"Here's your food, hun!" Evangeline chimed. She set the plate and coffee on the table and asked, "Anything else I can get for you?"

Natalie shook her head before saying, "No, thank you." She sipped at her coffee and let out a satisfied sigh as the drops of caffeine entered her system. The warmth coated her insides as she opened her eyes and looked up at Evangeline. "Was this coffee brewed in heaven? It is so delicious!"

Evangeline chuckled and said, "No, but it is my specialty. I bring my own coffee grounds to work because I can't stand the coffee they provide. You looked like you could use some quality coffee over the mud water this place has."

"Wow, thank you so much! This might be the best coffee I've ever had." Natalie took another sip of the liquid bliss as Evangeline left with a smile and a nod.

Natalie dug into her omelet, wanting to eat quickly so she could return to her room.  She still needed to work on her research, but she figured it would be best to avoid prying eyes.

As she finished her omelet, the bell at the entrance chimed, capturing Natalie's attention. She looked towards the front door and saw the man from last night. He looked less homeless but still sported messy hair and clothes that looked like they could use a wash.

The man sat at a booth closer to the entrance and did not spare a single glance in Natalie's direction. He was sitting at his table with his hands folded into one another, waiting for the waitress.

Natalie allowed her gaze to linger a little longer before returning to her food. Something about him gave her a weird feeling in her stomach that she couldn't seem to place. She wasn't sure if it was his appearance or his demeanor that made her uneasy. Shaking off the feeling, she scarfed down the rest of her eggs.

As Natalie began to down her cup of coffee, Evangeline walked up with her bill. "No need to rush, but I'm about to clock off, and I figured I should have you as my last customer. The next shift waitress is nice and all, but I like you. So take your time, and I'll be in the back getting out of this uniform." She began to walk off before Natalie called after her.

"Oh! I can pay now," Natalie said eagerly. "Here's the cash, and you can keep the change. Thank you so much! You have been so nice."

Evangeline smiled and took the money. Natalie

gathered up all her things and followed Evangeline up to the counter. "So," Evangeline began, "you got any fun plans for the day?"

Natalie took a moment to think of a response. Evangeline glanced up with a questioning look on her face. Quickly, Natalie spat, "No, I don't. Sorry! I'm still waiting for that coffee to kick in." Natalie let out a small chuckle that Evangeline returned with a smile.

"No problem, hun. I know how it is. Anyway, I hope you have a good day! See you around later, hopefully!" Evangeline hands Natalie the recipe before disappearing behind a door labeled *employees only*.

Natalie took the receipt and turned to walk out when she was met with a pair of sea blue eyes. She froze, taken aback at how close he stood beside her. She didn't even realize her mouth was hanging open until he looked at her with a quizzical brow and cleared his throat. Closing her mouth, she moved to get around him and out of the diner.

"Excuse me," Natalie said softly. The man didn't bother getting out of her way. Instead, he shot her a look that told her she was nothing more than an inconvenience. Natalie scowled as she brushed past him, giving him an aggressive shoulder tap before exiting the diner.

As Natalie returned to her room, she thought about that strange interaction and wondered why she was left with that uneasy feeling in her stomach again.

# Chapter 7

Natalie sat in her motel room at the small desk in the corner. She set her laptop on the table and began looking over the files once again. Before she could find a way to connect to the internet to infiltrate the black site's servers again, she needed to commit what she currently had to memory.

Looking over the files now, she didn't notice anything new. The documents highlighted the research and disclosed what they were looking for. Still, Natalie searched for the why. Why were these experiments being conducted in the first place? Why were members of the most unprotected demographic being taken and experimented on? What was the end goal? Natalie couldn't tell whether it was for war efforts or research.

One new piece of information she discovered was that the subjects were only sometimes tested in the experiments. Some were labeled as "unfit" to be tested. The weird thing was there are no accounts of what happened to them afterward. There was no indication of whether they were let go or subjected to other conditions that Natalie couldn't imagine.

One thing was obvious. As she speculated, the two agents who came to her house were directly related to the experiments. Despite their efforts to remain cordial at her mom's house, they seemed to take everything personally. Also, their initials appear to be mentioned a lot in the files. There is especially a lot of Agent J. included. They were either heavily involved as researchers or they were the orchestrators.

***

Natalie spent the rest of the day memorizing the files, taking in every ounce of information they offered. She only took breaks to pee or stretch her legs.

It wasn't until around 5 p.m. that she felt hunger pangs. She hadn't eaten since breakfast and had only been consuming water. Not feeling in the mood to go to the diner again, she decided to go to a convenience store. She'd pick up some snacks and maybe a stale pizza slice and then return to the room.

Natalie grabbed her purse, stuck a couple of twenties in her wallet, put on her shoes, and then walked out. The air was cooler than it was in the morning. Natalie debated returning and getting her jacket, but she saw the convenience store just across the street. Convenient. She made her way over to the store quickly. As she opened the door, a bell chimed. She was hugged by warmth as she stepped inside, grateful she had left her jacket in her room.

A worker shouted from somewhere in a back room, "Welcome in!"

Natalie browsed the aisles and picked a bag of Hot

Cheetos, sunflower seeds, and trail mix. She walked over to the cooler and grabbed a water bottle and a coffee for the morning. Looking at the hot food section, she decided she would get a pizza slice after all.

The door chimed as she got her food, drawing Natalie's attention. She looked up and stopped in her tracks. He was there. The man from the diner, who she figured probably wasn't homeless. She decided to stop referring to him that way. Instead, she settled for calling him a vagrant. She looked at him, and their eyes locked for what felt like an eternity. It was only a few seconds before he looked away and walked between the aisles. He was so tall that his head stuck out from on top of the shelves, but he kept his head down.

Regaining composure, she slid a slice of pizza into a container and walked to the checkout counter. She rang the bell sitting on the counter, and the store owner shouted again, "I'll be with you in a second!"

"No worries!" Natalie responded.

She stood there waiting when all of a sudden she heard another voice. "I wouldn't trust those pizza slices if I were you." It was him, and he was speaking to her.

Natalie turned around and said, "I don't have any other options at the moment, and beggars can't be choosers."

"That's a grammatically incorrect saying," he grunted with no emotion.

Natalie's eyebrows drew together, and the corners of her mouth pointed downward. "Regardless of any grammatical error," she said slowly, "I'm out of other options for food, so stale pizza it is."

"Why don't you eat at the diner? I've seen you there twice."

"I can't be a big spender all the time. Besides, I was hoping to avoid a certain unfriendly person tonight." She eyed him. "I guess I'm just all out of luck."

Before he could respond, the cashier popped out of nowhere. "Sorry for the wait! I appreciate your patience." The mysterious stranger walked off to do his shopping as the cashier rang her up.

After paying for the food, she moved to walk out of the store. Once she got to the door, she froze. She couldn't believe her eyes as the world crashed down on her. Across the street at the motel was a black SUV, identical to the ones parked outside her mom's house. She scanned the parking lot, and she saw them. Agent Jannis and Agent Bennet. They were standing near the main lobby of the motel. Her room wasn't too close but also not far away enough to where she could guarantee she wouldn't be spotted.

Feeling the panic starting to set in, Natalie slowly backed up into the store and suddenly felt something hard against her back. She turned around and saw him. He was looking at her with a furrowed eyebrow. She gaped at him, and the panic must have been written across her face because his features softened before he asked, "What's wrong?"

Natalie didn't know why, but her stomach flipped at his concern. This man was a stranger and had no business asking her what was wrong. It made her nervous that he was showing her any level of worry. She couldn't tell him what was wrong, but she saw an opportunity for an escape. Quickly, she came up with a lie.

"I need to get back to my motel, but I don't want to be seen by the front desk man. He gave me a bad feeling and made me uncomfortable when I checked in."

The man went rigid at her words. He glared across the street before taking her by the arm and walking out of the store. He pulled her to the side farthest from the front office, shielding her body with his own. Luckily for Natalie, this man was large and had no problem shielding her from view. He pressed her against him, and Natalie was frozen with fear and intrigue. The hardness of his body revealed that he was definitely muscular. She figured as much early, but being pressed up to him like this confirmed her suspicions.

As they were nearing her room, his grip on her body eased. Natalie separated herself from him, putting a comfortable distance between them. She fumbled with her keycard, aware of the way his eyes bore into her from behind. Once she opened the door, she turned to look at the man as she crossed the threshold.

"Thank you for that," she said, scratching her head. "I owe you one."

"Don't mention it," he said, leaning forward as he rested his elbow on the doorframe. "Maybe find a new place to stay if that creep scares you."

Natalie paused, wondering if that was an invitation. "Thanks for the advice. I'm actually heading out of town tonight."

Some emotion flashed across his face for a split second, but Natalie couldn't place what it was.

"Anyways, I better get packing," Natalie said, her voice reflecting her awkward feelings. "Thanks again."

"You're welcome," he said, finally. Wasting no more time, he turned and left without another word, his hands curling into tight fists before relaxing at his sides.

Natalie watched as he walked away, admiring his backside and how his long legs strode away from her.

Frustrated, Natalie closed the door. She felt stupid for how she reacted to his body's proximity. She hated allowing them to part ways without at least exchanging names. He did something so kind, and she ended their interaction like someone who had never socialized with another human being. It also frustrated her that she was feeling a sense of attraction for the stranger.

Remembering why he helped her to begin with brings Natalie crashing back to reality. They found her. They had been talking to the front desk man about one of two things. They either wanted a place to stay or were looking for her, the latter seeming the most plausible. Natalie was not sure what her plan was, but she started by packing. She gathered her clothes, silently cursing at herself for not doing laundry like she had planned earlier that morning. Her appetite from before was gone, so she shoved the food into her duffel bag. She recounted her money, setting aside enough for a bus ticket.

Instantly, Natalie froze, fingers gripping the bag and causing her knuckles to turn white. Her mouth dried as she stared at the blinking lights, panic threatening to consume her again. She reached into her bag, beside where she stored her laptop, and pulled out the tracking device. How she had missed it before, she didn't know, but there it was. It had a soft blinking red light, signaling that it was connected to a server somewhere and communicating her every move.

This was how they found her. Natalie thought back to her mom's house, trying to find any explanation in her memories for how this device could have been planted in her bag. Carter was the only person other than her to touch this bag when he packed her laptop. Other than him, she hadn't allowed anyone near it. She knew Carter would never track her. It was too dangerous, and he would never willingly put her in harm's way. Right?

Natalie couldn't think of any plausible answer to the millions of questions swarming her mind. She decided the best thing to do would be to destroy the tracker and keep moving. She threw the tracker on the floor and stomped on it repeatedly. She panted with each step, not stopping until the light stopped blinking. Panicking, Natalie searched her bag again, making sure there would be no other surprises like that again.

Once all her things were neatly put away, she looked out the window to see what nightmare was happening outside. She noticed that the SUV was gone. She didn't see the agents anywhere. Taking this as her one shot, she grabbed her bags and bolted out of the room.

Making sure the coast was clear, she rushed to the main office. As soon as she opened the door, her eyes met the concierge. She motioned to put the keycard on the desk, wanting to be quick. Before she could move her hand away, he slammed his hand to hers, preventing it from moving.

His eyes bore into hers. "Some men from the government stopped by. They showed me quite a pretty photo of you." He paused, waiting for a reply. Natalie just stared, her body shaking.

"I told them I've never seen you before," he said, his yellow teeth flashing in a wicked smile. "I don't do nice things for free, though. Your room is going to be extra."

He released Natalie's arm, rubbing his fingers together to tell her she needed to pay up. Scoffing, Natalie dug into her bag, ignoring her father's box, and found the extra money she had brought for herself. She looked up at the man, shaking her head at the exploitation.

"How much," she asked, her voice tight.

"Five hundred, darling," he said, holding his hand out in wait.

Natalie's face drained of color. She looked down, counting the bills in her hand despite knowing she didn't have enough. As she counted, her eyes looked from the money to the man. He was behind the counter. Without thinking too much about it, Natlaie darted out of the lobby before the concierge had a chance to stop her. He yelled after her, but Natalie didn't stop.

She ran as fast as she could in the direction of the bus station. Her bags hit her legs as she ran, making it uncomfortable, but she trudged on. She couldn't get caught right now. She still had so much information to uncover and needed to figure out how to connect to the CIA black site. She couldn't do that in prison.

As Natalie ran, she took in the small town one last time. She was sad she would never get the chance to explore for a few days. She also felt foolish for not checking for a tracking device sooner. They had no right to do this to her, and Natalie was determined to expose them. Now that she had ingrained the files she had into her memory, she could work on digging for more. She just needed to get out of here without being found.

Natalie made it to the station in one piece. She was cautious the entire way and was sure to watch for that SUV. Natalie walked to the sign with the bus times and read them over. She had fifteen minutes to stand there. During that time, the agents could drive by and spot her. Natalie didn't want to be a sitting duck, so she found a public bathroom and locked herself inside.

It smelt of stale urine and dust. Natalie let herself calm

down slightly now that she was this close to escaping again, and she let out soft and quiet sobs. Her breath was catching as she tried to keep her cries quiet, not wanting to alert anyone to her presence. She tried hard to fight the anxiety that was choking her from the inside out. Natalie hated that this was what her life had become, but she couldn't change it now. She needed to be strong for herself. For her mom. For Carter.

Natalie was a strong person. Her life had changed after having Carter be the one person she could be vulnerable around. He was there to pick her up, never letting her be sad or depressed. Now, Natalie knew she was on her own. She could only rely on herself, and thinking about how Carter makes things easier isn't helping.

Natalie composed herself and wiped off the tears that streamed down her cheeks. She took deep breaths, calming her mind, and then walked out of the restroom just as the bus pulled up to the stop. She quickly boarded the bus, keeping her head low, and found a seat at the back. Natalie stared out the window, relieved that she made it here safely.

Her skin erupted in goosebumps when she saw the SUV drive by. She sunk lower into the seat despite knowing they couldn't see her. Now that she knew how they found her location, she refused to let them get this close again. She double-checked the bus route, making sure it was taking her south to the location of the black site.

# Chapter 8

Natalie fell asleep thirty minutes into the bus ride. The adrenaline from her escape had worn off by the time the bus started moving, exhaustion taking its place. Her body crashed once her butt hit the seat, and she lost all concept of how far she had traveled.

Natalie woke up when streetlights started shining in her face. It had been close to sunset when Natalie ran. Now, it was completely dark outside, with only the bus lights and the occasional streetlights to light the way. She looked up towards the electronic sign on the bus to see where it was stopping next. Modoc National Wildlife Refuge. That was the end of the line. Natalie wasn't sure how long it would be, so she pulled out the cold slice of pizza from her bag and ate it.

As the bus came to a stop, she stood and picked up her belongings. She sauntered toward the bus exit, dropping money in the collection box as she passed the driver. She looked for a map at the bus stop that would tell her where she was compared to Klamath Falls. She couldn't be more than 5 hours away if it were still night out. As tired as she was of traveling, she needed to put more distance between herself and those agents.

Natalie found a paper map near the bus schedule post and saw that she was still too close to Klamath Falls. After finding another bus to take her even further south, she sat to wait for it. She just took a second to do some breathing exercises. She only had the one recent panic attack and refused to let it happen again. She couldn't afford to panic anymore.

It wasn't long before the bus showed up, and this one would take her as far as Plumas County. Natalie was unfamiliar with that area, but she figured the less familiar, the better. This is the last place the agents would bother looking for her. At least, that was the hope.

Natalie managed to stay up the entire bus ride. She felt a rush of anticipation as she realized she was getting closer to the black site, which meant closer to uncovering the whole truth of the experiments. She continued eating the snacks in her bag, making sure to keep rations because she didn't know when she would be able to get food again. At that moment, she wished she had bought more practical foods rather than junk. Still, she could never resist hot Cheetos. It must have been the Latina in her. Natalie was half-Mexican on her mom's side. Her mom had long, curly hair that complimented her tanned skin. She was on the shorter side, but that didn't take away from her feisty nature. Her dad, on the other hand, was tall. He was muscular from his time in the military and always sported a short haircut.

Growing up, her mom wanted to make sure she stayed connected with her heritage. They would celebrate Cinco de Mayo and even Dia de los Muertos despite their religious beliefs. Natalie didn't believe the dead relatives paid visits during Dia de Muertos, but it was nice to spend that time around family, remembering those who were no longer with her. Natalie's mom also raised Natalie around Mexican music and food. The food was the best part. Natalie was raised eating foods like cochinita pibil and tamales. That food exposure extended to Hot Cheetos, her mom's favorite. The love was passed down to Natalie, who liked her Hot Cheetos served with a bottle of Coke.

Thinking about something as trivial as a snack brought a smile to Natalie's face. It was the first smile about her family that she had since before she left. She held onto these memories, allowing them to shine like a beacon of hope in her darkness.

The bus screeched to a stop as it arrived at its destination. Natalie ensured all her belongings were organized before getting off the bus. Taking her bags, she exited the bus and took in her surroundings. Plumas County was beautiful. It was not as pretty as Klamath Falls, but that shows the difference between Oregon and California. Even in its forest areas, California is dryer, and the air isn't as fresh.

Fortunately for Natalie, dry air was what she needed. This time, she wasn't going to risk it in a motel. She was put in a vulnerable position to be spotted by the agents. A motel room is too risky. The agents can easily go to the front desk and show a picture of her like they had before. She was lucky the front desk man at Klamath Falls didn't expose her. She wouldn't always be that lucky.

Natalie decided she would go deep in the forest and camp out. She didn't have a tent, but it was summertime.

The worst thing that could get her were the mosquitos. And bears. Bears loved to wander the forests in California, but Natalie figured she would cross that bridge when she came to it. She could only focus on one bad thing at a time, and bears come second to federal prison.

According to the bus driver, the nearest town to the bus stop was a five-mile walk. She started her trek, knowing that she needed to find real food before looking for a good spot to camp. A convenience store wouldn't be ideal, so she hoped to find a grocery store in town. Of course, small towns tend to have the smallest grocery stores where people can be easily recognized, especially outsiders. No one would recognize Natalie, making her easy to spot as a stranger. She would stick out like a sore thumb. She needed to be in and out quickly to avoid unwanted questions and attention.

Natalie walked for miles. It was early morning, so it wasn't too hot, but it was still summer in California. Sweat was glistening on her face, and she was growing breathless. Despite her exhaustion, Natalie could still appreciate the beauty of the world around her. The trees were swaying in the little breeze the air was giving off. A slight breeze that Natalie was grateful for. The birds were also having morning conversations that brought a peaceful feeling to Natalie's mind. Nature always had a way of calming her and centering her. It was always the one thing besides Carter that could ease her mind when overwhelmed with anxiety.

Natalie made it to a cute little town, but it looked a little more run down than the town in Klamath Falls. It wasn't as touristy as Klamath Falls, which meant she would definitely stick out. These weren't people who saw hundreds of tourists coming and going. They were used to certain faces, and an outsider would be memorable. Natalie wasn't sure when the next town would come up, and she had to get into the forest so she could hide behind the tree coverage. Deciding that it was best to be in and out quickly, she went into the local grocery store.

Keeping her head down, she found the store and walked in. The door chimed as it opened, making Natalie cringe. So much for going unnoticed. Natalie looked towards the cashier, but the girl at the register had headphones on, and her eyes were glued to her phone. Hope sparked through Natalie, grateful that this girl was too preoccupied with her phone to notice a stranger.

Natalie made sure to be quick with her shopping. She stuck to food that didn't need to be cooked or refrigerated. She got some canned tuna, bread, and some fruit. Natalie was a sucker for grapes. After gathering all her food, Natalie went up to the cashier. The girl took a moment before looking up from her phone. She gave Natalie a once-over before scanning the items. This girl still had her earbuds and didn't bother looking at Natalie as she rang up the items. Usually, Natalie would be upset that this girl was being so rude, but given the circumstances, she was relieved. The girl paid Natalie no attention as she handed over the money and exited the store.

Natalie was confident that the girl wouldn't remember much about her. She was able to get in and out without too much attention being drawn to her. Now, she had to find a way to enter the forest and locate a place to camp. She figured it would be easy since the town was surrounded by trees. The forest was all around her, and she just needed to pick a direction to disappear in.

Natalie found a small alley next to one of the stores that seemed to lead into the forest. It seemed a little too convenient, but Natalie was desperate. She walked towards the alleyway cautiously. She scanned the surrounding buildings and didn't see anything alarming. As she began to walk up the alley, she heard voices coming behind her. Scared, Natalie ran up the path, and luckily, it led into the forest. Natalie stopped to hide behind a tree before looking back the way she came. Natalie wasn't sure why, but she got a horrible feeling from those voices. It might not have anything to do with her, but she had to be sure.

The voices started getting closer again. Natalie couldn't make out what they were saying, but they were walking into the forest from the alley. Like clockwork, two figures came into the clearing just before the trees thickened, and they stopped. They just seemed to be talking, both of them men.

They didn't seem to be the type to go to the gym. Not like her hot vagrant from Klamath Falls. These men were nothing compared to him. Really, no man paled in comparison to him, not even Carter.

Wait, what was Natalie thinking? She needed to focus her attention on hiding herself and not on comparing the different men in her life. Not that the broody mystery man from Klamath Falls counted as being in her life, nor did these men. The only man in her life was Carter. He was the only one who mattered, and Natalie needed to remember that.

Focusing back on the men, she noted that one was tall and lanky while the other was short and stout. The taller one was cowering as the shorter one seemed to scold him for something Natalie couldn't know. She still couldn't hear what they were saying since she was far enough away to see them. Whatever it was, they didn't seem to know about Natalie's presence. They weren't looking for her.

Natalie kept her body tucked behind the tree until they finished their conversation. She listened as she heard the footsteps growing fainter as they walked away, waiting for them to be truly gone before deciding on how to continue. Chalking up her worried feelings to paranoia and fear of being found, Natalie quietly walked deeper into the forest. Casting out her thoughts about those two guys, she focused her energy on finding a good place to set up camp. She didn't have to reach her destination tonight, but she wanted to get deep enough that she didn't have to worry about anyone finding her.

Natalie walked through the forest for the entire day. She is relieved when she finally finds a place to stop for the day. Her legs and feet were screaming at her as she allowed herself to collapse to the ground. Natalie only stopped a few times to drink water and eat a snack. Otherwise, she wandered deeper into the forest, not allowing her exhaustion to get the better.

The trees were a cover from the sky and the sun. While Natalie could tell the sun was still up, it was getting darker in the forest. She assumed it was nearly sunset, but there was no natural way for her to tell. She found a spot in the woods that gave her excellent tree coverage. She also was happy to get as much comfort as the forest floor was willing to offer. It was a spot that resembled a hut created by trees. Natalie was always amazed at nature and the Creator who sculpted it.

Natalie set up her camp, laying down one of her jackets as her bed. She didn't have a blanket or a tent, so she would have to make do. Maybe once she felt safer, she would return to town and look for a blanket. Until then, Natalie would have to live with what she has. She wasn't sure how long she would be in the forest, but she knew it couldn't be for too long. She needed to get closer to the black site and continue her digging. She needed to find a place with a library or where she could access the internet. She couldn't just connect her laptop because she would be found. She needed a safe way to connect to the CIA servers without it being traceable to her. If she could stay in the forest and then pop into town occasionally to do her work on a public computer, that would be great.

Deciding it was best to devise a plan in the morning, Natalie lay down on the forest floor and fell asleep to the sound of cricket and leaves rustling in the breeze.

# Chapter 9

The forest was kind to Natalie as she wandered through the trees for the next few days. As she explored the woods, Natalie looked for a water source. She needed a solid plan to obtain more files and couldn't risk being found in town before then. Leaving the comfortable area she had found on her first night, Natalie delved deeper and deeper into the forest. Her confidence in herself was wearing thin with each hour that passed, having yet to find even a trickle of water.

Natalie appreciated the coverage that the trees gave her. She didn't have to worry about sunburns, and the air around her was kept cool. It was still hot, but it was manageable. She was able to walk long distances without dying of heat exhaustion.

When she wasn't looking for a way to hydrate herself, she was eating through her continuously thinning food supplies. She managed to eat all the food that provided any amount of sustenance. Rationing food was never something Natalie was good at. Her hips and thighs were proof of that, though her thick thighs were a part of her body that she loved. Even if it meant she had to sport a little belly pooch, Natalie ate any and everything.

Unfortunately for Natalie, her love for food was not good, given her current dilemma. She needed to be smart about it and ration. While she was an avid hiker, she knew very little about hunting and finding food for herself, so that was not a likely option. Her lack of hydration and sustenance made it impossible for her to avoid town for much longer. Natalie decided to spend one more day looking for the resources before cutting her losses and heading back into town.

She managed to venture deep into the forest, her sense of direction lost in the thick trees. She tried her best to keep track of where she was, but she was unfamiliar with wandering off the trail and was lost almost immediately. Part of her determination to find the necessities in the forest was because she wasn't sure she would even be able to find her way out.

Natalie was in the middle of a lunch break, eating an apple she bought from the store. Apples weren't her favorite, but all of her grapes were gone. Natalie was mid-bite when she heard leaves crunching in the distance. Wondering if it was merely paranoia and she was simply hearing the crunching of the apple, she waited to see if the sound would continue. Surely enough, the noise continued, but it was far away. Quietly, Natalie gathered her things, packing the food in her backpack so she could take off in the opposite direction of the rustling. She hadn't seen any bears since being in the forest, but she wouldn't be surprised if they were out and about.

Quickly and silently, Natalie opened her backpack and pulled out her gun before slinging it back over her shoulders. She walked as fast as she could in the opposite direction of the sound. Every few feet, Natalie stopped and listened. She wanted to ensure she was going away from whatever was out there.

As Natalie paused, she heard the rustling grow faint, as if whatever was making that noise was distancing itself from her. Relief filled Natalie, and she took a breath and began walking away. It was with that single step that a branch snapped under her foot.

Natalie froze as her ears listened intently. The footsteps of whatever was out there stopped, too. It felt like an eternity passed as Natalie stood there. Her heart raced in her chest, and a sweat broke out on her forehead. Natalie hoped that whatever it was didn't hear the snap, but that wasn't likely.

Almost as quick as the snapping of the twig, Natalie heard the footsteps resume. This time, they moved in her direction, and they moved fast. She swore there were two pairs of feet, but there was no way to be sure. She didn't bother being quiet this time before breaking into a run. Based on the speed of the footsteps, Natalie knew there was no way she would outrun whatever was chasing her. She would inevitably be caught, but Natalie refused to stop, willing to fight.

Coming to a halt after running what felt like miles but couldn't have been more than fifty yards, she brought her gun up, ready to open fire if needed. She quickly tucked herself behind a tree, facing away from the direction in which she ran so she was out of sight. Natalie became silent and did her best to make herself small.

Running away from a bear is never a bright idea. It is

best to face the bear and make yourself as big as possible. Spread your arms wide and make loud, growling noises, hoping the bear will leave you alone. Wait… maybe that was how to fight off a cougar. Natalie couldn't remember as she heard the footsteps behind the tree she used as a shield. She pressed her back against the tree, looking up to the sky to find her salvation, and prayed to survive whatever encounter this would be.

Afraid to look, Natalie just stood at the tree, pressed as close to it as possible. She held her breath, fearful that her breathing would alert the predator of her presence. She shut her eyes and listened intently for any sign that it had found her.

There was no breathing or grunts that one would typically expect from a bear. Its steps didn't sound heavy like a bear, either. That brought some relief to Natalie. This was potentially an animal she could fight off. Of Course, there were other animals just as lethal as bears with light footsteps, so Natalie's relief didn't last long.

She finally made out what sounded like two pairs of footsteps. Not animal, but human footsteps. The people affirmed her thoughts as their voices broke through the deafening silence.

"Hello?" Asked one of the voices in a taunting tone. "We know you're here. Why don't you come out, and we can properly introduce ourselves."

Natalie heard the evil that laced his tone. Her skin prickled as she debated on what to do. She could try to run away again and be caught, or she could show herself and try to scare them off with her gun. She didn't have long to decide, so she figured self-defense was best.

Natalie made sure that her safety was off before stepping out from behind the tree. Her eyes met the eyes of the men who chased her, and her spine straightened at the realization of who was staring back at her. They were the guys who had followed her into the forest.

"Wow, he was right. She is a pretty thing to look at," said the shorter one. The taller one just nodded like a dog about to get a treat.

Natalie stood firm, refusing to show a shred of fear. She wanted to wince at the way their eyes bore into her. She didn't have to read minds to know that they were thinking vile things about her.

"Aww, missy," the taller one continued, "no need for the gun. Why don't you hand that over, and we can go somewhere nice and cozy to… talk." He reached out, motioning with his fingers for her to hand over the gun. His face wore a wicked smile, the yellow of his teeth causing Natalie's gut to wrench.

"Who are you," Natalie asked, her voice hard.

"We're just here to help you out. A nice girl like you shouldn't be wandering around the woods by herself," the taller one spoke this time.

"Who are you," Natalie repeated, her voice rising.

"We demand respect when being spoken to, girl," the shorter one said, his voice stone cold. "Now come with us nice and gently, or we'll just have to force you."

"I think she wants us to force her," the taller one countered. "She looks like the kind of girl who likes to be chased."

They both looked at Natalie with a sickening desire. It made Natalie step back from disgust. She had no idea who these men were or what their intentions were. All she knew was that she refused to be taken. She fired her gun at their feet, making them jump back in fear. They looked at her wide-eyed, but Natalie stared dagger back, her eyes narrowed.

"Kitty won't play nice," the shorter one sneered. "No problem. We don't have to play nice either."

The two men sprang forward as they approached Natalie, acting like rabid animals. Shocked by their sudden advances, Natalie fled in the opposite direction. She ran as fast as she could, hearing them follow quickly behind her. She wasn't going to be able to outrun them. She cut left before coming to a stop. She turned back towards them, her gun raised once more. As they approached, she fired off two rounds. She heard their panic yells before the world turned silent. Natalie's ears strained as she listened, hearing nothing but scurrying animals and birds flying overhead.

Natalie didn't know where they were anymore. She spun around, pointing her gun in every direction, waiting for them to come out of hiding. She wasn't prepared for the blow that struck her back as she fell on her face, her gun flying out of her hand. Natalie tried to crawl forward, but her legs were being held. She saw the world rotate as the man holding her legs spun her so she was lying on her back.

"Now, now, little lady," said the taller man, "you know you've been a bad girl. We gotta punish you now." He let out a sinister cackle as he held Natalie down with one hand. With his other hand, he worked to unfasten his belt.

Natalie bucked her hips and did all she could to get this man off her, but it was no use. He held her down with strength she had no power to fight. Tears started streaming down her face as she broke out into sobs.

"P-please," Natalie whispered. "Please don't do this."

He didn't acknowledge her cries for help as he started

yanking down her pants.

"Please!" Natalie's voice reverberated through the air, her throat straining as she screamed. "Someone help me!"

She shouted for help, knowing it was useless. She watched in horror as the man pulled down his pants and prepared to violate her in the worst way possible.

"What are you doing?" It was the shorter man. "You can't just take her here on the forest floor!"

Natalie felt relief was over her. She hadn't expected the other man to be her salvation. She hated that she was grateful for him.

"She's been bad. We punish bad girls." The taller man spoke like a child with a new toy. It was as if all intelligence exited his brain at the opportunity to take advantage of a helpless girl.

"Yes, we do, but we have to take her back to the agent. Then he'll give us our money, and we can punish her all we want."

Natalie's tears streamed down her face, paling at their revelation. They were working for Jannis. They had likely followed her into the forest that first night but lost sight of her. Now, they would take her back to that monster, and everything she had done would be for nothing.

Without warning, they lifted her. The shorter man came around and zip-tied her arms behind her back. He then pulled her pants back up for her, running his hands along the length of her legs before she was covered.  The feeling of his callused hands on her made her entire body tremble.

"Where's her gun," he asked.

"I don't know. It flew out of her hand when I tackled her."

"Forget it. We only need her anyway."

They each gripped one of her arms and began dragging her out of the forest. She refused to move her legs, making them tug her with each step. Natalie couldn't believe she had made it this far, only to be captured by two sadists. She did her best to fight their clutches but to no avail. She was being taken back. Natalie hung her head, tears trickling down her face and dripping from her nose as they led her out of the forest.

# Chapter 10

Natalie's cheeks felt stiff as streaks of tears dried down her face. Her breathing turned ragged, and her body shook as she fought to stay strong. Her anxiety was bubbling just below the surface, ready to spill over any moment. The men kept strong grips on her arms, and she was sure they would leave bruises.

Natalie wasn't sure how close they were to the tree line when they came to a sudden halt. She felt their grips tighten even more, their bodied bracing as if waiting for impact. Surprised, she lifted her gaze. Her eyes widened as she met the eyes of the cause of the disturbance. That was when she saw him. The stranger from Klamath Falls stood just ahead, his hand gripping a pistol at his side—her pistol.

"Who are you," asked the shorter man, his voice shaking with fear.

"Let her go," he said in a low rasp. That was all the beautiful stranger said before stalking toward them, each footstep promising death.

"She doesn't concern you," the shorter man said, his voice shaky. "Now, get out of our way and forget you ever saw us." The false confidence he spoke with was laughable. He had to know that there was no easy way of getting out of this.

The stranger's mouth lifted in a smirk. "I can't walk away when you have something that belongs to me."

Natalie wanted to fall to her knees at his words. She didn't know if he was talking about her, but she didn't care. She just prayed it was enough to save her.

"I don't know what you're talking about," the shorter man said, his fear more apparent than ever. "Now move aside!"

Natalie didn't have time to blink before the stranger sprang forward. He went for the taller man first, knocking him down by kicking through his legs. The taller man dropped like falling timber. The stranger then turned the gun towards the shorter man.

"Let her go," he said again, the growl of his voice rumbling through the deepest parts of Natalie.

The shorter man obeyed, dropping her arm. He stood there cowering in fear as Natalie put distance between them. The stranger fired the gun, the bullet grazing the ear of the shorter man. He fell back in surprise, screaming with pain. He touched his ear with his hand and saw the blood. He stood frantic. Deciding to preserve his life, he took off in a sprint toward the edge of the forest. The taller man followed quickly behind him, stumbling as he gained footing.

Natalie stood frozen, watching as they fled. She steadied her breathing as she looked toward the stranger who had saved her twice now.

The stranger stood with his eyes trained in the direction of where the men ran. His body itched to chase after them. He wanted to rip them to pieces for the way they treated Natalie. From the moment he found them and saw how her head hung low in defeat, his body filled with rage. He would have gone after them and killed them slowly, savoring in their screams, if Natalie wasn't standing there gawking at him. He turned slowly towards her, his eyes flashing with concern.

"Are you okay," he asked gently.

Natalie merely nodded her head. They studied each other for a long time. Natalie didn't know how to say thank you. She was in shock about what had just happened and didn't know how to move forward from here. The stranger motioned to give her her gun back. She hesitated for a moment before taking it. The men who had tried to take her left her bags on the ground. She picked them up, put her gun away, and slung them over her shoulders.

It was the man who broke the silence. "What are you doing in the forest by yourself?"

Natalie gaped at him, confused by his line of questioning. Why would he ask her that after what she had just gone through?

"I could ask you the same thing." She said, her tone harsh. "Why are you here, and how did you even find me?

He looked at her with a blank expression. "I heard the gunshots, and I followed the sound. While I was walking, I found your gun on the ground. Those men aren't very good at covering their tracks, so I was able to find you guys pretty easily."

Natalie paused at his frankness. Still, he didn't explain

what he was doing in the forest in the first place. Natalie thought about it for a second. It suddenly hit her. Maybe this man was actually homeless. He was finding a place to camp in the woods because he had nowhere else to stay. She felt the guilt of her assumptions wash over her in a wave of heat. Her cheeks burned red with her embarrassment and shame.

The man stared at her, no expression giving away his thoughts.

Stammering, Natalie said, "I-I'm sorry. I didn't mean to imply anything. I'm disgusted after what they tried to do to me."

He looked at her, a spark of amusement in his eyes. "I'm not homeless," he said, his lips pulling into a quick smile before returning to a stoic expression.

"I just like to travel. And I was just in Oregon passing through like you were, I'm assuming. I come out to these woods every summer to camp," he gestured around the forest as his gaze turned sorrowful.

"I'm sorry they attacked you. I'm glad I was able to get to you in time. They didn't touch you, did they?" His voice turned lethal.

"No," she said softly. "They tried, but... no."

His face was white with rage as he thought about what those two animals would have done had he not shown up when he did.

Natalie noticed the change in his mood and decided to change the subject.

"Well, I guess camping is better than being homeless," she said under her breath but loud enough for him to hear. "But if you're camping, why aren't you at a campground? This is the middle of a forest. I don't even think we're supposed to be here."

"I could ask you the same question. It can be dangerous to wander into a forest alone, especially with no trail or campgrounds. I'm used to it here, so I have no issue. But you don't look like you know your way around these trees."

Natalie sucked in a breath. He was right. She didn't know her way around. She tried her best to keep track of where she was walking, but she got lost almost immediately. She didn't know how deep into the forest she was.

Relenting, Natalie said, "I am a little lost, but I'm not here by accident. I was actually trying to camp on my own out here, and I didn't think it would be too hard." It was a lie, but she couldn't reveal the real reason she was out here and dying of dehydration.

Natalie licked her lips, feeling their dryness. She became increasingly aware of her appearance. Not only were her lips chapped, but her hair was a rat's nest on her head, her breath was terrible, and she'd been wearing the same clothes as the last time she saw this man. She really needed a shower.

The man assessed her. He didn't look her up and down. He didn't even seem to be judging her. He was just deep in thought as if deciding whether or not to help her learn how to camp or to take her back to town.

Natalie didn't have to wait long before the man gripped the strap of his bag that hung from his shoulder and walked in the opposite direction. He didn't say anything as Natalie stared after him, unsure what to do.

He kept walking as he shouted over his shoulder, "Well, are you coming or not?"

Natalie fumbled after him, doing her best to catch up. He wasn't walking too fast, but he had long strides. Tall people always had a way of walking annoyingly fast, which had always given Natalie a hard time when she had to keep up. If she weren't basically jogging, she would fall behind, and they would typically be none the wiser.

"Where are we going?" Natalie wasn't sure if he would give her tips on camping out in the wild or if he was taking her back to the town.

He was a man of few words, and it seemed he didn't particularly enjoy sharing details, not that Natalie was too bothered by it. She was lying to him about why she was there. If anything, she knew people were entitled to their secrets. Especially people she hadn't known for too long.

"I know of a place to get fresh water. I assume you're thirsty, given the chapped lips."

Natalie's cheeks reddened. Not just because of her appearance but because she was so inexperienced that this man could tell she hadn't found a water source. Natalie didn't like being the least knowledgeable person in the room about anything.

"Well, if I'm going to be sticking by you for a bit, do I get to know your name?" Natalie asked.

He glanced at her, a slight tilt in his lips showing for a split second before saying, "Elijah." His voice was raspy and deep as he said his name, as if it wasn't something he shared often. Natalie felt honored that he told her her name, feeling like only a few people were granted that privilege. Natalie got a sense of understanding in his tone. She couldn't share her name with people anymore. It would only take one person knowing her name for the CIA to find her. That was a change that she hadn't thought about until now. Hearing Elijah's hushed tone when he shared his name made her realize that she would need to be just as careful with her own name.

A question lingered in her mind. She knew why she had to keep her name a secret, but why did Elijah seem to want the same? They're strangers, sure. But a name shouldn't be a secret unless you have something to hide. Despite Elijah disclosing his name to her, Natalie had a weary feeling in her stomach. She didn't know this man or where he was from. For all she knew, he could be a dangerous criminal. But wasn't she one now, too?

Elijah continued to walk, feeling Natalie's conflicting thoughts in the way she looked at him. He didn't share his name with people often. He knew what a risk it was. Still, he was glad to tell her his name. It was an intimate thing to him. After saving her from those two monsters, his name was the least he could give her. He wanted to do all he could to make her feel safe.

They both found themselves in a very confusing situation. Natalie's weariness at not knowing this stranger was outweighed by one simple fact: she needed his help. She couldn't survive much longer in these woods without him. He could get her water, and since he was familiar with the surrounding area, he could tell her about any towns she could go to to continue her research.

Natalie let out a sigh. She had no choice but to trust Elijah. Besides, he had already helped her out twice now. The least she could do was be honest. Well, not completely honest, but honest enough to give him her name despite the danger it could bring her.

Ignoring the tornado of emotions swirling in her stomach at that moment, she opened her mouth and threw caution to the wind with one single word.

"Natalie."

# Chapter 11

Natalie's legs ached from how far Elijah led her into the forest. She felt a spark of apprehension shoot through her as the trees became denser around her, wondering if she were genuinely being led to a water source.

Remembering how helpful he had been to her was the only thing that kept her feet moving. Elijah had helped her back in town by helping her sneak to her motel room, no questions asked. Now, he had saved her from those two guys who were taking her, God knows where. He hadn't asked questions about that either. His help was something she wasn't soon to forget.

Natalie's feet were aching when she heard the faint sound of a waterfall. She had wanted to take a break from hiking a while ago but refused to break the silence that grew between her and Elijah after sharing their names. It was as if they had a mutual understanding of how dangerous it was and were using this long walk to a water source to assess each other.

Elijah studied Natalie from the moment he saved her. He scanned her body for any signs of harm. When he found nothing physically wrong with her, he observed how she walked beside him. He could sense her hesitance in following him. He knew he hadn't yet earned her trust despite saving her, and she was second-guessing her decision to go with him. He would let her leave if she wished. He wouldn't hold her captive as much as he couldn't stand the thought of watching her walking away.

As Natalie observed Elijah, she could feel his eyes continuously scanning her. She didn't feel the same sick feeling as when the two men looked at her, so she didn't say anything about it. Besides, she was staring, too. She found it challenging to keep her eyes off Elijah. She remembered how he towered over her when he stood behind her in the cafe and when he held her body close to his back at the motel. She thought about what it felt like to stand close to his body, feeling his muscles through his clothing as their bodies pressed against each other.

It was as if his Creator sculpted him to be a deadly weapon. His muscles accentuated his already large frame, making him appear even taller. He could kill Natalie as easily as snapping a pencil if he genuinely wanted to. He almost did just that to the two men. The fact that he hadn't resorted to such violence with her put Natalie at ease. As strange as it was, she couldn't deny the unspeakable warmth and security she felt at his brutality.

"I hear the water. Are we getting close?" Natalie asked with a raspy voice. Walking in silence for so long made the simple task of communicating more difficult than it should have been.

"Yeah, only a few more feet," he said, his tone filled with indifference.

Natalie looked at him with eyebrows raised, perplexed by his words. The water sounded close but not a few feet close. Typically, when you are close to a waterfall, all sense of hearing is lost as the crashing invades the senses. It wasn't until the trees opened up that she saw it. It looked like something out of a fantasy world. The swimming hole was large, like the cenotes in Yucatan. She recalled the beautiful underground lakes from visiting her grandma's village with her parents as a little girl. She loved her heritage and was glad for the memories as she allowed her eyes to take in the scene before her. The sparkly blue water glimmered as sun rays broke through the thick trees above. The water led into a break in the mountain that resembled a cave opening. Only it wasn't a cave. It was a waterfall. It was as if the mountain grew arms to keep the waterfall guarded from the world. The walls surrounding the waterfall answered Natalie's questions about why the waterfall's crashing was so faint. The sound was being muted by nature.

Natalie stared at the water and nearly fell to her knees at the beauty of it. Never had she seen something so beautiful, not even in the Pacific Northwest. Something like this was supposed to be impossible in the state of California. Nature is God's work of art that she was continuously amazed by.

Elijah looked at the wonder in Natalie's eyes. She watched as the beauty of the hidden oasis slammed into her, overriding any sense that told her to be reserved. He saw the way her eyes scanned the water and the formation of the mountain. The look in her eyes made her beauty multiply, and Elijah couldn't take his eyes off her. The very presence of her intoxicated him. She could bring him to his knees if she looked at him with the same admiration she used to look at nature.

Remembering she wasn't alone, Natalie found Elijah's eyes. He looked at her with such awe, his lips curved in a hint of a smile. With a blink of an eye, he looked away and started heading towards the water's shore. He had a tent set up and a fire pit that was put out. He had been here a while then, maybe as long as she had, even though Natalie didn't remember him being on the bus.

Following him to the small campsite, Natalie asked, "How long have you been here? And how did you find this place?" She scanned the water again, still not believing it was real.

"I got here about three days ago. A day after I saved you from the creepy motel guy." His voice had the same rasp that made Natalie's legs shake. "I've been in this area a few times. I found this place on my second trip here. I got lost after going too deep into the forest and just kept waking in hopes of finding people. I stumbled on this place, and it saved my life. Now I come here every time. No one ever makes it this deep into the forest without any trails to follow, so I don't think anyone else knows it's here beside me and now you." He looked at her with eyes that threatened death if she told another soul.

Natalie was impressed. She enjoyed hiking and being in nature, but wandering off the trail always gave her anxiety. This was her first time walking mindlessly through a forest, and she was almost immediately lost. Elijah, on the other hand, seemed like an expert. She was grateful for his skills in the wild. Curiosity settled into the pit of her stomach as she wondered how he had acquired the skill. Years of camping was one thing, but she couldn't forget his skill with the gun when he saved her earlier.

"Thank you for bringing me here."

"I didn't really have a choice, did I?" He asked, his voice clipped as if in annoyance.

"Well, you could have easily taken me back to town, but you brought me here instead. I don't know if you plan to kill me yet, but until I find out, I'm grateful."

"You didn't seem like you wanted to go back to town," he said kindly. "I assumed anyone insane enough to wander into a forest with no experience doing so must want to stay hidden."

He was a good guesser, apparently. Natalie didn't let him know that as she changed the subject.

"Are there parts of the water that I can't drink? Because I'm really thirsty, and I will consume the entire swimming hole unless instructed otherwise."

He let out a soft chuckle, saying, "Yeah, you can drink any part of it. The cleanest water would have to be near the waterfall, though. I also have a water filter if you're worried about it."

"Wow, you are prepared for anything," Natalie said incredulously. "I guess I won't take any chances and just use the filter."

He reached into his bag and grabbed a portable water filter. She allowed her finger to graze the back of his hand when he handed it to her. His breath caught in his throat, but he did not make eye contact with her. After realizing what she did, she snatched her hand away, muttered a quick thank you, and walked to the water.

As she filled up her water bottle, she scolded herself. She didn't know what compelled her to brush her finger across his hand. It wouldn't have meant anything if she hadn't lingered there longer than necessary. She noticed how his breath caught, making her cheeks redden almost immediately. Had she forgotten about Carter? The man who was back home taking care of her mother while she was here hiding because she was a fugitive. The man she was ready to marry at any moment when he decided to propose. She couldn't betray him like that.

Romance was the last thing that should be on her mind right now. She needed to stay focused on creating a plan. She still had no clue how close she had gotten to the black site or how she would find a way to get into the servers to obtain more files. She had a feeling Elijah might be able to help her. He knew the area and could point her toward the nearest town with local computers and internet access. Tonight, she would think of a plan to get everything she needed. She wouldn't give Elijah any ideas that something might be happening between them. There wasn't. They were strangers, and she just needed to get her head back into focus.

She finished up with her water bottle and walked back to the campsite. Elijah was moving his things out of the tent. Her things were gone.

Panic rose as Natalie asked, "What are you doing? Where's my stuff?"

Elijah didn't bother looking at her when he replied, "I put them in the tent. You can sleep in there for the night or however long you need to figure yourself out."

Natalie froze, shocked by the chivalry this man possessed. "You don't have to do that. I've been sleeping in my jacket for almost a week now. I can go for a couple more days."

"Don't worry about it. You take the tent and the air mattress. I'm not just going to let you sleep on the forest floor. I can see you're capable, but that doesn't mean I can't help you out."

Natalie stepped back. He wasn't going to stand down.

Not only that, but Natalie couldn't believe her ears. She wasn't used to people taking care of her if they weren't Carter. When he wasn't around, Natalie was on her own. It was the sad reality of her life. She learned to take care of herself from a young age. It wasn't anyone's fault, but once Carter came into her life, he made it possible for her to rely on someone else for support. He never let her do things on her own, and she loved him for it. Other than him, no one else bothered taking care of her. No one else thought that she might need a break once in a while.

Now, here was Elijah, a practical stranger who not only acknowledged her capabilities but offered her help. It was a small thing to do, but it meant the world to Natalie. Her eyes softened and threatened to tear up. When she felt most alone, there was a stranger being kind to her—this stranger she planned to use for information. Guilt began to form in Natalie's chest, and she stepped closer to the tent where Elijah stood.

As she approached him, his spine stiffened. Natalie wasn't sure, but she thought she felt a nervousness emanating from Elijah, like getting too close would cause him to shut down and close his walls. Not wanting that to happen, Natalie stopped a few feet away, looking at Elijah.

"Thank you," she said softly, "for everything. For saving me back in Klamath Falls and earlier today when the two men tried kidnapping me." She paused. "And now for helping me find water and stay hidden and for letting me sleep in the tent. You have been so nice to me and don't even know me."

He shifted on his feet. "Do I have to know you to be a decent human being?"

Ignoring his cheekiness, she continued. "If you like, we

can both sleep in the tent."

Elijah moved his arm up to scratch the back of his neck. "No, it's fine. There is only one air mattress, anyway. You take it, and I can sleep out here in my sleeping bag."

"Oh, okay... well, I'm going to turn in then. Goodnight." Natalie wanted to argue more, but she didn't want to make Elijah uncomfortable.

"Do you want to eat something before you go to bed," he asked, his voice sounding desperate for her company. He cleared his throat before continuing. "I made some food if you want some."

Natalie looked at him, feeling her stomach grumble in hunger. She was starving. She was also exhausted and wanted to sleep. Deciding it would be best to take some time to be alone, she said, "No, thank you. You've done enough for me. I just want to sleep now. Goodnight, Elijah."

He looked disappointed but nodded. "Goodnight, Natalie."

Natalie walked into the tent and zipped it up. She had difficulty calming her mind as she lay on the air mattress. Tomorrow, she had to ask Elijah about finding a town with solid internet connections. She was going to ask him to take her to town and hopefully find a library. Once she was there, she would have to get Elijah to leave her alone for a little bit so she could do her sleuthing in peace. Aside from procuring more files, her main goal was to uncover what was happening to the missing participants. These people were the ones that were taken but not used in the chemical testing. Where did they go? Are they dead? Did something else happen to them? Natalie needed to find out. Not only for her own curiosity but to help these people.

Tomorrow, Natalie would execute her plan and get Elijah to help her. One thing she was certain of was that she didn't want to manipulate him. He has treated her with so much care. Using him and lying to him is wrong. She couldn't tell him the truth, but she didn't have to be malicious. It would make her situation a little more complicated, but these were morals that Natalie couldn't sacrifice. They were too important to who she was as a person. She would find another way. Until then, Natalie slept with the sounds of the forest surrounding her.

# Chapter 12

Natalie awoke to the sound of a crackling fire and the smell of food cooking. She quickly got dressed and opened up the tent. Elijah was sitting at the fire pit, making eggs on a skillet over the fire.

Elijah looked up and gave her a slight smile before saying, "Good morning. Are you hungry?"

Natalie felt the hunger pangs as soon as the question left his mouth. "Yeah, I am, actually."

"Perfect. You can have these eggs. I have a couple more."

"Oh, if you're running low, I can find something in my bag to eat." Natalie thought of the crumbs of hot Cheetos and moldy fruit in her bag, and nausea took over at the thought of eating that. As much as she wanted to eat, she still felt distrust toward Elijah.

"I don't mind. I have to go into town anyway for more firestarter. I can pick up some food while I'm there, too."

Natalie perked up at this information, quickly saying,

"Oh, I was actually going to ask you about the town. I really need to find a library with an internet connection and computers. Would you happen to know anywhere in town or in a different town where I could find something like that?" He gave her the perfect opportunity to ask, so it felt natural to bring it up.

He stared at her for a beat before saying, "The town closest to us doesn't have much of a library. It's too small, and nobody reads anymore, so they haven't bothered with any upkeep. As for computers, there isn't a place where you can find one." A lie. He knew where she could find a library. Elijah didn't understand why she was looking for a computer, but he would withhold information for as long as she did.

Natalie deflated. "Well, is there any other town nearby that would have a library and access to the Internet?" Her voice sounded desperate. It was a detail that Elijah didn't miss.

"Why are you so desperate to go out in public," he asked suspiciously. "I thought you wanted to stay hidden. I would have taken you yesterday if I had known you wanted to go into town to find a computer." He sounded upset.

"No, I don't want to go into town. It's more that I need to. I need to find a computer to get something done. Trust me, the last thing I want to do is risk being found." She realized she said the wrong thing.

"Risk being found? What are you hiding from? What's so important that you need to *risk* going into town?"

This conversation was getting out of hand quickly. "No, I misspoke. I mean, I just don't want to be noticed by anyone. I enjoy my privacy." She said, her voice raising in pitch. The last thing she needed was for him to be asking a lot of questions, but she wasn't sure how to direct the conversation to go in her favor. "That's why I'm out here. To be alone for a bit. But I really need to find a working computer. I also don't feel comfortable telling a stranger about something private."

He flinched at her words. "Well, if you want to be alone so badly, I'll take you into town, and then you'll be on your own."

Crap. That was the last thing Natalie wanted. She needed him and his campsite and his waterfall. They offered her a way to hide from the CIA after entering their servers again. There was no way to do it inconspicuously. Now that she had already hacked them and stolen their files, they were likely waiting for her to do it again. She needed a place to hide. This was the perfect place for that. She had to turn this conversation around quickly.

"Listen to me," she started, "You aren't understanding me. I am out here to be alone, yes. But I like it here. And I enjoy your company, as broody as it is," she said, her sarcasm falling flat. "I'm grateful for all the help you have given me so far. Please, help me with this one thing. It's important that I find a library with Internet. I can't say why, but trust me when I say it's important."

He stood at this. "I am not going to help you unless you tell me why. What, do you run some blog or something? Do you need to contact someone? What is so important that you need Internet access?" He was raising his voice now.

Natalie didn't understand why he was so against her needing the internet. Why was he being so defensive? Most importantly, why would her contacting someone be such a bad thing? Not that she needs to, of course. Is he scared she's going to tell people about him? Whatever it was, it was starting to frustrate Natalie, but she couldn't back down.

"No, I don't run a blog, and I'm not trying to contact anyone. I am… working on a research project." It wasn't entirely a lie. "I just need to do some quick research, and then I'll come back here. Not that I owe you an explanation or anything. Besides, you shouldn't even have any opinions. It's not your business."

"It's my business enough for you to ask me for help. But fine. I can help you find a library as long as I get to see what you're researching."

"What? No way. It's not any of your business. What does it matter to you anyway?"

"It matters to me because this place is my sanctuary. I don't need you writing a blog post about it. About me." He said that last part in a hushed tone. "So if I'm going to help you, I'm going to make sure you're doing what you say you're doing."

Now Natalie was more confused. He wasn't homeless, he just liked camping. If he was camping, why did he want to stay hidden? He didn't want people to know where he was. This revelation left Natalie feeling troubled. It reminded her of the reality that she didn't know who Elijah was. He was kind towards her, but what if that was just a facade? Natalie decided she would make it her business to find out whatever he was trying to hide. She couldn't be camping next to someone she didn't know or trust.

"I told you, I'm not trying to contact anybody. My research is private. You can come with me to the library, but I can't let you see what I'm researching."

Elijah paused to think. He was determined to uncover

what Natlaie was hiding. Natalie was tense about the whole situation now. What if he knew something? No, that was impossible. He saw the agents in Klamath Falls. He didn't seem to recognize them or question their presence. Of course, he assumed Natalie was hiding from the concierge. Regardless, his desperation to stay hidden couldn't be his only reservations about helping her find a library. Natalie had a feeling there was more to it.

"Fine. I'll help you, and I won't peek at your research under one condition. I get to see what you type in the search bar. I won't look at the trails you follow or anything else. But I get to see the realm of possibilities of what the research could be about. Deal?"

Natalie's brow furrowed in confusion, but she said, "Yeah, okay, sure. But what does that even matter to you?"

"Just say thank you and get over it." His response was clipped.

Natalie just nodded her head, her mouth hanging open slightly. Elijah walked away towards the water, leaving Natalie there with the burnt eggs that they had both forgotten about amidst their arguing.

Elijah's mind was spinning. Why was she so determined to do research, and why was she being so secretive about it? Elijah began to feel like he made a mistake in bringing her here. He made a mistake in telling her who he was. She was going to expose him. He didn't know who she was, only that she was the most beautiful thing he had ever seen. He cursed at himself for falling for her eyes. She was going to be the end of him. Everything he had worked for up until this point was all for nothing. He wasn't sure how he would prevent her from turning him in, but he had to think of something.

As Elijah walked, he plotted his next move.

***

Natalie hid in the tent after the argument with Elijah. It bothered her that he was so persistent in knowing about her research. She understood his fear that she would share the location of the swimming hole and, by extension, where he was. The little oasis in the middle of the forest was his secret paradise. If the world learned about it, they would destroy it, as people do with anything beautiful. Natalie also understood his desire for privacy because she wanted the same thing. The last thing she wanted was for her location to be known.

Still, as much as he was entitled to his privacy, it gnawed on Natalie's brain. She should understand more than anyone the need to remain under the radar. Still, it felt off that Elijah had that desire, making Natalie feel more and more suspicious about him. She would figure out his motivations eventually, but for now, she had to focus on getting back into the servers.

Feeling suddenly aware of the grime on her skin, Natalie urged herself to find a way to shower. When she arrived here the night before, she wanted to clean the dirt and sweat off her body, but she wasn't sure where the safest place was to bathe out of Elijah's eyesight. She decided it would be best to shower close to the waterfall, hidden behind the walls of the mountain.

Natalie exited the tent and took a quick scan to find Elijah. He wasn't there. She hadn't heard him walk off but hadn't seen him since he stormed off after their argument. He probably went to town to get more food, like he said he was. Cursing herself for missing the opportunity to find Internet, Natalie started towards the water. Walking straight into it, she waded her way towards the waterfall. The water went up to her chest, so she didn't have to swim.

Natalie didn't bring a change of clothes with her since there was nowhere to put them next to the waterfall. She would just wash herself in her clothes and then change out of them back inside the tent.

As she arrived at the waterfall, the sound of the crashing water began to echo off the mountain walls, which formed something of a cave. Natalie wouldn't be able to hear herself if she tried to talk. Allowing the sound of the falls to invade her senses, Natalie bathed herself in peace.

Peace. It was funny that was how she described her feelings in that moment. Nothing about her current life was peaceful. She was far from her mom, not knowing when she would see her next. She was far away from Carter, the man she had such a bright future with before these experiments threw her plans off the rails.

Carter. She missed him so much. She thought of him often and wondered how he was handling her being gone. Natalie was beginning to forget what it was like not to have to worry about anything because Carter would take care of it. Of course, now she had Elijah, who was taking care of her, but in a different way. He let her sleep in his tent and helped her evade government agents.

Elijah would be the perfect companion right now if it weren't for his unabating need to question her about her research. He wanted to look over her shoulder as she typed out her research topic. It seemed paranoid on his part to feel the need to do that. But if Natalie had been honest with herself, she would probably have behaved similarly if the roles were reversed. The last thing she wants is to be discovered. For whatever reason, Elijah shared the same reservations. The least she can offer him is a hint of what she's researching.

Elijah has been nothing but friendly and kind to her up until their conversation earlier. He has gone out of his way to help her and has even brought her to his personal oasis so she could get water without having to go to town and risk being seen. Everything about Elijah says that he's a gentleman who is willing to risk his own comfort to help others. It's an attractive quality in a man.

Natalie began thinking about how Elijah's mouth threatened to smile whenever she said anything witty. She thought about how he looked at her when he first brought her into the little oasis, how his blue eyes sparkled like the ocean on a warm summer's day when he talked about this swimming hole. She felt like she could understand him at his core and related to his desire to remain guarded and hidden from the world.

Even after their argument earlier, she couldn't deny the pull she felt that drew her towards him. She thought about his muscular body and how it didn't make sense that someone who camped so much was so sculpted. She understood that anyone who spent most of their time outdoors would have higher levels of athleticism than anyone else, but he was built. His muscles were huge, and they made Natalie feel like a bug he could easily squash. It was like he spent hours lifting weights and training, but that didn't make sense either. It just added to the mysteriousness that radiated off of him, like a second skin.

Carter was built, but even he seemed small in comparison to Elijah.

What was she thinking? Carter was the love of her life. What was she hoping to gain in comparing him to Elijah?

No matter Elijah's superior sculpted body, Carter was the one who had always been there for her. Carter was the one who helped her rebuild her life after her dad died. Carter has been there for everything. Elijah was a stranger she just met.

Natalie couldn't believe she had let her mind wander to such a forbidden area. Thinking about Elijah like that wasn't helpful at all, especially since he wasn't as perfect as her mind was trying to convince her he was.

Wanting to feel peace again, Natalie pushed the thoughts of Elijah out of her mind. She allowed the sounds of the waterfall to overtake her senses once again and finished her shower.  As she made her way out of the cave's opening, she spotted Elijah on shore stripping off his clothes. He got down to his underwear before stepping into the swimming hole. Natalie felt her face redden as she watched him wade into the water. It wasn't until he spotted her that Natalie's spine straightened, and she decided to start moving again. They met halfway, the waterfall now only partially muting the sounds around them.

"Hey, I was just cleaning myself up," Natalie said shyly. Her voice sounded strange after the roar of the waterfall filled her ears.

She found it hard to make eye contact with him after all her thoughts about him under the waterfall. It felt like she was invading his privacy if she looked at how his eyes sparkled. She wanted to ignore how good his body looked when wet, his muscles looking more pronounced as they flexed with every subtle movement he made. Natalie felt guilty for where her mind kept going. Carter was like a distant memory now that she'd seen what Elijah looked wet and half naked.

"I was just about to do the same thing. I left some food by the fire if you're hungry." His voice was rough, and his words clipped, but he didn't seem upset. She knew then that he built his walls back up. He didn't trust her, or at least he was deciding if trusting her was a good idea. Natalie understood, not trusting him entirely either. Still, she couldn't ignore the sting.

"I'm sorry about earlier. I don't want you to think I have any malicious intent. It's just that my research is really private, and I could get in trouble if anyone sees it." Natalie didn't know why she brought this up again while they were both wet in the swimming hole. It wasn't the best place to talk about this, but that made her want to do it more. She would do all she could to be able to look at him like this a little longer, even if it meant starting up another argument.

"I don't really care about you getting in trouble," he said, emotion absent from his face. "I'm gonna see what you're researching, or you're not getting to a library."

"What does it matter to you?" Natalie's voice was beginning to rise. "I just want to know why you care so much about my research. It doesn't make sense why you're this adamant on seeing what I'm doing."

"Because I need to make sure to protect myself. I don't know you. You're a stranger. I'm helping you, but that doesn't mean you won't screw me over." He shifted on his feet, his frustration evident.

"How would I screw you over," she asked, throwing her arms up in frustration. "You're right. We're strangers. We know nothing about each other. I appreciate that you're helping me, but please tell me, in what ways would I screw you over?"

His hands tightened into fists as he stepped forward. "I

can't have you compromise my location," he yelled.

He moved one hand to his hip while the other pointed at her. "I knew I should have stayed away from you, but I took pity on you because you clearly don't know what you're doing on your own."

The words stung, but Natalie couldn't get what he said first out of her mind. *I can't have you compromise my location.* He said it like he used that kind of vocabulary often, like he was trained to speak like that. Weariness began to build in Natalie's stomach. She started bringing everything into question. His helpfulness. His inviting demeanor. What if it was all a ploy to find her? To expose her.

Natalie stopped herself. Her mind was spiraling with trust issues. She had just gotten done thinking about how she understood him, how she recognized his distrust and understood why he would be weary of her. She stared at him, her mind coming to a decision that she might come to regret.

Elijah must have read Natalie's sudden change in her face because he said softly, "All I mean is that I don't want people to know where I am or how to find this place. I enjoy my privacy, and the last thing I need is people coming here and ruining it."

Natalie studied him for a bit before replying, "I understand that. I value my privacy, too. You can't expect me to tell you every detail of my life when you aren't willing to do the same."

Elijah stood there, just staring at her.

Natalie continued, " You are a complete stranger. A helpful stranger, but still a stranger. My research is very sensitive, and I can't divulge all the details simply because you want to know."

Elijah straightened. Natalie was stubborn. She wouldn't be honest with him, no matter how hard he tried. Sighing, he said, "Fine. Pack your things. I'm taking you back to town."

Natalie felt her entire body fill with panic. She might have just found the one person on this earth more stubborn than she was. He turned to walk away.

"Wait," Natalie said, her voice panicked. "Please, don't take me back. I can't risk being seen."

Elijah turned back towards her, his eyebrows furrowed. "Tell me why." It was a demand. Natalie had no choice. She needed to be honest if she wanted to remain under his protection.

The wariness still there, Natalie said, "I'm researching the CIA." She didn't wait to see his reaction as she continued. "I uncovered some experiments that a unit within the agency has been performing. They're disgusting and inhumane experiments that I can't even begin to explain. I need to find more information on them so I can expose the agents involved. That's why I need to find a computer."

Elijah looked at her, the color drained from his face. He didn't know what to expect, but this was not it.

Natalie felt like she made a mistake. "You think I'm crazy. That, or you want to turn me in. Either way, just forget about it. I'll be out of here in the morning." Natalie moved to turn away from him, feeling nauseous. She told him everything and risked everything. She didn't know what compelled her, but she felt in her core that she could trust him. Clearly, her gut was wrong.

"No, wait!" Now, he was the one sounding panicked. He gripped Natalie's wrist as she made her way out to shore. "Please don't go. I want to help you." His voice was soft now. Before, Natalie thought his helpfulness was suspicious, but now it only confused her.

"What," she asked slowly.

"I don't think you're crazy. I want to help you."

He could see it in her eyes that she was becoming increasingly weary. He let go of her wrist, and before she could utter a response, he said, "I'll take you to find a library tomorrow. Please don't forget to eat." As if what just happened was no big deal, he turned and waded toward the waterfall without another word.

Natalie watched him go for a minute, confusion filling every cell in her body. Slowly. She made her way out of the water and didn't bother eating the food he had set out before zipping up the tent.

# Chapter 13

Natalie tossed and turned all night in anticipation of leaving the forest. She didn't know when she ended up falling asleep, but once she did, she fell into a deep sleep where she dreamed of her mom and Carter. She woke up missing them and was on the verge of tears.

Natalie sat up, startled by the noise. Her dream quickly left her memories as she rubbed her eyes and remembered where she was. She put her pants on and then peeked outside of the tent through a section she had unzipped.

Elijah was awake. He was cooking food over a fire. The air smelled of fresh dew as light from the morning sun attempted to peek through the trees. Natalie could tell it was still early in the morning since the sun wasn't hot, and the forest around was dim under the shades of the trees. There wasn't enough sun to cast any shadows.

Natalie zipped the tent closed before Elijah noticed she was there. Today, he was going to take her to a library, or so he said. Natalie still wasn't sure if he was lying about the library, but she had no choice but to trust him after last night's conversation.

Taking a couple of deep breaths to avoid a panic attack, Natalie made her way out of the tent. Elijah noticed her immediately, watched her exit the tent, and close the tent flap.

They stared at each other for a beat before Elijah spoke up. "I made some breakfast before we go. I know it's early, but I figured the earlier we get going, the sooner we can be back."

Natalie nodded, the consideration he put into her plans surprising her. "Thanks, but I'm not hungry." Natalie's words were clipped. She sat down on a log close to the fire. It wasn't cold outside, but the warmth of the fire felt like a nice blanket wrapped around her. It was comforting.

Elijah noticed Natalie's tone of voice, slightly flinching at her words. "Oh, okay. I can save the food for when we get back." He spoke softly as if trying to diffuse whatever fire was burning inside Natalie.

"Where exactly are you taking me? You said there wasn't a library in town."

"Right, there isn't," Elijah started slowly, "but there is a library in a town going west. It's a decent size, plus they have computers."

"How do you know that? You originally told me that you didn't know where we could find an internet connection."

"I went out yesterday to scout the surrounding towns. That's why I was gone all day. I found a town that's about an eight-hour walk west from here.

That sounded uncomfortably close. Elijah had told her

that no one had ventured this far into the woods before, but if it were only an eight-hour walk from here, surely someone would have found this place before.

"I thought you said we were deep in the forest. Why is it so close to the town?"

"I think you're underestimating how far away an eight-hour walk is, especially with breaks in between. Anyway, that's why I was wanting to leave early. I would have laid out the game plan to you last night, but you locked yourself in the tent."

"I was tired," Natalie said quickly. "We should get going then if this is going to be an all-day excursion."

"My thoughts exactly."

They broke off to make sure all of their things were gathered. Natalie went back into the tent and dumped the contents of her backpack on the ground. After picking out everything she would need, she packed her bag. She made sure she grabbed her laptop, charger, flash drive, and a couple of snacks. She took her gun out of her backpack, sliding it into her belt at her back. She didn't think she would need it, but she couldn't be too safe.

Stepping back into the opening, Elijah was standing there waiting. He was wearing a pair of black cargo shorts with a tank top. The shirt clung to his body as if it were too small to contain the muscles underneath. The tank top accentuated his shoulders and back as it framed his body. Natalie caught herself staring and quickly looked away, hoping her eyes would find anything else to land on. She was unsuccessful as she ended up meeting Elijah's gaze. He had a smug smirk on his face that vanished almost immediately.

"You ready to head out?" He asked, amusement laced in his voice.

"Uh… yeah, let's go," she said, cheeks pink.

As they left the small touch of paradise that Natalie had come to appreciate so much, unease flooded Natalie's senses. She was leaving the safety of this swimming hole with a stranger. This stranger was more than capable of turning her in. There was no way of him knowing who she was, but there was still a slim chance. Natalie tended to think of the worst-case scenario. Some might have called it paranoid, but she called it being prepared. Prepare yourself for the worst, and you won't be disappointed. They were words to live by, especially right now. The last thing Natalie wanted to do was trust Elijah and have him screw her over. That disappointment would be something that she wouldn't recover from.

As they walked through the forest, Natalie took the time to admire nature. The trees were tall around her, the tops of the trees seemingly miles up. There were rays of sun that peeked through, lighting their way as they trampled through the forest. Natalie heard birds twittering as they flew by, singing joyfully. It starkly contrasted how Natalie felt, but it was a beautiful sound nonetheless.

Elijah kept pace ahead, glancing back at Natalie every so often to make sure she was able to keep up. He knew he had long strides and did his best to keep a slow pace. Every time he glanced back at her, he noticed how she admired the forest around her. She looked at the birds and the trees with such awe it made him want to smile.

He knew there was no way he could fall for this girl. She was working to bring down the CIA. He had no issue with that, but she would leave him once she discovered his secrets. He would be left with a gaping hole in his chest as he would have to watch her walk away. Still, he couldn't help but imagine what it would be like to hold her face in his hands. To pull her into a deep kiss and let his hands explore her body. He wanted to feel every inch of her and discover the points of her body that brought her the most pleasure.

Elijah knew he was crazy for her, but he continued to deny that he had already fallen for her.

They walked for twenty minutes in silence. They were going west, Natalie assumed. Her sense of direction was lost quickly after she herself was lost. She felt like she had given Elijah too much control over this situation, and it was beginning to grow her anxiety.

"Which way are we going?" Natalie broke the silence, her voice gravelly after not talking for a long time.

Elijah glanced in her direction before saying, "West." So much for having a conversation.

"How do you know? I feel so disoriented. It's like we're walking in circles."

Elijah said nothing as he revealed a compass in his left hand. Natalie snatched it from him, shock written all over her face.

"Have you had this the whole time?"

"Yes."

"Why didn't you show it to me?"

Elijah gave her a confused look before saying, "You never asked."

"I have been feeling like you're leading me to my death this whole time. It's nice to know you were at least telling the truth about which direction we were going." That was the wrong thing to say.

Elijah stopped and turned toward her, his eyes shooting her a look that threatened to bring her to her knees. His eyebrows were furrowed, and his forehead creased as he looked at her. Natalie noted how his blue eyes darkened. He looked lethal, but it wasn't fear that Natalie felt in her core. She stared back, waiting for him to say something. Natalie didn't know why, but she had the sudden urge to kiss him. His lips were tilted down in a look that made him look angry, but also hurt. She would do anything to take that look off of his face.

Before she could step forward and risk everything, he said, "It's nice to know that I was *at least telling the truth about that*. What is that supposed to mean? Is there something you need to say to me?" His voice was filled with a calm rage.

Natalie hadn't realized her words came out like that. She hadn't wanted to give him the idea that she didn't trust him, but she let her words slip.

Not wanting to back down, Natalie allowed her stubbornness to shine through. "Actually, yes, there is something I need to say to you." Natalie stepped a couple of inches closer to Elijah, anger radiating from her. "I told you everything about my research and what I'm actually doing here. I have disclosed information that could get me arrested if not killed. What have you given me in return? Nothing. For all I know, you could be working with the CIA and be taking me to turn me in."

Elijah's eyes showed skepticism as he said, "You're right. I could be taking you to turn you in. You don't really know that. I guess you're just going to have to trust me."

"Like I said, I don't trust you. You haven't given me the slightest reason to trust you. I'm probably better off finding this library on my own."

"No, you're not. You'll just get lost. And watch what you say about trust. I have given you safety, shelter, and food. Not once have I put you in danger. In fact, I've saved you more than once now. If those aren't reasons to trust, then I don't know what you want from me," he finished, his tone lethal. He didn't like that Natalie didn't trust him.

She noticed his displeasure and decided to use it to her advantage. "Just because you went out of your way to be nice doesn't mean you don't have malicious intent. You could be keeping me alive just to end up killing me for your own sick pleasure, for all I know."

"You're still on that? I already told you that-" Natalie cut him off.

"-that you don't trust me. Isn't that rich coming from someone who is so bothered that I don't trust him?" Natalie felt a sense of accomplishment. "Trust goes both ways, Eli. How do you expect me to trust you when you can't trust me."

Elijah went silent for a beat, thinking about whether he was actually going to fall for this and give her what she wanted. She wanted her privacy, just like he wanted his. It was the least he could do to grant that to her. And something about how she called him *Eli* seemed to appeal to his better nature. He also had to admit that she was right. She told him everything, and he had given up no information about himself.

Elijah had his hands on his hips as he looked up toward the sky, leaning on his left leg. He finally let out a sigh and said, "Fine. I'll leave you alone to do your sleuthing. I'll keep watch outside of the library and let you know if we need to get out." His voice was calm. Any anger that was there before was now gone, replaced by understanding.

Natalie felt victorious. "Deal." She paused for a second

before softly adding, "Thank you."

"Let's keep walking. We've wasted time standing here arguing." His voice was back to the stony indifference.

Natalie hated when he would close up on her after revealing more than one emotion to her. He enjoyed staying closed off, which was fine. Natalie didn't need to be open and honest with this man. But she couldn't explain the hurt she felt when he would shut her out after letting some emotion show. It shouldn't bother her, but it did. Even though she distrusted him, she wanted to be closer to him. She wanted them to have a deeper relationship. It confused her, and she tried her hardest to deny it.

A part of Natalie wanted him to open up to her. She couldn't do anything but understand why he was closed off because she was, too. That same part of her that wanted to know everything about him wanted to share everything with him. Maybe it was because she hadn't gotten to be honest with anyone in a while. She craved the closeness that she used to have with her mom and with Carter. The loneliness of being a fugitive was drawing her to Elijah more and more every day. The more she fought it, the more it was on her mind.

Natalie followed Elijah through the forest, her satisfaction from winning their argument no longer there. She was glad she would be able to hack the CIA without someone looking over her shoulders. That part was always the end goal. What she didn't like was that Elijah wouldn't even look in her direction. They weren't speaking, and the silence was killing her.

Natalie craved a conversation but remained silent and took in the beauty of nature around her as they walked through the forest.

# Chapter 14

They walked for six and a half hours, stopping every so often to rest and to use the bathroom. They didn't speak much unless it was Natalie asking how much longer they had to walk or Elijah letting her know of a change in direction. Mostly, they traveled west, taking random turns to cut across bodies of water or avoid being out in clearings.

The trip was going smoothly, and Natalie's earlier feelings of uneasiness almost wholly disappeared. There were moments when she wanted to strike up conversations, but she was scared they would break out into another fight. She seemed only to be able to talk about things that would lead to an argument, which was unfortunate because he was her only option for a companion right now. She was also confused about her feelings and unsure how to navigate them.

Walking for so long in silence was awkward, the tension between them as thick as honey. Their anger towards each other, along with something else, is what fueled the tension. Natalie couldn't put her finger on it, but she felt an unspoken tug every time she looked at him. She knew he was feeling the same thing. She could see it in his eyes whenever he dared glance in her direction. Despite their hostility, there was an unexplainable attraction. Natalie didn't want to acknowledge it. She tried to distract herself from these feelings by admiring nature and thinking of a game plan once she got her hands on a computer.

It wasn't as simple as opening Google and searching "CIA illegal experimentation." That wasn't how hacking worked. She had to find a way to download programs on the library computers that would give her access to the CIA databases. It wouldn't be easy if the computers were as old as Natalie pictured. It would probably take a lot of time to get them to start up and to get into their software. After breaking into the database, she wouldn't have much time to extract the information before her location was discovered. Natalie needed to be in and out as fast as she could, not knowing how quickly they could get to her once they found her.

Natalie began to worry about how much of an asset Elijah was going to be for this. He was aware of the urgency she needed for this to be a success. It was common sense that hacking into a government agency was highly illegal, and they could get in heaps of trouble if caught. Natalie mostly feared that he would slow her down, panicking at any sign of danger. He didn't seem like the kind of person to react badly, but she couldn't be too sure.

Endless possibilities were circling Natalie's mind when Elijah said, "We're about ten minutes away. Do you need to rest before we get there?"

Natalie jumped at his voice. She was deep in her thoughts and forgot he was even there for a second.

"Sorry," he said quietly, " I didn't mean to scare you."

"No, you didn't scare me," she started, "I was just spaced out. But no, we can keep walking. I just want to be in and out." Her voice had a shred of urgency laced into it, and Elijah noticed.

"Why do you suddenly seem anxious? You've been waiting to do this for days."

Natalie was taken aback by how accurately he could guess her emotions. Not even Carter was able to do that. He only knew when she was having an anxiety attack when she was in the middle of displaying symptoms.

Brushing off the feeling of being seen, she said, "I'm not anxious!" A lie. She was in a constant state of pushing down her anxiety to the depths of her core until she couldn't feel it anymore. "I just don't want to draw attention to myself. In small towns, people tend to recognize outsiders."

"I know what you mean. But there's no rush here. Everyone seemed to mind their business when I came by yesterday. They didn't seem interested in knowing strangers."

"Well, that's a good thing then." The tension Natalie felt in her shoulders loosened a little. "What are you planning on doing while I'm doing my ... research?"

Elijah's brow lifted. "So you can have your privacy, but I can't have mine?"

"No! I was just-" Natalie stopped. Elijah had an amused look on his face. He was messing with her. "Ha-ha, very funny. No, I was just curious where I could find you when I'm done."

"I'll just be hanging outside of the library, keeping watch."

"Oh, okay." Natalie felt bad. He would just wait on her while she was in the library. Of course, she was the one who wanted to come here so badly. He was bringing her here out of the kindness of his heart. Maybe she judged his intentions too harshly.

"Well, I'll try to be quick so you're not waiting for me for too long," she added, guilt ever apparent in her voice.

Elijah grinned at her and said, "Don't worry, Natty. If I get lonely, I'll just come and find you."

Natalie felt the blood rush to her cheeks. No one ever called her Natty. Not after her dad died. That was his name for her. She wanted to speak up and tell him never to call her that again, but something about how he said it brought her a sense of calm. Not to mention, his voice itself was comforting. And his words. *I'll just come and find you.* It was like a secret promise that made Natalie's stomach do flips. She knew he just meant it at that moment, but Natalie felt like no matter where she was in the world after today, he would always find her. She wasn't going to escape him. She didn't want to escape him.

Natalie gave Elijah a soft smile, but she didn't dare speak. Her voice would come out in a high pitch, and she would give her feelings away. She couldn't let him know how he made her feel. Not with Carter waiting for her back home. Especially not with the illegalities of what she was about to do.

They went the rest of the way in silence, reality coming into view in the form of the town. She was about to hack into the CIA, and there was a chance she wouldn't walk away this time. She choked down her anxiety, not wanting it to hinder their mission and not wanting it to show in front of Elijah.

***

As they walked through town, Natalie scanned the buildings and streets. There were quite a bit of people out, and no one noticed when they came out of the forest. The buildings were their original brick, and it seemed like this town had been here for a while. Given the amount of people here, it was a touristy town where new faces were in a constant rotation. That gave Natalie a good feeling about being here. Even if anyone noticed her, the likelihood of them remembering was unlikely.

Elijah led the way to the library like he was a town resident. Natalie knew he was accustomed to this area, but it still shocked her how he knew his way around pretty well. Natalie didn't bother mentioning it as she followed him. Her surprise didn't last long, given his sense of direction in the woods. He clearly had an impeccable memory when it came to directions.

Natalie loved the town. It was such a cute place, and it looked like it belonged to a different time. Natalie would love to add this to a list of places to visit with Carter. The thought sent a shot of pain through her heart. Any chance she would have to live an everyday life with Carter was gone. It hurt that such a small thought brought her world crashing down again. Any high she was on as she walked left her with every step she took as she kept walking, knowing she would always be alone now. She wouldn't allow herself to think about normalcy as long as she was running from the CIA. Natalie trailed Elijah through town, not allowing her emotions to take over. He came to a sudden stop, and Natalie crashed into his back.

"Hey!" Natalie shouted. "Why did you-" she stopped as

she looked up and saw past Elijah. There was a large building that was several stories high and a block wide that said *Public Library* above the double doors. It was huge. And from what Natalie could see through the windows, it was up to date and in constant use by those who came to town. The tourists kept this library up and running, allowing it to keep up with modern technology. Natalie's hope rose as she realized she would be able to do her job more efficiently than she initially believed.

Her relief must have shown on her face because Elijah said, "Wow, I don't think I've seen anyone so excited to see a library before."

Her eyes looked to him, "You must not surround yourself with the best people then." Natalie couldn't contain her smile.

"I guess I don't, but I'm glad I'm starting too." His face softened as he spoke, studying the smile on her face.

Natalie looked back at the building, her cheeks turning a deeper shade of pink. Elijah was right; she was excited. But not for the reason he suggested. She was eager to get her hands on the computers and get to work. She wasn't going to have to make do with a dinosaur. She would be able to handle updated computers and work two times as fast as she initially thought. Natalie was excited to wreak havoc on the CIA database and steal all their files on the experiments. She was going to expose them, and the technology in that library would help her do it.

"Okay," she said, finally looking back at Elijah, "I'm going to go in and get to work. Since the computers look more up-to-date than I originally thought, I should be in and out quickly. I'll need two hours tops, and then we can get out of here." She felt her face heating as she spoke to him.

Elijah nodded his head as he said, "Okay, sounds good. I'll just be sitting out here if you need me. Hope you find what you need, cheeks." His voice was drenched with sarcasm.

"Excuse me," Natalie asked, a shy smile on her face.

"Your cheeks turn red when you're nervous. I also like how big they are." He said, a playful smirk on his face.

Natalie rolled her eyes, but couldn't help but smile. "Whatever Elijah. I'll be quick, I promise."

Elijah waved her off, and Natalie turned towards the building. She opened the double doors and was hit with the air conditioning from inside. It felt amazing on her sweaty skin. Natalie didn't realize how hot it was outside until that moment and felt terrible that Elijah was sitting out in it. He could come in and just in a different area than her.

Allowing guilt to guide her emotions, Natalie peeked her head out of the library and scanned the street for Elijah. He was sitting in what little shade there was beside the building.

"Eli!" Natalie called. "Why don't you come in? It feels great in here."

Elijah stood and stepped towards her. "I thought I was supposed to stay out of your way and keep watch."

"Well, I figured letting you be in the library couldn't hurt. Plus, I feel guilty letting you be out in the heat when a perfectly air-conditioned library is right here." She stood to the side and motioned for Elijah to walk in.

The moment he stepped inside, he let out a heavy sigh. "This feels amazing. Thanks for not letting me suffer out there."

Natalie chuckled, "You're welcome. Besides, I can still loathe your presence without leaving you to die from heat exhaustion."

Elijah allowed a small smile to spread across his lips. "Okay, well, I'll just be over at the Cafe."

"Okay," Natalie said, "I shouldn't take too long."

"Alright. See you."

Natalie watched Elijah briefly walk towards the cafe area before turning towards the computers. There were about five rows of twenty computers. Natalie picked one that was farthest to the entrance, which still gave her a good view of anyone coming in and out.

She sat down in the office chair, powered on the computer, and got to work.

# Chapter 15

Natalie only had a short period of time to hack into the CIA black site servers, locate the correct database, find the information, and get out of town before her location was compromised. She couldn't waste any time reading over each document. She would have to transfer them to her laptop and flash drive and go through them later.

As soon as Natalie sat at the computer, she took out her laptop and plugged a flash drive into the library computer. Once her laptop connected to the internet, she downloaded her software onto the computer. She could extract it from the computer when she was done to remove any evidence that she was even on it. The last thing Natalie wanted to do was leave a trace. Even the agents finding the exact computer she was on could lead to her.

The first thing Natalie did was head over to Google Earth and locate the black site. She froze for a moment, stunned at how close she had come to it. She would be able to connect directly to its network and enter its servers that route. Hacking into the CIA was not an easy job. It's actually impossible. Or at least, it's supposed to be. Doing it from Portland had been tricky since she had no direct connection to the servers. Traveling to California was the best decision she could have made.

Natalie used to joke about hacking the CIA all the time in her coding classes. It was only supposed to be a joke. On the night Carter told her about the conspiracy theory of the experiments, Natalie got curious. She tried for hours to break into their servers, but couldn't figure it out. She was about to give up and close her programs when the firewall began to open up. Her hacking script had broken through. Actually, she didn't break through at all. It was as if she was let in. Natalie found a back door into the CIA database. It was an opening that must have been forgotten about because the way she could slip past all of the security measures and get into their servers was too easy. Now, Natalie knew precisely where that backdoor was, and as soon as she found it, she was in.

She quickly navigated through all the departments of the CIA until she was in Jannis' unit. She located all his unit files and inserted herself into their servers and programs. There were more files than last time. They hadn't paused their experiments after finding her. They kept going. Natalie felt her rage bubbling in her core. The thought of more people suffering made her sick.

Having tagged the documents she had already stolen, she could locate any new documents and break through their encryptions more quickly than the last time. She took every file and every document that would bring these guys down. She was able to locate the original files for all the documents, including the ones she already had. Those had no redactions, and she could see everything.

Natalie came to a folder that she hadn't been able to break into last time. She decided to save this file for last since it seemed to have more complicated encryptions than the other files. She had the feeling that this folder had all the information about the people who were taken and unaccounted for in the experiments. This folder had to have the answer to what happened to them. Natalie got to work. Aware that her time was running thin, Natalie worked fast to try to break through the encrypted file.

Using the program Python, Natalie chipped away at the encryption and security measures in place to keep this information secret. She tried different hacking scripts that she knew to try and break through to the file. There was no doubt in Natalie's mind that the agents added their own encryption separate from the CIA's to ensure their information stayed buried even from their superiors. It was stubborn, but so was Natalie. She wasn't going to quit until it was her only option.

Determined, Natalie inputted code after code. Nothing was working. She couldn't be here any longer without the risk of being found. Natalie wasn't sure how much time she had, but it wasn't much. She wanted to scream and rip her hair out. This file was as impossible as getting into the CIA was supposed to be. This file had no back door. It was airtight, and she couldn't get past the walls and walls of security surrounding this single file.

"Hey, Natalie, how's the internet sleuthing coming along?" It was Elijah.

Natalie snapped her head up, and her eyes met Elijah. He looked at her like she was crazy. She must have looked crazy. Her hair was frizzy from all the times she ran her hands through it, gripping it in frustration. Her eyes must have been bloodshot from refusing to blink until she got through the file.

His eyes went from her to the screen. Natalie didn't know what to do, so she told the truth. "I can't get through this file. I have all the other ones, but this one has an impossible encryption. I need a little bit more time to get through it." She spoke as if this was completely normal.

Elijah looked at her again, concern filling his eyes. "You're going to have to leave it." A statement, not a question. "We need to go now. You're out of time. I saw dark SUVs pulling up to the library."

Natalie didn't stand. "No, I need to get into this file. This is important."

"It won't matter if you get caught." He said urgently.

Natalie looked at him, confusion written all over her face. "I'm not going to get caught. I have a few more minutes to get what I need. I need to get past this encryption."

Natalie looked at the screen and tried creating different scripts on the spot. It wasn't easy, and it was basically trial and error at this point. There was no way Natalie would hack through in just a few minutes.

"Natalie, we need to go. Now." Elijah was all but screaming at her now.

She looked up at Elijah to tell him to back off when something in her peripheral caught her attention. She looked out towards the entrance to the library and saw him. Agent Jannis. Close behind him was Agent Bennet. Natalie's stomach dropped.

Quickly, she began closing up the doors she opened in

the CIA database and extracting her codes and programs from the library computer.

"You need to hurry up!" Elijah said in an urgent whisper.

"I'm going as fast as I can," Natalie said through clenched teeth. She spent too much time here. She shouldn't have tried to get into the file today. She should have taken what she could get and returned for the other file another day. Now, she was about to be caught, and there was no one to blame but herself.

Just as the last trace of her left the public computer, Natalie disconnected her laptop from any internet connection and server, ejected her flash drive, shoved them both in her bag and stood.

Elijah looked at her like he needed to tell her something but didn't waste any time. He grabbed her arm and moved her behind the bookcases of the library. The agents had just entered the library, and a small army was walking in behind them. They b-lined for the computer lab as Elijah continued to tug her deeper into the library. Their bodies were touching as he held her close to avoid being found. Natalie didn't know what he was planning, but he moved with a sense of purpose. They hid between the shelves, Natalie unsure of how this would play out.

There was no way they were going to make it past these cops. She was done. After all she went through to stay hidden, it was over. Natalie cursed herself as she followed Elijah through the library. That was when she saw it. An emergency exit door. It wasn't being covered. A sparkle of hope ignited inside Natalie, causing her to move toward the door.

"Don't," Elijah whispered to her. He gripped her hand and pulled her into his body again. Her back was to his chest as he whispered, "We can't leave that way. Even if it doesn't look like it, they'll have all the exits covered."

His voice had a rasp that made Natalie's stomach flip. She didn't like how his voice made her feel at this moment. She was seconds away from being arrested, and this man was making her brain fuzzy when it was supposed to be on high alert.

"What do you suggest we do then?" Her voice was shaky, her desires unable to stay hidden with how her body moved into him as she spoke. She hadn't meant it to be flirtatious, but that's how it was received. She felt Elijah's body go rigid behind her.

His voice a deadly calm, he said, "What we do now has nothing to do with what I plan on doing to you once we make it out of here alive." Natalie didn't know if it was a threat to her life for getting him into this situation, but that didn't stop her core from heating and the blush that invaded her cheeks.

"I mean," she said softly, "what do you think we should do to get out of here?"

"I know what you meant, cheeks." She could hear the smirk that he spoke through. She spun around to get a look at his face. "We're going out the front door. But I need you to trust me." As he spoke, he pulled a ski mask over his face. He was insane. There was no way they could leave through the front door. It was basically suicide.

"We can't leave through the front door. They are surrounding the entire place, and no one is getting out of here. It's on lockdown!" It was true. Everyone in the library was being herded into the center. Agents were marching through the shelves and finding everyone. It was only a matter of time before they saw them crouched between the shelves. They were sitting ducks at this point.

"We're going to leave through the front door, and you're going to trust me."

Natalie didn't have time to respond before Elijah put her in a headlock. She felt as he slid his hand down her back. When his hands arrived at her lower back, he gripped the gun she had secured in her belt. She felt the cold metal press against her head. He was holding her gun to her head. Natalie tried to fight out of his grip, but he was too strong.

He leaned down and whispered in her ear, "Trust me, Cheeks, I'll get us out of here." She heard the smirk in his voice.

Despite herself, Natalie felt that warmth that appeared whenever Elijah spoke return to her core. She tried her best to struggle by clawing at his one hand that wrapped around her throat, but it was no use. She wasn't leaving his grip until he allowed it.

Elijah began to lead Natalie toward the clearing, ensuring a wall was behind him at all times. The last thing he needed was to be attacked from behind. Natalie didn't know what his plan was, but whatever it was, it was mad. He was going to be stopped, and she was going to be arrested. This was the CIA. They were highly trained agents who knew how to neutralize any threat.

Elijah seemed to understand their slim chances of survival as he raised his gun, passed Natalie's head, and fired off her weapon. She froze. She didn't know what Elijah had planned, but she didn't expect him actually to fire the gun. She hadn't expected the gun even to be a variable in this situation. His shot fired true as he hit an agent in the head. He went down like he was nothing.

The gunshot drew the attention of all the other agents, all of them drawing their weapons and aiming them at Elijah and Natalie.

Natalie had never had a gun pointed at her before. Now, she had one at her head and about six others pointed at her, all by individuals who most likely had incomprehensible skill with a gun. Even Elijah. He barely aimed and still managed to hit the agent in the head as if it was nothing. Natalie's dad was in the military. She knew what skill was needed to shoot a gun. She used to train with her dad before he died, growing skilled in the art of firearms. Her mom didn't like guns, so Natalie stopped training after he died. Still, she knew how skilled someone had to be to be able to hit a moving target, especially one as small as a head.

The fear that Natalie felt was unlike anything she had ever experienced. The only comfort was the fact that Elijah's body was still in close contact with her. She felt safe with him even if he held a gun to her head. He wasn't the actual threat to her, Natalie realized. It was the CIA.

She felt Elijah lower his head to her ear before whispering, "Keep struggling. It's motivating me."

Natalie's cheeks burned red, and she feigned a struggle. She could never get over the rasp in his voice. He sounded as if he wanted to devour her while simultaneously being gentle and caring towards her. It was getting harder and harder to deny her feelings for him. Even as he held a gun to her head, her conflicting feelings were beginning to merge together to become the same thing.

Pushing those thoughts to the side, Natalie kept her head down, not allowing herself to look around. The last thing she wanted was to lock eyes with Agent Jannis and Agent Bennet. She needed to behave like any other civilian who was caught up in this unfortunate situation. She acted as if she was trying to get out of Elijah's grip, clawing at him while pushing her body against him in protest.

He moved closer to the front of the library, still ensuring that a wall covered his back. He stopped when he was a few yards from the exit that two CIA agents were blocking. The rest of them were spread out as if to corner them. Natalie only let her eyes scare the floors to see where their feet were. She did her best to keep her face out of sight, her curly hair blocking most of her face from the view of any onlookers.

Natalie was given no warning when Elijah's voice boomed from behind her. "Now that I've gotten everyone's attention, I'm going to walk out of here, or I'm going to kill this girl. If anyone even attempts to step towards me, a bullet goes straight to their brain after one goes through hers." His voice was strong, not like anything Natalie heard from him before. "Does that sound like a problem?"

The silence was loud, and the tension was thick as Elijah's actions were being assessed by the agents. Before Natalie could start pretending to fight again, she heard someone take a step forward before clearing his voice.

# Chapter 16

Natalie's stomach dropped. If this man recognized her, any chance of her escaping would go out the window. She had to find a way to hide her face without making it obvious that she was being intentionally secretive. Thankfully, Elijah shoved the gun into the back of her head, forcing her to look down as the man took his first step. She didn't have to try hard at all when this psycho behind her was doing all the work for her. She would scream at him later for the way he was treating her. For right now, she had to endure it.

The man stopped walking, not wanting his actions to be why someone else died. There was a silent beat before he spoke. "I don't know who you are since you have your face hidden like a coward, but I can guarantee we aren't here for you." Agent Jannis' voice was firm. "So why don't you put the gun down and let the girl go."

Elijah could be just as arrogant. "No, I don't think I will. Like I said, I'm walking out of here, and you're not going to follow. Since it's not me you're after, I'm sure that won't be a problem."

The way he spoke sounded nothing like the man she had been sleeping next to for the past couple of days. Natalie didn't know what to make of it. All she did was continue to struggle while they compared sizes.

"See, the thing is, I can't just let you leave. You pulled a gun, killed one of my men, and now you're threatening the lives of every innocent life in here. All of a sudden that makes you my problem." Every word that Jannis uttered was filled with arrogance.

"I'm sure you can turn a blind eye. The CIA tends to do that quite a bit anyways, right?"

Natalie blinked at Elijah's words. How had he known that it was the CIA? She didn't notice that they had identifying uniforms on, but she could have missed it. He could have simply assumed they were CIA since she had revealed to him the truth about her research. Still, she couldn't help the sudden wariness she felt at his words.

"What the government does is no business of yours," Jannis continued, not questioning how Elijah identified them. There must have been someone around that had a jacket on or something.

"Actually, it is when it's keeping me from living my life. So again, let me out, and everyone lives. Well," he chuckled slowly, "Mostly everyone." He motioned to the man whom he had already killed, the lifeless body lying untouched.

"Or, I can just have my men open fire on you."

"Now, you aren't going to do that because you wouldn't risk the life of an innocent. That would look bad on your precious agency."

Agent Jannis must have taken another step forward

because Natalie heard another gunshot. It rang in her ears, but she didn't see who was hit. All she knew was that it wasn't her or Elijah. She heard the body hit the ground as Elijah returned the gun to her head, the heat of the weapon ironically sending chills down her spine.

Agent Jannis didn't respond to that. Instead, it was another familiar voice that spoke up.

"Let them out." Agent Bennet said, murder lacing his every word. "Don't follow them."

Elijah began moving towards the front of the door, never forgetting to keep his back covered from the agents who all surely wanted to put a bullet in it.

Agent Bennet spoke up again. "Don't think you're getting away. We will find you."

Elijah didn't bother responding as he exited the library. He held the gun to Natalie's head the entire time, not letting her go until they were a few blocks away and he was sure no other agents were within eyeshot. He pulled her into an alley, allowing a moment of rest before heading back into the forest.

The moment Natalie felt his grip loosen, she pulled herself away, turning to look at him. He had a smug look on his face as he offered her gun back. Taking it back from him, she started furiously, "What. Was. That?! Why on earth would you put a gun to my head? Why didn't we look for an easier way out? You thought the best plan would be to make a big spectacle of us? Everyone is going to recognize us next time!" Natalie was screaming as that last question came out.

She wasn't done. "I cannot believe you would do that to me. Where in your mind did you think pressing my gun to my head would be the best idea? Ugh! I can't believe you right now!" Natalie was red in the face with anger, pacing back and forth as she ripped into Elijah.

Elijah grabbed her arm and pulled her deeper into the alley, the tall buildings towering around them. He started, "I got us out, didn't I? Like I said, I would. How about a thank you?"

"You want me to thank you? You are insane. You killed those people. How do you expect me to be okay with that?"

Natalie wasn't allowed to feel disgusted by Elijah before his body came over her. He forced her back to hit the wall, bringing his arms up to surround her head. He towered over her, making her feel so small. He could quickly kill her just as he killed the agents in the library.

"Don't act like you didn't get a rush from all of that." His voice was low and husky like it always was when he spoke to her. "I felt that way your body reacted when I pressed the barrel of your gun to your head. You loved it in that library. Your life was in my hands, yet you felt safe, didn't you?"

Natalie didn't respond. She just stared at him, her mind conflicted because he was right. She liked how her stomach turned into butterflies when he wrapped his hand around her neck and pressed the gun to her head with his other hand. She did get a rush from almost getting killed by the CIA but survived by finding a way to escape. It was wrong. She shouldn't be feeling those feelings, and it was that reality that she couldn't handle.

"And I killed those agents because it was the only way for me to get us out of there. One of them had to die. The other one was because that pompous ass couldn't follow directions. I don't enjoy killing people, but I'm not sorry I did it. That whole agency can burn for all I care."

The question from before popped up in her mind at his

words. How had he known they were CIA? And now, why did it sound like he had pure hatred for them? Not just any hate, but one that stemmed from experience.

Elijah was scanning her face, probably seeing the wheels turning in her head. He didn't give her a chance to say anything. "I honestly didn't think that would work, but I got us out. Now, we should go before they start looking for us." At his words, he lowered his arms and backed away from her. He motioned with his arm for Natalie to start walking towards the forest's edge from where they entered the town.

Natalie stared into his eyes as she moved past him, not daring to speak. He kept pace behind her. Natalie heard the cock of a gun. She snapped her head around and saw him scanning their surroundings, his own gun ready.

"You had your own gun this whole time," Natalie asked in a sharp whisper.

Elijah glanced back at her over his shoulder, a devilish smirk on his face, before replying. "Yeah. What about it?"

"Why didn't you use your gun to hold me hostage back there?" A valid question, Natalie thought.

"Because," he started, his voice gruff, "I thought it would be more entertaining to make you fear for your life with your own weapon instead of mine. It felt… poetic."

"How was it poetic," Natalie asked.

"Poetry can be provocative, don't you think?"

Natalie wasn't prepared for his words, tripping over her feet and almost falling on her face. Elijah chuckled before returning to his prowling stance.

He carried the weapon like he had training. His muscles flexed as he gripped the gun and walked with tactical stealth behind her. It reminded her of the way her father carried his firearms. Elijah wasn't some amateur.

She wanted to match his awareness, so she steadied her grip on her gun. The handle still had the lingering warmth from when he held it to her head, from when he killed those men. She feared the darkness that would consume her the longer she thought about what he had done, so she shoved thoughts away.

His words from the other day came into her mind instead. *I don't want you to compromise my location.* The way he phrased that sentence struck Natalie as odd. It made her question just who this man was. With everything that had happened since then, Natalie was sure she had no idea who Elijah was or where he came from.

They reached the tree line and holstered their guns.

Looking down at her, his face clear of emotion, he said, "I still don't understand this situation and how you got caught up with the CIA, so when we get back, you're going to explain it to me." In his voice, there was no room for argument. "We're going to have to run to make sure we stay ahead of them. They can't drive cars in the forest because of the thickness of the trees, but they'll move fast. I don't think they know that the girl I was holding was the girl they were looking for, but they'll figure it out soon. Now, can you run?"

"Yes, but I just have one question." She said, her voice shaky.

"No time for questions. You can grill me all you want when we return to the waterfall. There's coverage there, and like I said, no one knows about it. We'll be safe there."

Natalie nodded her head. She didn't have the mental capacity to argue with him right now. The shock of what she had just gone through was starting to invade her mind. She almost died. She was on the run from the CIA. Elijah wasn't who he said he was. Her mom. Carter.

The panic was starting to set in, and Natalie couldn't help it. She began hyperventilating. She felt as though her lungs were closing up, and she shouldn't get enough air in to keep her standing. A sweat broke out on her forehead, and her heart began pounding in her chest. Natalie gripped her throat as her eyes found Elijah.

"Natalie?" The control and assertion were absent from his voice, replaced by concern.

He looked terrified, not sure what was happening to her. He reached for her, catching her as she collapsed to the ground.

"Natalie," he yelled, panic now accompanying the concern. "Natalie, breathe! Please!"

Natalie didn't respond. Her eyes were closed as she tried so hard to breathe, but she couldn't think about anything other than the panic.

"Natalie, look at me! Look at my eyes." Elijah was losing it.

Natalie opened her eyes, finding Elijah's. The moment her eyes met his blue eyes, Natalie could feel the panic start to pull back.

"Yes, just look at me. I've got you. I'm here. You're safe." He held her body close as he continued to speak these words of affirmation and support. "Do you feel that? Do you feel how I'm breathing? Copy me. Breathe like me. You're safe with me, I promise. I won't let anything happen to you. Just breathe. Copy the movements of my chest."

Natalie listened. She felt how his chest moved up and down as he breathed, and Natalie did her best to replicate the movements. The air began to fill in her lungs again. Her breaths were ragged and uneven, but she was breathing again.

The panic began to subside, and she continued looking at Elijah's eyes. They were as calm as the sea after a hurricane. When she looked into his eyes, she didn't see what he did in the library. She didn't see how he held the gun to her head. She just saw safety. She saw security.

Natalie's breaths began to even out, and the panic in Elijah's voice was gone as he said, "There you go. Just breathe. I've got you, Cheeks." The concern was still there.

Natalie looked at him and said weakly, "I'm sorry."

Elijah raised a brow in confusion. "You're sorry? Don't say that. You have nothing to be sorry for."

"I just get panic attacks sometimes. After what just happened, I couldn't stop it. I usually have better control over them. I just - I'm sorry."

"Stop apologizing." His voice was firm now. "You had a panic attack. It's okay. You don't have to be in control all the time."

Natalie just stared at him. He wasn't freaked out or bothered by her attack. He didn't even seem inconvenienced since they were in the middle of trying to get away. He was accepting and understanding. That wasn't what she expected at all.

Before she had the chance to argue why she should apologize, Elijah said, "Come on, let's get back. We have a lot to talk about, and it's better to do it where it's safe."

Natalie nodded her head in agreement. Her panic attack wasted more time. The guilt flooded her mind as Elijah helped her off the ground. He made sure she was okay before taking off in a run into the forest. Natalie let the guilt remain as she ran after him.

***

They ran the entire way back. Natalie wasn't accustomed to running for so long, so Elijah allowed for short breaks. They stopped only so she could catch her breath and rehydrate before continuing. Elijah allowed Natalie to set the pace but never let her stop running. Natalie fought hard to keep her legs moving. She knew that if she allowed them to slow down, the chances of them getting caught would increase. Natalie wasted enough time as it was, so she did her best to keep moving.

Elijah would check in with her whenever they stopped for a water break. He would ask about her panic levels and if she was good to keep moving. He was adamant about getting back, but not if it was going to be detrimental to Natalie's well-being. Natalie assured him that she was fine each time and that they could keep moving. She didn't want to stop. She was just as anxious as he was to return to their haven by the waterfall. She kept her legs moving, ensuring she no longer slowed them down.

They made it back to the swimming hole at sunset. They arrived quicker, not only because they were running but because Natalie recognized the way they came from. Elijah still directed her on where to go, but Natalie could make out some of the areas where they rested.

Along the way, Natalie asked Elijah about any tracks they might be leaving, afraid of being found by the agents. He assured her that he would go back out and cover any trace they left. His priority was getting her back to the safety of the campsite. After that, he would head out.

They arrived at the thick treeline that separated the

outside world from their safe haven. Natalie wanted to fall to her knees in relief, her feet aching from the journey. They walked through the trees, and Natalie headed straight to the water. Dropping her bag on the way there, Natalie didn't care that she was fully dressed. She walked to the water and lay down, allowing her whole body to float on the surface. Her legs were noodles, and she didn't want to use them anymore. She floated in the water for a long time, just feeling the way the water carried her body along the surface. She began to smell something good coming from the campsite. Raising her head, she saw that Elijah had made food. She mustered up the energy to move out of the water and walk over to him. She sat next to him, closer than she probably should have. He handed her a plate, and she took it.

Without hesitating, she ate.

# Chapter 17

The forest was calm the day following the library incident. The birds and small animals were the only noises for miles. The tree coverage shielded the heat of the California sun. The forest floor was filled with residual warmth, not too hot or cold. Natalie spent the following day alert. She was convinced that the agents were out there right now, searching for them. Everything about their escape was sloppy, and the fact that they even got away shocked her.

Elijah had gone out after they ate, just like he said. He was gone through the night as he covered their tracks and made new ones to throw off the agents. Natalie worried about search dogs, but Elijah told her the waterfall would cover their scent. Natalie gave him a piece of her clothing to allow him to create a new scent trail, just to be safe. Once he returned early in the morning, he told her it was done and that he hadn't spoken another word since. He has managed to make breakfast but has avoided her otherwise. Natalie wasn't sure where he went, but she felt like he left to get away from her.

They haven't had a chance to talk about what happened in town. Natalie still didn't know where Elijah learned to use a gun, and Elijah still didn't know what information Natalie obtained. She was burning to know who he was and where he came from. It wasn't that she didn't trust him, because she did. After he managed to get them out of the library, her trust for him had grown deeper. Still, she wanted to know more about this man she was suddenly attracted to—another thing she felt needed a discussion.

She felt his words to her after they left the library, and how her body reacted to his deep and raspy voice needed some explanation. She needed to voice her feelings so she could understand them. She thought about Carter and what he would have to say about Elijah. She began to ponder their differences, comparing and contrasting their personalities and appearances.

Natalie was swarmed with guilt for doing such a thing. She knew her feelings for Elijah were wrong. She knew she should stay away from him. He probably knew it, too, with his sudden avoidance of her.

Natalie sat in the tent after breakfast, drowning in her thoughts. Natalie was beginning to go out of her mind with worry and dread. He assured her they would talk once they returned to the waterfall. Instead, he left her alone. She didn't expect them to dive into the nitty gritty right away, but she expected more than deafening silence. Maybe he was scared of his own attraction. He seemed to enjoy the excitement that came with holding a gun to her head. He couldn't take his eyes off her after they left the library, and he held her up against the side of the building with a ravenous hunger. He seemed invested in her up until… her panic attack.

He was so attentive when she had her attack, but he's been icy ever since. Her panic attack freaked him out. He saw that she had something wrong with her. Natalie had to hide her attacks her entire life. Anyone who had ever been a witness to her anxiety attacks always treated her differently afterward. Her teachers would send her to the nurse or make her leave the room during 'particularly stressful lessons.' Her friends would stop inviting her places because they wouldn't want to trigger her accidentally. Everyone treated her like a fragile girl who couldn't handle anything.

It had almost driven Carter away. He did his best to be there for Natalie, but one particularly nasty episode happened on the anniversary of her father's death. They had been dating for a few years now, so her panic attacks were nothing new to him. They were watching TV shows to keep her mind off of the day. Her mom was locked in the room like she always used to do on this particular day. Natalie and Carter were cuddled up on the couch with a popcorn bucket, binge-watching Breaking Bad. It was one of their favorite shows to watch together.

Back then, anything could trigger Natalie. Despite all the years of therapy, she could never get a good handle on her triggers. Thanks to her mom, she wasn't having as many attacks as she used to.  She had a way of calming her like no one else did. After they started dating, Carter was able to pick up some of the tips. Now, he was a pro, too.

They had just finished an episode when an ad popped up. Natalie didn't have the luxury of having a no-ad subscription, so they had to endure it. Typically, they would make out during the ads, but Natalie wasn't in the mood that day. She was sad and hurting, so she stared at the TV blankly when the ads were playing. Her mindless stare at the commercials was interrupted when an advertisement for the US Marines came on TV, forcing Natalie into focus. As the commercial played, Natalie's heart rate grew. Her breathing became shallow as she started to pant. Her anxiety and panic began to take over, and she couldn't stop it. Carter noticed immediately, and he rushed to turn off the TV. He knelt in front of her as she stayed seated on the couch, ignoring as the bowl of popcorn went flying off his lap when he stood.

Carter would always do the same thing to calm her. Depending on his position, he would run his hands up and down her arm or leg. He would talk to her calmly and tell her that she was okay. He would then try to get her to breathe regularly. He would run his hands through her hair and give her soft head scratches as a way to calm her down. On a typical day, it was all Natalie needed. On the anniversary of her dad's death, it wasn't enough.

Natalie's panic attack peaked as the commercial prompted the viewers to *sign up for the Marines today*. Her body was shaking, and her heart was pounding in her chest. Natalie's eyes were filled with tears as she hyperventilated. She felt like she was having a heart attack with the way her heart was racing. With her inability to get a good breath in, Natalie collapsed onto the couch.

"Natalie!" Carter screamed. He didn't know what to do. He had never seen her have one this bad. He lifted her into his arms and sat on the floor, holding her as she shook.

"Just breathe, baby. Breathe with me. You're going to be okay." Carter was on the verge of tears. He could do nothing more than just let Natalie ride it out.

As quickly as it had started, the panic began to subside. Her breathing slowed, but her body still shuddered with the terror. She had sweat beading on her forehead. Looking up at Carter, she saw nothing but pure anger on his face.

"Carter… I'm so sorry." Natalie's voice was weak.

Carter placed her on the couch gently before standing up and facing her. Natalie would always remember his following words.

"What the hell was that," he asked, voice sharp with anger. "I thought you were going to die. Do you understand how freaked out I was? Why on earth wouldn't you calm down? You're typically fine if I say those stupid words to you! Do you understand what you just put me through?"

Natalie's tears blurred her vision. She closed her eyes as she spoke, "I'm so sorry, Carter. I don't know why that one was so bad."

"I thought you were going to therapy to get all this fixed."

"I am, it's just hard. I promise it won't be that bad again."

"Good, because I can't take it anymore." Those were Carter's last words before he stormed out of her house.

Natalie cried by herself for hours after that. He was right, wasn't he? He must have been so scared for her. She had to learn to suppress it so she wouldn't scare him away.

Natalie could reply that day in her head and remember every detail like she had it written on the back of her hand. She remembered how that single moment had motivated her to fix herself. She didn't want to lose Carter. After all, he was the only person who knew how to keep her calm. She sought him out in the days following his outburst, hoping for forgiveness. He apologized for yelling at her but emphasized how he meant every word. Natalie assured him that she would invest more time and energy in improving her anxiety. And that's what she did. She made it better. She learned how to suppress it. She had fewer and fewer episodes. Now, she could identify when her panic would start and know how to stop it. Carter had helped her get there.

Now, here she was with Elijah, and she had forgotten everything. She forgot that she needed to stop her attacks, that she needed to control them. After the library, she lost control of her emotions and had an episode in front of him. One that he was forced to help her through. Afterward, he had done his best to avoid her, just like everyone else in her life. Just like Carter was so close to doing.

The thought that her panic attacks were the cause of this sudden rift tore at Natalie's heart. He was the only person to give her company right now. Natalie thought about the attack and how she had apologized after she had been able to calm down. She knew what he would be thinking. She knew how mad he must have been since she slowed them down again. She had apologized for the inconvenience she was causing. Natalie hated this anxiety disorder that had been nothing but a hindrance.

As she thought, the words Elijah spoke to her came to mind. Words that she had never heard from anyone. *Stop apologizing. You don't have to be in control all the time.* Not even Carter had said those words to her. Natalie knew that she didn't have to worry about anything with Carter. That he would take care of any and everything. Still, he had never spoken to her like the way Elijah did.

Confusion clouded Natalie's thoughts. Indeed, he was avoiding her because of the attack. But if he was, why had it been so reassuring? It didn't make any sense to Natalie. She decided she was done waiting for him to come to her. She needed answers, and she needed to know why he was suddenly ignoring her.

Natalie stood and exited her tent. As soon as she stepped out, She ran into something hard. The tent kept her from falling back, but she was now pinned between a rock and a hard place. The hard place being Elijah's body. She looked up at the skyscraper of a man. He stared back with amusement in his eye.

He took several steps back to give her some space before saying, "We need to talk."

***

They sat by the fire pit that still had a lingering smell of the fire from earlier that morning. Elijah sat across from Natalie, knee bouncing up and down as he thought of how to start this conversation. She wanted to ask him if he had food prepared, but she didn't think now was the time. Besides, after they talked, she could make her own food. She didn't need him to make her every meal of the day.

Elijah sat facing the swimming hole, and Natalie sat to his left. Natalie studied his face, hoping to find an explanation in his eyes, but his gaze avoided hers. He stared at the water, biting his bottom lip as if trying to find a way to begin the conversation. The tension was thick between them, making Natalie shift in her seat. So many words hung between them, but she didn't know where to start. She had a feeling Elijah felt the same way.

Feeling the need to fill the silence, Natalie cleared her throat. She looked over at Elijah, who was already staring at her, a ghost of a smile on his lips.  He returned his eyes to the water and began.

"Sorry that I've been MIA this morning," he said, still refusing to look her in the eyes. He spoke in a gravelly monotone that bothered Natalie.

"That's all I get," Natalie asked, irritation evident. "You've been avoiding me ever since we've been back. I deserve an explanation for why you've been so cold towards me."

Natalie was more upset than she first believed. She didn't really deserve anything from Elijah, but the tug from deep in her chest told her otherwise. Besides the obvious attraction, something between them made Natalie feel like he was hers. They belonged to each other. It made no sense, but it did.

"I haven't been avoiding you?" He said questioningly. "I've just been out gathering food."

"You haven't said a word to me since we got back. We were supposed to talk about... everything that happened." Natalie's voice quieted.

"We are going to talk about it. I just needed some time to process it."

"How much time?"

Elijah stopped. He just looked at Natalie, an apology hidden in his blue gaze.

"I haven't been avoiding you," he said again. "You had a panic attack after we left the library. I just -"

"You just didn't know how to deal with it." Natalie cut him off. "You can't talk to me because you don't want to trigger another one. I've heard it all before. Just forget it."

Natalie went to stand, but Elijah quickly grabbed her arm, preventing her from rising.

"No, no. You have it all wrong." His voice was firm but calm. "I've wanted to ask you about the files since we left the library."

Natalie settled back down and waited for him to speak again.

"You had a panic attack at the tree line." Natalie stirred, but Elijah kept going. "I thought it was my fault. I thought holding a gun to your head caused the panic attack. At first, I stayed away because I didn't want to make you uncomfortable. I promise it had nothing to do with your panic attack. I don't think you're weak. If anything, I don't think I've met anyone stronger. It was all about me. I can't live with myself if I make you feel unsafe. So I've just been making your food and then heading into the woods to keep watch for any agents. I just wanted to give you space. I promise."

Natalie just stared at him, stunned. How did this man keep saying things that made her stomach do flips? She was speechless as she allowed the morning to play over again in her head. He made her food and kept her fed. She didn't have to worry about going out and finding food because he provided for her. She had given the agents a few moments of thought, but she didn't dwell on them. She had felt safe since returning, except for the fact that her only companion wasn't talking to her. But he was right. He had kept taking care of her. He had given her space.

The space is what drove her crazy, though. She wanted to talk to him. She wanted him to tell her she was normal. Her mind was reeling from his silence. But it wasn't about her. He had kept his distance, not because he thought she was weak, but because he felt he was the bad guy here.

Natalie looked into his eyes as she said, "Thank you."

Elijah looked down on her with tender eyes. He reached his hand over and stroked her cheek with his thumb. It took everything in Natalie not to lean forward and kiss him. She wanted to feel what his mouth felt like against hers. Instead, she grabbed his hand for her cheek and brought it into her lap, where she held it.

Looking back at him, she explained, "My attacks have always weirded everyone out. They started after my dad died." Her voice cracked, but she continued, letting her head look down. "Back then, anything could set me off. After I started dating my boyfriend, he became my rock."

Elijah tugged his hand back, but Natalie barely noticed. She was too focused on her following words.

"He was the only one who ever bothered to help me besides my mom. After a really bad attack, he convinced me to go back to therapy, and it got better. I'm pretty good at stopping the attacks before they start, but sometimes I lose control. When I lost control with you, I thought you were like everyone else. I thought I freaked you out, and you wanted me gone."

Natalie finished speaking and folded her hands together. It was then that she noticed she wasn't holding hands with Elijah anymore. She turned to him, and he had a sour expression on his face. Natalie had a sinking feeling in her stomach and wasn't sure why he looked so upset. She closed her mouth and looked back down, on the verge of tears.

"Thank you for telling me that." Elijah's words were soft. "I'm sorry people made you feel like you were different for having panic attacks. It's nothing you should feel bad about. At least, that explains why you apologized after your episode ended. As I said before, you never have to apologize for that. Anyone who makes you apologize for your anxiety isn't worth your time." He smiled at her now, the sourness in his face gone.

"That's new to me," Natalie said. "I've always had to apologize for making people uncomfortable. Even my boyfriend." This time, Natalie noticed the shift. She looked at Elijah, and now he was seething. "What," she asked.

"He made you apologize," he asked, his tone violent.

"Well, it was my fault. I had an awful episode on the anniversary of my father's death. Carter, my boyfriend, freaked out about it. I scared him, and he thought I was going to die. After that, I returned to therapy because he would have left me if I hadn't fixed my anxiety. I couldn't lose him." Natalie spoke with a finality that made Elijah stand.

"Do you hear yourself?" He was almost yelling. "You had an attack on the day your dad died. He made you apologize for it. He made you feel guilty for having an emotional reaction to something traumatic that happened in your life. Not only that, but he made you think he would break up with you if it happened again. That doesn't sound wrong to you?"

Natalie stood now. "If I had only known how to control my anxiety levels, he wouldn't have had that reaction. It was my fault, and I fixed it."

"Natalie, I'm sorry, but that's the stupidest thing I've ever heard. You aren't stupid. You're smart. You should be able to piece together that your boyfriend is a jerk."

"You don't even know him!"

"I don't need to. I've heard enough. If I ever meet him,

I'll kill him." He said it in a low voice. Stepping closer to her, he continued, "I'll kill anyone who makes you feel guilty about having emotions. They aren't something you need to apologize for. They aren't a problem that needs to be fixed. When you have an anxiety attack, you need support. Point, blank, period."

Natalie just stared at him. He was bold for saying all of that. Natalie wanted to be angry. She wanted to keep arguing. She wanted to scream in his face how much she loved Carter, but she didn't. She just stood in silence because a part of her knew that Elijah was right. She knew that something about Carter's reaction to her attack was wrong, but she refused to think about it. She refused to think badly about him.

Instead of arguing, Natalie spoke softly. "Can we change the subject?"

"Gladly," Elijah said, his voice still filled with irritation.

Natalie would think about Carter later. Right now, she needed to know who Elijah was. She refocused her mind and remembered what they needed to talk about. The files. The CIA.

Elijah started the conversation. "Did you get everything you needed at the library?"

Natalie sucked in a breath before answering, "Yea, I did, except for that last file." She was still upset about it. She knew the contents of that file had a vital piece of information that she feared she would never get her hands on.

"I'm sure that one file isn't going to make a difference. You should have enough to do what you need to, right?"

"I hope so."

"How did you get involved anyway?"

Natalie looked at him. He was leaning in, listening

intently. She told him everything. She told him about the conspiracy and about the agents coming to her house. She told him about running away and how she needed to uncover all the secrets this unit was trying to keep buried.

She told him about the files and everything they held. She told him about the missing population of people who were kidnapped but unaccounted for in the experiments. She told him about the files that she had found in the library. She hadn't gone through them yet because she wanted to ensure everything with Elijah was okay. She actually wanted to go through them with him, though she didn't admit that.

"Okay," Elijah said. "That's a lot to process, but I get it now."

Natalie couldn't help but smile. "I didn't realize how much work being a fugitive would be."

Elijah smirked before saying, "Well, I don't know if I need to say this, but I won't turn you in."

"I didn't think you would turn me in since you killed those agents."

Elijah didn't respond, his body going taut.

Natalie smiled before saying, "Thank you." She paused. "Going back to you killing people, where did you learn to use a gun?"

Elijah let out a laugh. "I've been waiting for that question. Unfortunately for you, I don't know if I'm ready to share that story quite yet."

"I told you all my secrets today, and you can't tell me where you learned to use a gun? Who are you, Elijah?" Natalie spoke in a playful tone.

"Walker," Elijah said, his voice hesitant.

"What?" Natalie stopped, perplexed.

"My name is Elijah Walker."

Natalie knew immediately what he was doing. It was his secret. The identity that he has worked so hard to keep hidden. Giving his first name was hard, she remembered. It was hard for her, too. But his last name? She never thought she'd hear it.

Smile returning to her mouth, Natalie replied, "Walsh."

# Chapter 18

The rest of the day was calm after their conversation. Natalie was still unsettled at Elijah's refusal to explain his gun proficiency. It was not something she would forget about.

The following day, Elijah went out and hunted before Natalie awoke. They ate breakfast together but spent most of their time apart. Elijah would ask Natalie about the files occasionally, but she hadn't looked at them. Truth be told, she wasn't looking forward to discovering what the new documents held. She had managed to uncover unredacted documents and break through each encryption that protected them. She now had the opportunity to learn the whole truth about the experiments, and she found herself to be nervous. She knew she needed to act fast but wanted to remain ignorant of the facts for just a little while longer.

Elijah was beginning to suspect that Natalie was purposefully avoiding her research. She hadn't touched her laptop since they were at the library. He could only guess how disturbing the information she found would be, so he hadn't pressured her to look at them. Despite what Natalie was studying in college, what she was likely to see wouldn't be easy to look at.

Elijah would wait as long as she needed to look over the papers. It was her research and her burden to bear. She needed to be at the top of her game to make sure whatever needed to be done was done right. He would be right beside her, ready to help her if she needed him to.

Luckily, they had time for Natalie to mentally prepare herself. Given that lives were at stake, it wasn't a lot of time, but it was enough to give her space for a few hours. Once she was ready, they had to act fast. The last thing he wanted was for her to have another panic attack. Of course, he would be there for her if she did.

Elijah didn't know why, but he felt like he always wanted to be there for her. He wanted to be the person she went to for help. When she told him about Carter, a primal instinct to protect her filled all his senses. He hated how this boyfriend of hers treated her and made her feel like her panic attacks were an inconvenience. If Elijah ever saw Carter in person, it wouldn't end pretty.

Elijah had this sense of protectiveness over Natalie that he couldn't explain. He had just met her, and they were still practically strangers. But he couldn't help that he was drawn to her like a magnet. He couldn't control how his body reacted whenever he saw her. She could just be sitting there, and Elijah would get the compulsion to pick her up and ravage her. He wanted to know what she tasted like. He wanted to see every detail of her body and learn what parts he needed to touch to drive her crazy.

From the moment he saw her in Klamath Falls, he knew he wanted her. Her attitude with him in that diner was enough to drive Elijah insane with desire. When he helped her avoid the agents, he wanted to follow her into her motel room so badly. He had wanted to push her on the bed and touch every inch of her body. Leaving was the hardest thing he had ever done. When they met again in the forest, Elijah knew he needed to ensure she didn't slip away again.

That was why he brought her to the little oasis in the forest. He couldn't let her go. Even with everything he had done and where he came from. He knew he didn't deserve her, but he needed her. He needed her close by. If she ever found out who he was, she would hate him. She would never trust him again. So he had to keep it a secret.

Divulging his name to her was a bad idea, but he loved hearing his name on her lips. He would love to listen to what it was like when she moaned it.

When? More like if. He had to accept that he might never study her body as he would like. If she discovered who he was, it would all be over. Yes, giving her his name wasn't the most brilliant move, but it was done. He had to accept the consequences, whatever they may be.

***

The feeling of looking at the papers was growing. Natalie had avoided them as much as she could, but she knew that time was of the essence. She didn't have the luxury of waiting weeks to look at these papers. Innocent lives were being taken, and she needed to do all she could to help them. The anxiety that would come with it wasn't avoidable. No matter how much Natalie prepared herself, she knew it would never be enough.

Natalie was out in a clearing, practicing her shooting in the warm afternoon. She hadn't fired her gun in so long that she forgot the level of calm it brought her. When she was shooting, her mind cleared, and she didn't have to worry about anything.

She had a voice in her mind telling her it was time to look at the documents. She was trying to muster up the courage to get out her laptop and look. It was eating away at her, but her anxiety prevented her from completing her work. The anxiety fueled her procrastination, and her procrastination fueled her anxiety. It was a vicious cycle that was nearly impossible to get out of.

Natalie kept her focus on the way the gun recoiled with every bullet fired off. The sound of each gunshot rang through her ears, and the smell of gunpowder burned her nose. Each shot found its mark, hitting empty cans that Elijah had set up for her. The clinking of bullets meeting aluminum worked to ease her anxiety.

Natalie fired a couple more rounds before deciding it was time to look. She returned to the oasis and found her backpack in the tent. Making sure her laptop and flash drives were there, she went and sat by the fire. She took out her laptop, opening it to the sound of the crackling embers. Thankfully, she had the brilliant idea to charge it up at the library and then turn it off before they made their great escape.

She powered on her laptop and got out her flash drive. She looked around as if anyone was there to sneak up on her. She only saw Elijah cleaning his gun at the edge of the tree line. After their conversation, she asked if he knew of a nearby area where she could practice her shooting safely. He had shown her the clearing she had just returned from, but she waited a day before going. She still wondered about his marksmanship but knew he wasn't ready to discuss it. Despite her frustration, she didn't press him about it.

Looking back at her laptop, Natalie began.

Natalie compared the redacted and unredacted documents, starting with the files she already had. The redacted ones had false information on them that made their experiments seem less severe. The documents lacking redactions exposed their actual dealings.

As Natalie knew, they were kidnapping people in the homeless population. They targeted those in larger cities that were overridden with homelessness. Portland, Los Angeles, Chicago, and Seattle, to name a few. They would take them in small increments at a time to avoid detection. They would transport them to the testing sites and remain discrete by labeling these human beings as *cargo*. Once they were in the facilities, only those leading the experiments were allowed inside.

As soon as the victims were secure in the facilities, they were separated by race, age, and gender. Once the different populations were established, they were then weighed. This is where some of the people went unaccounted for. It seemed that younger individuals were the ones going missing from that data. Not all who went missing were young, but many of them were. There was no documentation on what happened to them or whether they were a part of the experiments. As far as Natalie could find, they were still considered missing despite not being a part of the experiments. They weren't let go. They were simply gone.

The rest of the people were then put through different experimentation trials. Different chemical weapons were tested on them. They were injected with chemicals involving Sarin and Tabun. They were exposed to gases like Zyklon B and mustard gas. After exposure, the reactions were recorded.

Sarin was a nerve agent that caused paralysis, loss of consciousness, seizures, and cardiac arrest in the worst cases. If medical treatment is administered quickly after inhalation, it results in severe neurological damage. Long enough exposure to it could cause death within ten minutes. The production of this poison was outlawed in the 90's.

Tabun was another nerve agent that caused similar effects, as well as vomiting and loss of vision. The strength of this liquid is not as severe as Sarin's, but it is still considered a chemical weapon that was outlawed at the same time as Sarin. They are both considered G-series nerve agents, meaning German scientists initially created and synthesized them.

Mustard gas is a chemical compound released in microscopic liquid droplets that cause painful blisters and severe burns to the eyes and skin. This sulfuric agent is another illegal chemical that became regulated in the 90s. There is little other use for this chemical weapon other than warfare.

Zyklon B is the worst of all. It is an agent that is made up of hydrogen cyanide. This chemical was created in Nazi Germany and used to murder over a million people in the Holocaust. It caused excruciating pain to the participants. It made breathing almost impossible for those who were exposed, and it even caused severe seizures. No one who was exposed to it survived. Though the most deadly of the four, this chemical weapon is legal in some areas and still in production.

Natalie was sick from the new details. She was disturbed by what her government was putting these people through. A government that was supposed to be there to protect its people. Not only were these tests inhumane and unethical, but they were absolutely illegal. Every single one of the chemicals they were testing was banned as far back as the Chemical Weapons Convention, save for Zyklon B. That fact confused Natalie since Zyklon B was the gas used in the Nazi concentration camps to kill thousands at a time. How the CIA got their hands on such weapons, Natalie didn't know.

Why they were testing them was even more of a mystery. In the documents, they wanted to see how different demographics reacted to the chemicals. They tried to expose the participants enough to see the effects. The aim wasn't to kill. It was to test. If they could avoid death, they would. Still, Natalie didn't know how these things could be happening. She couldn't comprehend how anyone could do such terrible things to another human being.

The rest of the papers had each participant's information. They indicate the names of each subject, their family history, and how each specific person reacted. The documents also had the names of each agent responsible for these innocent people's suffering. Jannis and Bennet.

Natalie was going to find joy in exposing them. She was going to enjoy watching their world crumble as the world discovered what they were doing. She would make sure the destruction of this organization ended in ash. Natalie would be sure that their pain was worse than that of the unwilling participants. She would end them with a smile on her face and Elijah at her side.

Elijah. Natalie came out of the trance that she had fallen under while looking over the papers and looked around for him. He told her that he would help her. She needed to show him everything she found. It wasn't exactly that she needed him. No, she wanted him to help her. She liked that she didn't have to do all this alone. He was there offering to shoulder some of the burdens with her. It was refreshing to know she wasn't alone anymore.

Natalie stood and walked over to where Elijah was still cleaning his gun. He just had the one pistol he had pulled out as they left the library, and he had been sitting over at the edge of the treelined, cleaning it since before Natalie began sifting through the papers. She spent at least an hour looking at everything.

As Natalie approached him, she asked, "How long does it take for you to get that thing cleaned?" Her voice was teasing.

He jumped up, startled by her voice.

"Sorry," Natalie laughed. "I didn't mean to scare you."

He looked at her with a mischievous look in his eyes. "You didn't scare me," he lied. She did scare him. He was so focused on his gun that he hadn't noticed her walk up. "I just wasn't expecting you to sneak up on me."

"I wasn't sneaking. I just wanted to come get you."

"Oh yeah? What's up?" His voice was riddled with curiosity.

"I looked at the files." Natalie's voice was suddenly quieted, her face falling as she spoke.

Elijah stood up, worry written all over his face. "Are you okay?" He asked with such concern that it caused Natalie to take a small step back.

"Yea. I'm okay. But what they're doing... It's awful." Natalie had to stop talking. She couldn't get everything out without her voice breaking.

"Okay. Let me clean up this, and we'll review it together."

Natalie nodded.

Elijah turned around and bent at the knees to collect all his gun parts. With a skill Natalie had never seen, he put every piece into place. Not even her father was that quick at rebuilding his guns. Elijah was done in a blink, and then he stood and approached Natalie. His neck craned as he got closer. Natalie always forgot how much taller he was than her. He towered over her like a tree does a squirrel. She looked down, unsure if she should turn around and walk back towards her laptop for him to follow or let him lead her.

Elijah took her hand and brushed a strand of hair behind her ear before bringing her chin up to look up at him. Their eyes met, and it took every cell in Natalie's being not to fall to her knees. He looked at her with a hunger she had never seen before. She melted into his touch, feeling every ounce of warmth his body radiated.

Elijah's lips parted as if to kiss her. He inclined his head down for a second before pulling back too soon. He couldn't kiss her right now.

"Show me the files," Elijah said, his voice barely a whisper. He spoke with such tenderness. Natalie let a small breath escape her lips as she pulled away from his touch. She turned and walked away, feeling his stare burning into her back.

The desire to kiss him remained there as they arrived by the fire. They sat in different chairs as Natalie opened her laptop and started from the beginning. Any feelings of desire vanished as they began to dive into the files together. Natalie was thorough with what she showed

Elijah. She made sure he knew every detail. She made sure he was aware of everything happening and how important it was to get these documents in the public eye.

They looked over the documents for another hour before Natalie had to put them down again. Elijah seemed to be disturbed by all the information as well. They sat in silence for a while, the sparks of the campfire the only noise between them. Elijah was shocked at what he saw. He knew that the things Natalie found were terrible. He knew what the agents were doing at the testing facilities was awful. Going through the details made him realize it was worse than he could ever imagine. He felt sick.

Natalie sucked in a deep breath and stood from her chair. She looked towards Elijah, waiting for him to look up at her before she spoke. Slowly, Elijah met her gaze, sorrow and pain flooding his eyes.

"I'm going to clean up," Natalie said quietly. "I need to wash away everything I just read." She released an exasperated sigh and walked off toward the water before Elijah could respond.

# Chapter 19

Before she got into the water, Natalie stripped down to her bra and underwear. She didn't care if Elijah saw her. She needed to wash herself of all she uncovered today. This was why she held off on looking through the files. She knew how she would react. Her mind swam with thoughts of the people who were deemed unwanted—the people who were seen as undesirable by not only the CIA but the whole of society. Homelessness was seen as a burden rather than something to be fixed. Society didn't want to "deal" with them, so they were pushed to the side, forgotten. It broke Natalie's heart. Those whom the world deemed unworthy were now being taken and treated like lab rats. For what? For the sick curiosities of demented minds. There was a reason these weapons were illegal. There was a reason why the entire world put laws in place to prevent these weapons from being created and used. How the CIA got away with this and remained under that radar was beyond Natalie.

The water was warm as Natalie waded through it. She swam towards the waterfall and let the sound of the crashing water fill her mind. She didn't want to think about the experiments anymore. She tried to forget them, if only for the night. The water splashed on her skin as she neared the waterfall. She dunked her head under, her ears deafening as the water surrounded her. She held her breath as she stayed submerged and allowed her body to calm.

Her lungs began to yearn for air, so she resurfaced. She wiped the water from her eyes, and when she opened them, her eyes met Elijah's. Natalie let out a small scream as she backed away. She hadn't expected him to follow her.

"Hey," Natalie yelled, "Why would you scare me like that?"

Elijah's lips tilted up in a smirk. "Sorry, I didn't mean to. I just thought you could use some company."

"I kind of just wanted to be alone. I need to clear my mind from everything." Natalie spoke quietly, barely audible next to the waterfall.

"Yeah," Elijah said, his voice softening. "I know what you mean. Can I join you, or do you want me to leave?"

Natalie's eyes scanned him before she nodded. "You can stay," she said. "Being alone with my thoughts isn't all it's cracked up to be anyway."

Elijah chuckled at that. He walked beneath the waterfall, only half his body submerged underwater. He wet his hair and then came back out. Natalie just stood there watching him. The water dribbled down his body, accentuating every sharp edge of his muscles. He ran a hand through his wet hair, his biceps flexing with the movement.

Realizing she was staring, Natalie turned away. She threw her head back, letting her hair get wet before coming back up. As she stood, she said, "Thank you for being here. It's nice not having to be alone."

Elijah met her eyes, coming closer to her. "You'll never have to be alone again. I'll be here for as long as you want me."

Natalie smiled. "I don't even know how I could get through all this alone."

"I thought you were trying to get your mind off everything," Elijah said, slowly creeping closer.

"I am," Natalie said, her body tensing at his nearness. "I just -"

"Don't bring it up." Elijah's voice was low but firm. "We're trying not to think about everything we just looked at. I could have gone my whole life without knowing the sick things they were doing. Let's enjoy a small moment of peace."

"Hey," Natalie said, her voice playful yet defensive. "I'm just trying to show gratitude." She paused. "But you're right. My brain always needs to be working. I can't just forget for even a second, no matter how much I want to."

Elijah was getting dangerously close now. "I'm sure I can be of some assistance in that regard."

Natalie met his eyes again. He was so close to her, their bodies practically touching. She tried her best to prevent any sinful thoughts from entering her mind, the task becoming more challenging with each breath.

"Yeah," Natalie said breathlessly. "It's a good thing you're here."

"So," Elijah said as he moved his face down, becoming nose to nose with her. "How should we start our distractions?"

Natalie allowed her head to tilt up towards him. This time, she was the one moving closer. Her skin prickled at their proximity. She finally allowed their bodies to make contact. She looked longingly into his eyes, dragging her fingertips along his arms. She enjoyed the way his body tensed at her touch.

"I think…" Natalie started.

She didn't finish her sentence. Wasting no time, she sprang forward, crashing her mouth into Elijah's and letting her desire for him consume her. She didn't want to think about what she was doing. Natalie knew if she thought too much about it, she would stop this from happening. She just wanted to feel his lips on hers.

Elijah wrapped his arm around her back, eliminating any gap between them. His other hand gripped the back of her head, his fingers tangling in her wet hair. His movements made Natalie's breath hitch as he explored her body with his hand. He separated the kiss, eyes burning into Natalie's as if he were seeing into her soul.

"I hear you loud and clear, cheeks," he whispered, his last words before he brought his mouth down on hers.

The kiss was gentle, Elijah kissing her like she was the most delicate flower he didn't want to ruin. Natalie's lips were soft as they brushed over Elijah's.

They pulled away for a moment, allowing themselves to make eye contact. The yearning in Natalie's eyes was all Elijah needed to pull her back into a deeper kiss. This time, he didn't hold back. She wasn't a delicate flower that needed protecting. She wasn't a fragile thing that couldn't handle herself. Natalie was strong. She was enduring. Everything about her radiated a will unlike anything Elijah had ever encountered. So he didn't kiss her like she was fragile.

He gripped her hair as their lips clashed. Natalie's hand reached up to find Elijah's hair, her other hand pressed firmly on his chest. She was in awe of how solid his body was. His muscles felt amazing under her hands. Their mouths worked together in a dance that only they knew the steps to, the crashing waterfall acting as their music.

Elijah allowed his hands to explore Natalie's body. He took in every curve of her body as his hands passed over her. He touched the soft skin of her neck before moving down to the curves of her breast. He lingered there for a moment, relishing in every part of her.

His hands continued to travel down, feeling the way her waist curved inwards and then out again as he got to her hips. He loved the way her body was shaped. He got a rush of hunger as he felt for her butt. He squeezed it hard before releasing her hair from his other hand. Then, without breaking their kiss, he reached down to her thighs and lifted her up. Natalie gasped at the movement, their wet bodies collided again as Elijah lifted her. She wrapped her legs around him, and both hands gripped his hair now.

Natalie could feel any negative thoughts dissipating as she kissed Elijah. The feel of his hands on her was all she could think about as she held onto him with her legs. She had one hand gripping his hair now as she let her other one run down his chiseled back and over his arms. She wanted him to feel just as desired as he made her feel.

As their kisses deepened and their desire grew, Elijah slipped his tongue into her mouth. Their tongues grazed each other, and Natalie let a soft moan slip from her throat. This only encouraged Elijah. He broke away from their kiss and moved his mouth down her chin and onto her neck, causing goosebumps to erupt all over Natalie's skin. He kissed her neck, causing her to grab onto him harder. The harder she pulled on his hair, the more he kissed her.

He left marks on her neck as he kissed and sucked. He moved down to her breasts, Natalie leaning back, allowing him access to the rest of her body. He kissed every part of her that was possible in this position.

He kissed his way back to Natalie's mouth, his passion for her apparent as he lowered her down to her feet. Natalie's hair was messy, and one of her bra straps fell off her shoulder. Elijah admired his handiwork, craving her more. Seeing her messy hair and swollen lips increased his desire for her. He longed for every part of her.

As their bodies separated, Natalie stared at Elijah. She wanted nothing more than to take him to the tent. She wanted to feel every part of his body on her. Her desire was at an all-time high. She looked up and down his body, seeing how much he wanted her too.

"Tell me what you want," Elijah said, his voice husky.

She was so swept up in her desire that she paid little attention to the voice in her head telling her to stop. The voice she knew so well and typically listened to. However, these circumstances weren't typical, so she pushed away any conviction. She had never been with a man before, wanting to save herself for the man who would be spending his life with her. Right now, at this moment, Natalie ignored that. She knew it was wrong, but being here with Elijah felt right.

"I just want you," Natalie said, her voice breathless.

"Get out of the water and go to the tent," Elijah said, his voice filled with desire. "I want you comfortable when

I devour you."

Natalie was stunned at his words, but she obeyed. She made her way out of the water, Elijah following close behind her. She felt like a fly caught in his web. He was the predator, and she was the prey. His body was close behind her as she neared the tent. He gripped her neck from behind, spun her around to him, and pulled her into another kiss. Their tongues swirled around each other. The way he kissed her was unlike anything she had ever experienced. It was flooded with passion and longing. Everything about how he kissed and touched her made her feel seen and wanted.

He pulled away from their kiss but kept his mouth close, barely touching hers.

He still gripped her neck as he said, "Get in." His breath warmed the area behind her ear.

Natalie nodded as he released her. She ducked down into the tent. She stayed facing the inside as she heard Elijah enter. She heard him zip the tent close before she felt the firmness of his body press up against her back. Natalie knew one thing at that moment. She wanted him, and nothing would stop her from getting what she wanted. She knew it was selfish. She knew she should stop it and seek comfort in God, but she didn't care.

Elijah's hand ran up her body as he leaned down and whispered in her ear, "You smell so good, cheeks."

Natalie gasped.

"I can't wait to feel the way your body reacts to mine." Gripping Natalie's waist, he spun her around to bring her face to face with him. "I can't wait to make you scream my name."

Natalie could only stare at him, her breathing becoming shaky with every word he spoke. She felt the way her body responded to his words, the way her core heated with every syllable he uttered.

"I'm going to ruin you, Cheeks. I am going to devour you until there's nothing left but pleasure. You wanted me to help you forget. It would be my honor."

Goosebumps erupted on her skin at his words. Giving him one final kiss, she laid on the bed, and Elijah began.

# Chapter 20

Elijah wasn't in bed when Natalie woke up. She half expected him to be lying underneath her, but he was gone. Natalie sat up on the air mattress, with nothing covering her body except for a couple of blankets. She brushed her fingers across her lips and remembered everything that happened the night before.

Her body could still feel the way Elijah touched her. She could feel the pulsing in between her legs as Elijah stayed true to his word. He absolutely devoured her. He had worshiped her body and made her feel like she was the only woman in the world who ever existed.

Natalie felt the reality of what she had done slam into her. Everything she believed in and hoped for in her future marriage was gone. She couldn't believe she had allowed last night to happen. As much as she wanted Elijah, as much as she craved every part of him, she couldn't believe it. For years, Carter had tried to be intimate with her. He asked constantly until she told him she didn't want to do anything until after marriage. He had agreed reluctantly.

Natalie had solid convictions. She wanted to save herself for marriage. She liked the idea that no one would share her body except her husband. That is what sex was designed for, to be had between a husband and wife. This wasn't a belief that she thought was bad. It was actually quite beautiful. She didn't know how it had escaped her so easily. She wasn't sure what exactly came over her, but she couldn't hold back her lust. Everything she believed in slipped her mind the moment she saw Elijah in the water.

He hadn't known she was a virgin. He hadn't known her beliefs. She hadn't told him. She didn't know if he would have behaved differently if he had known, but she didn't want to find out. She took responsibility for what happened. She wanted it. She wanted him. Despite everything she believed in, she couldn't resist him. She shifted as guilt began to settle in her stomach. It wasn't even the fact that she had basically cheated on Carter. It was the fact that her morals were now compromised.

Natalie felt that any shred of her credibility as a believer went out the window. Shame roiled within her, her guilt threatening to consume her. She had willingly ignored the convictions and chose her pleasure over what was right.

Before the guilt and the shame could consume her, she leaned into Him. She humbled herself and acknowledged that her mistake did not define her worth. She sought the redemption that was hers. She prayed for the forgiveness that was already hers to have. She leaned into her Savior's grace rather than run from it, even though sin had taken control. She could imagine the arms that wrapped around her in comfort and love as she sought forgiveness and found a way to forgive herself. She then decided to tell Elijah everything. She would tell him what had transpired between them couldn't happen again, not for her lack of desire but because she wanted to stay true to herself and her beliefs. She slipped, but that didn't mean she had to keep falling.

Aside from the fact that she wanted to remain true to herself, they needed to focus on the CIA. They had to remember what they were working towards. They couldn't get distracted by the desires of the flesh when there were more important things to worry about.

Natalie got out of bed and got dressed. She was sure Elijah was out getting food for their breakfast. Once she found him, she would talk to him.

The fire was dying as she exited the tent. Elijah started the fire before going hunting every morning. Natalie must have slept in longer than she thought since it was already beginning to die. She added a couple more logs to the fire before sitting down in one of the folding chairs.

She grabbed her laptop from the other chair. She had left it there before going into the water last night. She had forgotten about it after everything that happened last night. The distractions worked. Opening her laptop, Natalie began to scan through the documents again. She needed to write a type of manifesto that she would publish along with every file she had. She needed to write a clear explanation for what these files were and how she had them.

It wouldn't be hard to convince people about what the CIA was doing. Getting it out in the media without being stonewalled would be hard. Media outlets were hesitant to publish anything that might make the country look bad. If the world saw what the government was doing, it would threaten national security. Natalie had to be very careful with how she got these papers out.

She had only looked over a few files before Elijah emerged from between the trees, carrying freshly caught fish. All he had on was a pair of jeans being helped up by a belt. He was shirtless, letting his muscles darken under the California sun. Sweat glistened on his shoulders and chest. Natalie couldn't help but stare at him.

Elijah caught her staring and looked down at the ground with a smirk forming on his mouth. He knew she enjoyed looking at him. He enjoyed seeing her body tense in reaction to seeing him. He hadn't planned on being shirtless when she woke up, but he was glad he was if only to watch her squirm.

Natalie realized she was still staring as Elijah approached. She diverted her eyes back to her laptop screen before saying, "Good morning." Her voice was soft and warm.

"Good morning, cheeks. Sleep well?" He had a mischievous tone in his voice.

Natalie couldn't help her grin as she said, "Yes, I did. Best sleep I've had since being here. You?"

"I slept alright." His voice was monotone, but the look in his eyes was playful.

Natalie chuckled softly before asking, "Where did you get the fish?"

Their little oasis was the only body of water nearby, but there were no fish in it. He had to have either found another body of water or gone to town.

"I hiked to the top of the waterfall this morning. There were some fish up there, so I caught a few."

"Wow, that must have been pretty."

"It was." There was a new sparkle in his eyes. "I could take you some time if you want."

His invitation made Natalie's breath hitch. "I'd love to. We can do all that after we get these papers published." She motioned to her laptop.

"Of course. How about I make you a promise? As soon as we get those files out in the world, I'll bring you back here, and we'll go on that hike. I'll show you around this place so you can be as familiar with it as I am."

Natalie felt her chest tighten. She would want nothing more. "That sounds pretty great. I don't know if I'll ever come back here, though."

Elijah's brows furrowed as he tilted his head in question. "Why not? You could come back if you want to. I want you here."

"I just… I have to go back to Portland. To mom and to-" Elijah cut her off.

"Carter." His voice turned lethal. "You're going back to him." Not a question.

"I don't know," Natalie said, running her hands through her hair. "I haven't thought about what will happen once this is over."

"How can you go back to him? After everything he's done to you." His voice quieted. "After last night."

She had hurt him. Natalie shook her head, not wanting to fight. "I didn't say I was going back. There's just a lot to discuss. Speaking of which, we need to talk about last night."

Elijah's spine straightened as he got on the defensive. "Don't worry. It won't happen again."

Natalie's head snapped to him, shock on her face. "What?"

"That's what you want, isn't it? You just needed the

distraction, and now that it's out of your system, you're done? Don't worry, I get it."

Natalie stood at that. "No, you don't understand. It had nothing to do with getting it out of my system."

"What was it then? A way of getting revenge on your prick boyfriend?"

"No! I wanted it to happen because… because I like you." Her voice quieted as she spoke those last words. "I was a virgin."

Elijah's eyes went wide. It was done. She said the words. There was no going back now.

"W- what?" His voice was nothing more than a whisper.

"I haven't had sex before. Not even with Carter. I- I was planning on waiting until marriage."

Elijah took a step towards her. "Why didn't you tell me?"

"Because I wanted you. Badly. I don't know what came over me, but I only know that I wanted last night to happen."

"But now you regret it." Again, not a question.

"No," she said, releasing a breath. "I don't regret it. But I don't think it should happen again because I would still like to wait until after marriage. It's something that I've believed in my whole life. It's still important to me. I know what we did can't be undone, but that doesn't mean I have to keep doing it."

Elijah let her words sink in. He had no idea she was a virgin. He would have never touched her the way he did if he had known. He would have asked more questions. He would have respected her morals. He felt guilty for not realizing it. He enjoyed her so much, but he would have wanted to know everything first.

"Okay," he started, "It won't happen again."

"Thank you, I-" He cut her off again.

"It won't happen again until I make you my wife."

Natalie's eyes widened. "Excuse me?"

"You're mine, Natalie, not just because of what happened last night but because of everything. From the moment I saw you, I knew you would be mine. It was just a matter of how. I was willing to let you go back at the motel. I figured if it were real, we'd meet again. Then I saved you in the woods, and I knew. I don't plan on letting you go. And I am sorry about last night. I would have stopped if I had known about your beliefs and feelings. It would have been hard, but I would have stopped for you. You're important to me. So I promise I won't touch you in that way again until we're married."

Natalie just looked at him. He spoke with such certainty that Natalie almost agreed to every word. But she couldn't. There was so much lying between her and Carter. There was so much to do with the CIA. She couldn't think about Elijah and his beautiful words right now.

"Elijah," her words were a whisper, "I need time to think."

"Take all the time you need. You're worth waiting for."

She couldn't handle his words right now. She stood and walked to the water. Her appetite left her with every second that passed between now and the words he had spoken. The conversation went nothing like she had planned. She had expected him to be enraged at her decision. She expected him to argue with her. To say things like *we did it once. What's one more time?* Those are the kinds of words Carter would say. But Elijah wasn't Carter.

When she got to the water's edge, she sat down, allowing her toes to be covered by the shallow water.

Carter was her high school sweetheart. He was the person who helped her after her dad died. He helped her through college. He was the man she was going to marry. But he was controlling. When they began dating, he took over every aspect of her life. He decided what she ate and drank and when she went to bed. He called her anxiety a problem and an inconvenience and forced her into therapy. He encouraged her to hide her emotions because they made him uncomfortable. She went to the college he had gotten his scholarship so he could still take care of her. She figured it was convenient, but he had orchestrated it to be that way. He fought tooth and nail to get her to have sex with him, saying, "If you love me, you would do this." He used that manipulation to try to get her to be intimate with him, though it never worked. Everything in her life, up until the CIA raiding her house, was decided by him. And she let him. It was easy that way. But it wasn't what was best for her. Her independence and autonomy were lost to his constant need to be in control.

Elijah, on the other hand, was different. He let Natalie make her own decisions. He protected Natalie without question. He helped her through her anxiety instead of making her bury it deep inside. Sure, he held a gun to her head, but he did that to help her escape the CIA. He gave her the mental breaks she needed instead of occupying every second of her life. He had made her feel whole. Elijah accepted her desires. He heard her out and listened to her. He didn't throw her actions back in her face. He took everything she said and planned his next move to accommodate her better. Elijah showed her what it was to be genuinely cared for and loved.

The water was surrounding Natalie's feet as she came to her decision. It hadn't taken her days or weeks. It had taken only a few minutes before she came to the realization. Elijah was hers. She couldn't deny her feelings for him anymore. There was a reason these desires were there. There was a reason why she got lost in his ocean-blue eyes whenever he looked at her. Elijah was it. He was the person who had been designed to go through life with her. She loved Carter, but his love was toxic. His love was only meant to control her. She did have one thing about him to be grateful for, though. He packed her bags.

Natalie rose to her feet and walked over to where Elijah was cooking the fish. He glanced her way for a second before returning to his cooking.

"The fish is almost done." His words were clipped.

"Okay," Natalie said softly. "I just wanted you to know something. I decided I'm not going back to Carter."

Elijah turned to face her, the hope in his eyes in contrast to the tone of his voice as he said, "Did you, now? Well, good for you." He turned back to the fish.

"I actually decided that if this all ends well, I want to come back here and take you up on your offer for that hike."

Elijah didn't turn this time, but Natalie could hear the smile in his voice as he replied, "It would be my pleasure, Cheeks."

# Chapter 21

The next day was spent working and eating. Elijah kept Natalie fed as she compiled a dossier about the experiments and everything she had uncovered. She wanted to send all the information to the news outlets, hoping they would report it as breaking news. Natalie planned on posting everything to Reddit and Wikileaks, but she needed to ensure that people saw what was happening. She couldn't just hope they went viral.

There came a point when they needed a break from the subject matter. The documents highlighting the atrocities that the experiment group was being subjected to were heavy, and Natalie couldn't stomach it for too long. Elijah took Natalie to the clearing, where he set up his makeshift shooting range. Elijah wanted to see for himself where she was at with her shooting skills. Natalie had only gone the one other time and was excited to clear her mind of everything they had been working on.

It was mid-afternoon, and the sky was overcast, the air

a biting chill as they stood getting their guns ready for practice. Natalie was dressed in biker shorts and a hoodie, her legs taking the cold in full force. There was no sound of birds as there had been in previous days, probably staying sheltered to avoid the cold.

Elijah was staring at Natalie, never thinking loading a gun would be attractive until he saw her do it. He kept true to his words and didn't initiate any sexual contact. They still kissed and cuddled, but that was as far as their touching went. They were both burning in their flesh, but they restrained themselves. If it ever got to the point of crossing the line, Elijah would end it and take a walk in the woods. He had more control than Natalie did. It made her feel good to be wholly respected without complaint.

Elijah grinned as he loaded his gun. "I like how you load your gun," he said, his voice playful.

Natalie looked at him, a smirk appearing on her face. "Thank you. I forgot how much putting the bullets in the magazine hurts my thumbs."

Elijah chuckled. "You just need to develop calluses. The more you do it, the less it will hurt."

Natalie nodded as she smiled. "Thank you for bringing me out here."

"Well, I couldn't go another day without seeing you shoot. I have to see what pointers I can give you."

"I don't need any pointers. I'm probably more skilled than you are."

Elijah tightened at her words. "I can guarantee that isn't true," he said darkly.

Natalie blinked in confusion but decided to brush it off.

She cocked her gun. "Let's get started then."

They practiced shooting for about half an hour before

Natalie had an itch to finish her dossier. Elijah was utterly impressed at her skill with a gun. He assumed she would be all talk, but her dad had really trained her well.

They returned to the camp, and Natalie sat down to continue her work.

Natalie was close to finishing her dossier. She knew that she and Elijah needed to devise a plan on how they would publish and share the files. Elijah has been helping by compiling a list of news outlets to whom she could send her evidence.

Natalie turned towards where Elijah was sitting. She stopped to admire him momentarily before saying, "Can you come here real quick? We need to talk."

Elijah raised his eyebrows as he walked over towards her. He said nothing as he sat down and waited for her to start.

"We need to figure out our course of action for getting these papers out," she started. "I think the best place to get everything out would be the library."

Elijah stiffened.

"I know, it's risky. We don't know if agents are still patrolling the area, but it's our best bet. It has guaranteed connection, and now I can get everything out quickly."

"No," Elijah said, his tone violent.

Natalie waited for him to elaborate on his statement, but he didn't. He just stared at her with a hardness she couldn't decipher.

"What do you mean no," Natalie asked, trying to match his tone,

"You aren't going back to that library. It's too risky."

"It's the only place with a good enough connection to the internet to do. What we need to do."

"They'll find you. I won't let you put yourself in

danger."

Natalie was shocked. It was not like Elijah to get in the way of her plans. He had been so supportive of her decisions, and he never showed any sign of disagreeing with her approach. She looked at him, worry beginning to invade her mind.

Elijah continued, his voice strained, "I couldn't live with myself if something happened to you."

Natalie shaking her head was her only response.

Elijah let out a sigh as if relenting. To Natalie's dismay, he didn't, saying, "If the library is the best place, let me go in and do it."

"What?" Natalie stood at that, her voice angry. "What do you mean to let you do it? Why would you say that?"

Elijah stood as well. In a calmer voice than before, he said, "I'd rather they take me and you be safe. I'll share the documents, and if it comes to it, I'll be the one they take."

"It's my responsibility, Elijah! This is everything I've worked for. Why are you trying to take it away from me?" Natalie was yelling now.

"Because I love you!" Elijah stepped back, panting at the words he just let out. "I love you, and I can't stand to think that something will happen to you."

Natalie stared at him, speechless. She had only ever heard Carter utter those words to her. Hearing Elijah say them was supposed to feel different. She wanted to tell him she loved him too. She wanted to run into his arms and kiss him until her lips were swollen. But hearing him say them now, in this moment, in these circumstances? Natalie looked down at her feet, taking deep breaths to calm herself. She wanted to make sure her following words came out calm and collected.

"Carter said those words to me, too. He used them to manipulate me to do what he wanted, never thinking of what I wanted. He used those words when he doubted my capabilities. He'd used those words to take away every choice I had for myself. I'm sorry, Elijah, but I won't let you do that same thing to me."

Elijah's face paled. "Cheeks, wait," he said, voice desperate. "I didn't mean-"

Natalie put a hand up, interrupting him. "Save it. I'm going to do this my way. You don't have to help me if you don't like it."

Those were her last words to him before walking off into the forest.

# Chapter 22

Natalie didn't stop walking until she was at their makeshift shooting range. She needed to clear her head from the argument she just walked away from. She hated to think that Elijah was using the same manipulation tactics that Carter had once used on her. She wanted him to be different. She wanted him to acknowledge her strength and let her do what she needed to do. She couldn't be with someone who doubted her anymore. She thought he would be different, but wanting someone to be something they weren't didn't make them different.

Natalie allowed the sound of gunshots to fill her senses. She lost herself in the feeling of the gun recoiling with each shot fired off and the smell of gunpowder that surrounded her. Her mind had been racing from the confusion at Elijah's reluctance to let her publish the files and the manipulation tactics he was trying to use. Natalie wasn't convinced he did it purposefully, but she didn't care. He knew everything about what she had gone through with Carter, and he still did it.

Natalie hadn't noticed that she had unloaded her magazine, her gun clicking with each sob that came out of her. Tears were streaming down her face, both in anger and sadness. She knew she needed to go back and sort everything out, but she needed her space right now. She appreciated that he didn't come after her. At least he did that one thing right.

Natalie began reloading her gun when there was rustling in the woods. Natalie snapped her attention away from the bullets and towards where the noise came from. She expected Elijah to walk through the trees at any moment, but he didn't come.

Feeling concerned, Natalie finished loading her gun and chambered a round. Getting into a defensive stance, she watched where the sound came from and waited. Her mind went to Elijah's words when he first brought her here. *No one knows about this place. No one comes this deep into the forest.* Those words comforted Natalie as she waited, the cold breeze brushing her hair across her face, gun at the ready.

The comfort didn't last long as she saw someone emerge from the tree line. It wasn't Elijah. She pointed her gun at the stranger and waited until they walked through the trees. Natalie froze as Carter's face came into view.

She couldn't believe her eyes. There he was. The man she was meant to marry. The man she decided never to return to. He was standing there right in front of her in the place where she had been hiding. The place Elijah had told her was unknown to the outside world.

Carter scanned his surroundings until his eyes fell on Natalie. The relief overshadowed the concern in his eyes.

"Nat!" He sounded so happy to see her. "I can't believe it's you."

Natalie didn't say anything. She just kept the gun pointed at him. How had he found her?

"N-Nat. Put the gun down. It's me!" He spoke through a relieved smile, but his words were strained. He was scared.

"How did you find me?" Her voice was almost lethal.

"Put the gun down, babe. I'll explain everything." He began walking towards her.

Natalie stayed firm, keeping her gun raised. "Stop! Don't come closer. How did you find me?"

"I followed you, Nat." He said this as if it was a sufficient explanation. "I couldn't stand the thought of you being out here alone. You need me. You can't do this by yourself. Your mom encouraged me to come too. So I followed you."

Natalie wasn't shocked at his lack of faith in her, but his words still stung. He didn't think Natalie was capable of taking care of herself. This only fueled Natalie's anger.

"Why haven't you shown up since before right now?" It didn't make any sense that he followed her. They would have crossed paths before now. She'd been gone almost a week.

"Because I was following the agents as they followed you. They led me to this town about 7 hours from here." It was eight hours, but she didn't correct him. "They have agents all over that town looking for you. They've had search parties going for a while now. I heard about something that happened at the library. That they almost had you, but some guy showed up and shot some of the agents." Elijah. "Anyways, they all think you ran into the forest to escape. I figured I would search for myself."

"How did you wander this far into the forest?" Natalie was not backing down. She needed answers.

"I just kept walking. I slept on the forest floor, and I ran out of food. I was about to turn back, but I heard the gunshots." He pointed to her.

"You're lying," Natalie said. "Why would you run towards gunshots?"

"I swear I heard it," he said, ignoring her assumptions. "Please, Nat. Put your gun down, and let's talk. I've missed you." His arms were raised in surrender.

Natalie kept her sights trained on him as she looked into his eyes. There was nothing there but relief and that love she knew so well. Her grip on the gun softened. She lowered the gun and let her hands fall to her sides. She still gripped the gun as Carter walked towards her and gathered her in a tight embrace.

Despite herself, she hugged him back. She missed his smell and the feeling of his arms wrapped around her. He was everything familiar to her, and she felt like she was home.

He pulled away and motioned to kiss her. This made alarms go off in Natalie's head. She pushed him away and held the hand without the gun between them.

Hurt flashed across Carter's face. "What? I can't kiss my girlfriend?"

Natalie paused before saying, "No. You can't."

He let an unsettling grin creep onto his face before saying, "Come on, Natalie. Don't you love me? Didn't you miss me? Kiss me." His voice became harsher with each word.

Natalie wasn't going to fall for it this time. "No. I'm sorry, but I don't want to. It's good to see you, but I need time."

Carter looked like he wanted to argue, but he remained silent. They just stood there, the tension in the air thick, before he said, "So, how's the research coming along?"

Reality slammed back into Natalie. She forgot Carter knew why she was here. She forgot he was there when the agents threatened her. Still, something about the way he spoke made Natalie uneasy.

"It's progressing." She wasn't going to divulge anything. She still wasn't sure if she trusted him.

"That's it? You're not giving me anything else? Come on. You always tell me about your research."

That was before she realized what kind of boyfriend he was. "I just don't feel comfortable sharing it with anyone." She left Elijah out of their conversation.

Elijah. He didn't know Carter was here and was this close to their secret swimming hole. Natalie needed to find a way to get back to him without Carter following. She now wished Elijah had followed her.

"Come on, I know that's not true." Carter's words broke through her thoughts.

"What do you mean?" Her words were laced with worry.

"I know you've been here with that killer. The one who killed the agents. You two have been here, sleeping together. Working together on your research. I know Natalie." His voice was unsettlingly calm.

"How did you-" He cut her off.

"Is that why you really left," he asked accusingly. "To shack up with vagrants? I can't believe you would give it up for someone like him. After everything I have done for you, you do this to me?"

Natalie couldn't stop the shock from forming on her

face. She lifted her gun to point at him again. She didn't know what to say. Carter had known everything, yet he only showed face now when she was exposed and alone. She had to get away from him.

"What's wrong, Nat? Cat got your tongue?" He said arrogantly.

"Carter," Natalie started, "You need to leave."

"No, you need to come with me."

Natalie just shook her head.

"You're coming with me, Nat. You're going to leave that guy and come home with me. We'll sort everything out with the CIA later. Let me get you home safe to your mom." His voice transformed from arrogant to caring in a matter of seconds. It was unsettling.

"No, Carter. I'm not going with you," Natalie did her best to strengthen her voice.

"Nat, please. You don't even know this guy." Carter was talking with such a convincing voice. He sounded genuinely concerned like he was looking out for her. "I just want to make sure that you're safe. Your mom is worried. Please, just come with me. We can do this together like we always have."

At his words, Natalie's eyes turned into daggers. "No, Carter. We have never done anything together. We have always done things your way. It was always your decision. There was never a conversation. Whatever you decided was what we did, regardless of my feelings. Not anymore." There was a finality in Natalie's voice that sparked rage in Carter's face.

"Natalie, you're acting crazy. I'm the one you trust. I'm the one who is looking out for you. I know what's best. Now let's go."

"I said no. Now, how about you get out of here before I

force you out of here," she said,   training her sights on him.

Carter stepped back, the anger not ceasing. "You're choosing to stay here with *him?* With that fugitive?"

Face draining of color, Natalie asked, "What are you talking about, Carter?" She didn't believe a word he said. "I'm the fugitive here. And you will be too if you don't leave. Please go back to my mom. Tell her I'm okay." Her voice was pleading.

"Nat, you don't know this guy. He's not on your side here. I'm the only one who is. I'm the only one you can trust. Just come with me."

"No, Carter. I don't want to go with you. And I don't want you here."

"Nat, please. I can explain everything once we leave."

"No!" Natalie was shouting now. "Carter, we're done. You can't control me anymore. I won't let you manipulate me. Now leave before I kill you."

"He's working for them!" Carter shouted.

Natalie froze. She didn't believe it. Carter didn't say what he just said. It wasn't real. There was no way Elijah had been lying to her this whole time. He killed those agents back at the library. He promised to help her. To love her.

She didn't want to listen to Carter anymore. She needed to get out of here. She needed to get back to Elijah and make him tell her everything he had been keeping from her. He would explain everything, and Natalie would realize Carter was spouting nonsense. She wouldn't allow Elijah to jump around his answers anymore. She wanted truth.

"Carter," Natalie spoke, her eyes moving to him. "You need to leave."

Carter stilled. "B-but Nat. That man is-"

Natalie cut him off. "That man is the only person I trust right now. I don't trust you. I don't believe you. Now leave before I put a bullet in your brain."

The color vanished from Carter's face as Natalie raised her gun at him again. He just nodded and slowly walked to the tree line. Once there, he sprinted into the forest.

She waited a beat, wanting to make sure he was truly gone, before sprinting back to the camp.

# Chapter 23

Natalie made her decision. She picked Elijah. But there was still so much he hadn't told her. There were things that she questioned about him that he hadn't yet answered. She didn't know where he came from. She didn't know how he was so skilled with a gun or how his actions at the library were successful in getting them out. She asked him once, and he didn't tell her. She thought allowing him to share it in his own time would be best.

Now, she needed to know. Carter had found her and started spouting these theories that made no sense. He called Elijah a fugitive. He said Elijah was working for the agents who were hunting for her. Natalie ran back to the swimming hole in the cold morning air to find out the truth.

Her trust in Carter was close to nonexistent. Still, she knew him. He wouldn't have said those things if there wasn't even an inkling of truth in them. Elijah needed to explain himself if Natalie was going to continue working with him. She knew that she could send him away with a simple command. His feelings for her were intense enough to give her that power over him. He knew it, and she knew it.

She arrived at the camp and found Elijah cooking food by the fire. He noticed her coming into the campsite and turned his head to look at her. Seeing that she was running, he stood and approached her. He wasn't allowed to get too close before Natalie pulled out her gun and pointed it at his head.

"Talk," Natalie said again, her voice firm.

"Natalie...," he said, raising his hand in surrender and freezing where he stood.

He was confused. Something happened when she was out. She looked like she had just gone through something intense. His heart ached at the crippling anger she flashed at him.

"Tell me everything," she said, her voice still angry. "Tell me why you're so good with guns. Tell me how we got out of that situation back at the library. Explain why I just ran into Carter, and he accused you of working with the CIA." Natalie was screaming at him when she reached the end of her sentence. Tears were brimming in her eyes as she feared deep in her heart that Elijah had betrayed her.

The color drained from Elijah's face at her words. Carter found her. Elijah wanted to curse at himself for not following her after she stormed off. He knew she needed her space, but if he had known Carter would show up, he wouldn't have left her alone for one second.

How Carter knew who he was, Elijah didn't know. He knew there would be no way of getting out of this conversation. Carter implanted seeds of doubt in Natalie's mind. He had to tell her everything now. He knew getting the words out wouldn't be easy. Recovering from the hatred she'd feel towards him afterward is what he would never get over.

"Okay…" Elijah said after a moment of silence. "I'll tell you everything. But please put the gun down."

Natalie shook her head, keeping the gun raised. "I won't put it down until you explain yourself." Until she trusts him again.

Elijah stepped towards her, causing Natalie to tighten her grip on the gun. He only moved around to one of the chairs so he could sit. Natalie remained standing.

"Okay," he started. "My name is Elijah Walker. I'm a former technological expert working in the Special Activities Department of the CIA. I was pulled out of my unit to come on staff for a higher-up agent." He paused. "Agent Jannis."

Natalie fought back tears as Elijah revealed his true identity. He had told her his real name, a factor she knew was risky for him. But he knew about the experiments. He had worked for the monster who started them.

Elijah continued, keeping his gaze away from the disgust in Natalie's eyes. "It was my job to set up the cyber security for his unit and ensure that all of his dealings were classified with the highest clearance. I was in his unit for a month."

Natalie was in tears at this point. She couldn't hold them back. He had lied to her. He had kept these vital pieces of information from her. Carter was right. She knew nothing about Elijah. The ease he had with lying to her and evading the truth this whole time is what hurt her more. She trusted someone who was working for the man who was hunting her. She disclosed every secret, every detail of her research to him. She shared a bed with him and spent her days falling for a man who had been lying to her and telling her half-truths.

Shaking her head, Natalie said, "I trusted you," her voice cracking.

Elijah stood. "Natalie, I am not working for them anymore. I promise. Please just let me explain."

Natalie couldn't speak, so she just listened.

"I was only supposed to be there for a limited time. I was told that all I had to do was set up their security, and then I could go back to my unit in spec ops. Agent Jannis started making me file everything. He was having me put encryptions on every document he uploaded. I wasn't sure why he needed so much extra security until I looked at one of the documents. After I saw what he was doing-" his voice broke. "They were kidnapping people, Natalie. And the ones they weren't testing the weapons on…" He stopped. He just started shaking his head.

Natalie stopped crying. He knew what was happening. He knew what happened to those people who went unaccounted for.

Suddenly, everything started to click. This entire time, Natalie believed she had found a random backdoor into the CIA database. She thought she was lucky to make it past the firewall and into files. To the file that was impossibly encrypted.

"It was you," Natalie spoke in a whisper.

Elijah just looked at her, his head nodding softly.

"You let me in. You opened up that back door. All along, it was you who helped me get all those initial documents. And at the library, you left the door open for me. But how?" Natalie was utterly stunned.

"I was working on downloading some of the files onto

a hard drive—specifically, the ones about the people who were deemed *unfit* for experimentation. Then, I saw your codes working to take down my security. I wasn't sure what or who was doing it, but I could tell someone was trying to hack in. I hoped that whoever it was would find everything and expose those sick agents. I knew they would come after me after I stole their file. So I opened the door, and I never closed it. I took the file, and I ran."

Natalie, at last, lowered her gun. She just stood there staring at Elijah. He was working for Jannis and Bennet. Carter got one thing right. But how had Carter known? Natalie didn't want to think about him right now. She would figure out Carter and his motives later. Right now, she needed Elijah to answer one last question.

"What was in the file you stole?"

Elijah looked at her with somber eyes but didn't answer her question.

"Elijah. You are the reason I couldn't get into that file. You took it. Tell me what was in it. Please. It's the last and probably most vital piece."

Elijah nodded and stood. He walked over to his bag and took out a hard drive.

"Everything you want to know is on here." He extended the drive towards her. "I don't want to look at that thing ever again."

Natalie stepped forward, reached out, and took it. He moved to grab her laptop from where she had left it after their argument. She sat in a chair and plugged the drive into her computer. She then met Elijah's eyes. She looked at him with a question lingering in her eyes. He gave her a look that dared her to ask it.

"Did you know who I was when you first saw me? When we-" She couldn't finish her sentence. She couldn't ask it because if he had known who she was all this time, she would feel that betrayal all over again.

"No." He said, his voice firm again. "I didn't know who you were when we met. When I saw the agents back at the motel, I thought they were there for me. I genuinely thought the concierge was why you needed to hide, so I hid you. I didn't care if they saw me. I just wanted to protect you." Natalie smiled at that. "I didn't know you when we ran into each other in the woods. It wasn't until you mentioned your research that I began to suspect. The events at the library confirmed my suspicions. But no, Natalie. I didn't know it was you this whole time. After I found out, I didn't think I could tell you who I was. I thought you would hate me. So I just kept it to myself."

Natalie nodded and then reached a hand up to caress his cheek. She gave him a kind look before saying, "Thank you for telling me all of that."

He leaned down to kiss her, but she pulled away.

"I'm sorry, but I can't. Not right now. I just... I need time."

Natalie looked back down at her laptop screen. As soon as the icon popped up, she opened the file. She finally looked at all the documents she had been trying to get for so long. The one that Elijah had this whole time. Not allowing her heart to ache at the fact that he had kept this from her, she started searching for answers.

Natalie had only ever been able to speculate what was in the file. She came up with her own theories about where the missing participants could be. She thought they were taken to a different unit to have various experiments run on them. She thought they were taken out of the country and let go, away from anything they knew.

Nothing she thought of was what actually happened. The participants who were deemed "unfit" were sold. They were sold off to human traffickers. The CIA agents took measurements of each participant and separated them by least and most desirable. The most desirable being primarily young women and a few men with average to low BMIs. They were loaded into a van and taken to warehouses where they would be auctioned off to the highest bidder.

The file had photos of each person who was being sold like property. They were given numbers in place of their names. They were given tattoos on their arms that labeled them"fit for sale." The rest of the files were receipts. They specified who purchased them and how much was paid for each person.

Natalie was sick to her stomach. She couldn't believe what she was looking at. This was the file that they had all those extra encryption on. Now she understood why. Agents Jannis and Bennet were working with human traffickers to fund their experiments. They promised a product in exchange for funding. It was sick. It was twisted.

Natalie shut her laptop and broke out into sobs. She wouldn't stop the tears as they streamed down her face. It was wishful thinking to believe these people were being released once they were deemed unfit for the experiments. She hoped that they were being spared the cruelty of chemical weapons. Instead, they were being forced into sex trafficking and being brutalized in ways that Natalie couldn't even imagine.

This is what Natalie was going to school for. She wanted to go to school to work alongside law enforcement to stop these things from happening. She would have never imagined that the government she was driven to help was the same one aiding this sick organization.

Natalie cried for so long that she didn't notice when Elijah came and knelt in front of her and wrapped his arms around her. He pulled her head into his chest, and his hand ran up and down her spine. His other hand held her head firmly to him. She cried into his chest until no more tears were left.

***

Elijah hadn't said anything the entire time he comforted her. He was just there, willing to be anything Natalie needed. He would burn the whole world down for her if she asked. For now, she just needed to cry. She needed to escape all the frustration that this morning had brought her.

The moment Natalie told him about Carter, Elijah wanted to hunt him down and kill him. He wanted to kill him for playing mind games with Natalie. Carter was nothing but a coward that he would take joy in dismembering. But he wouldn't do a thing to him unless Natalie gave the okay. He would allow Carter to exist if it meant Natalie would be happy. Besides, he had his own atoning to do. He had told Natalie he loved her. He meant every word, but his timing couldn't have been worse. She took it as manipulation, and Elijah couldn't deny it. It was his intention, and he would do all he could to make it up to her, even if it meant she went to the library to publish the papers.

Regardless, Elijah was glad to tell Natalie everything. He had been wanting to come clean for days now, ever since he took her to bed. Ever since she chose to stay with him the morning after. Still, he didn't for his own selfish reasons. He didn't want her to hate him.

Now that everything was out in the open, Elijah could breathe. She didn't hate him. Her trust in him was damaged, but it was nothing he couldn't patch up again. Now, he just held her close, allowing her to cry. He wasn't going to rush her. When she was ready to make a move, she would say so. Until then, he would be here.

Elijah still didn't know how Carter knew everything. Thinking that Carter was wandering the forest doing who knows what made him uneasy. Whatever he was doing, Elijah would find out later. He was sure Natalie thought the same thing based on how her gun lingered on the spot he ran towards.

Elijah gave Natalie head scratches as her sobbing slowed. They still needed to figure out a plan, but Elijah would bring that up later. She had just gone through hell, and he needed to ensure she was ready to continue.

He pulled away from her, using the tips of his fingers to tilt her head back. When her eyes met his, he gave her a look as if to ask if she was okay or if she needed more time. She gave him a soft nod. At that, Elijah rose and walked over to the jackrabbits he had hunted earlier that morning.

"You hungry?" He asked.

Natalie merely nodded and cleared away her laptop and the hard drive. She put away everything that reminded her of the documents and stashed them in the tent. Then she sat back in her chair and watched Elijah as he cooked, knowing that would be the last meal he cooked for her.

After she ate, she was going to run.

# Chapter 24

The morning air was foggy when Natalie woke up. She silently got dressed and gathered all her belongings. Elijah had slept outside, understanding she needed time before welcoming him back into her bed. She allowed him to make her food one final time before hiding away in the tent, avoiding him the rest of the night. The crisp air hit her as she unzipped the door to the tent. Careful not to make too much noise with every step she took, she made her way out of the campsite. Taking one last look at the place she felt had become a part of her, she walked out.

Natalie couldn't trust Elijah anymore. She had no choice but to leave and carry out the rest of her plan alone. He had kept something important from her, and whenever she asked him about it, he avoided anything resembling the truth. She felt so betrayed. She knew Carter was a liar and manipulative, but she never expected Elijah to be the same. She expected Elijah to be better. She wanted him to be better. She knew then it didn't matter how badly you wanted someone to be better for you. People were sinners and deceivers; that is the truth of humanity. She knew the only one she could trust was God, a fact she had lost sight of.

Natalie ran through the forest, leaving Elijah behind at the place that she thought was what heaven might look like. As she snuck away, she heard voices begin to surround the oasis. Natalie was glad for the fog and the darkness of the late summer morning hiding her from sight. She realized then that these people were agents preparing to infiltrate the campsite. There was no doubt in her mind that Carter had told them where she was. He had to be in communication with them if he knew about the secrets Elijah kept from her. Anger and hatred threatened to curdle her stomach at the thought of Carter betraying her like that.

Natalie walked as quickly as she could without giving away her location. She planned to go to town and hopefully gain access to the library. She needed to circulate the location of the black site so she could include it in the manifesto she would send out. She was also curious about it and wanted to see it for herself. If she could make it there and find a way in, she would get a first-hand account of what was happening in the experiments and increase her credibility with news agencies.

Now that she left Elijah, she needed to find a new place to stay. She didn't know how long the CIA would look for her after she exposed them, so she hoped to find somewhere comfortable enough to hide for a few days.

As she walked, she felt bile fill her stomach at the thought of everything she and Elijah went through. She gripped a tree with one arm and bent over, clutching her belly with the other. She retched as tears rimmed her bloodshot eyes. She had fallen so deeply for Elijah. She knew that everything he did was a lie. None of his feelings were real. None of his promises were real. Guilt swarmed through Natalie as it hit her. The sex wasn't real. He didn't want to marry her. He was a fantastic agent in the CIA if he was able to convince her that there was a possible future between them. She gave up her virtue for this liar. At least she now understood how he had easily gotten them out of the library.

Natalie couldn't stop the tears from falling anymore. She sobbed into her hands, knowing that she'd let herself be used like that. It seemed that she had a type—men who manipulated and used her.

The anxiety was growing, and Natalie could feel it. Natalie straightened, wiping the tears from her eyes. She prayed to the Lord, asking for forgiveness again and the strength to carry out the rest of her task. Taking in a few deep breaths, she avoided the onset of an anxiety attack. She could allow herself to feel later. Natalie needed to get to the library to find directions to the black site.

Natalie shook off all the negative emotions that were filling every one of her senses and returned to her trek through the woods. She could better recognize the town's direction than on her first visit there. She knew the general direction, and she was able to spot familiar landmarks.

Half an hour into her walk, Natalie heard twigs snapping. Natalie whirled in the direction of the sound. She reached into her bag and drew her gun, preparing for any sign to shoot. The fog continued to surround her feet as she scanned her surroundings. She knew the agents had surrounded the camp and had likely touched base with Elijah. There was a chance he knew where she was going and told them.

The footsteps came quickly, Natalie whirling to see who was trying to sneak up on her. She froze when Carter came out from behind the trees. Natalie's hold on her gun tensed as she watched him stalk towards her, a look of satisfaction on his face.

"What are you doing here," she asked.

"No, hello, Nat? Running away changed you," he said, a relaxed smile spread across his face.

"Answer me, Carter." Her voice was firm now, her temper rising.

"I just wanted you to know that I took care of everything. You're free to come home now."

"What are you talking about?"

"I made a deal. Now, let's go." He motioned for her to come towards him.

Natalie stood her ground, not faltering. "Tell me what you did," she yelled.

Carter sighed. "I traded that man and all your research for your freedom. They have him. Now, we need to turn over all your papers, and we can go home. We can put this whole thing behind us."

"How could you," she said, her voice breaking. "Do you know what they're doing to those people? I can't just let it go on, Carter!"

"Yes, you can. You will because you're mine! I will bring you home with me even if I have to force you."

As he said his last words, there was a rustling in the trees. Natalie's attention went to where the noise was coming from, and she almost fell to her knees at who she saw. The two men who had chased her before walked into the clearing, wicked smiles plastered across their faces. They stood next to Carter, the sight turning Natalie's stomach.

"Hey there, sweetheart," the shorter one said. "Miss us?"

Natalie didn't waste any time. She turned and ran in the opposite direction from where they were standing. She ran through the fog that covered the ground. The morning sun attempted to warm the world around her, but it was no match for the coldness of the forest.

Natalie knew there was going to be no way she would outrun them. She didn't hear them following her, but she could sense they weren't too far behind. She knew what was going to happen. They were going to take her. They were going to erase every trace of the files from the face of the earth, and no one would know what atrocities the government was practicing.

She couldn't let that happen. She ran until she found a tree larger than the others around it. Natalie picked the tree because she would be able to recognize it if she ever came back here again. She hoped she had enough time to do what she needed to ensure the CIA never got their hands on her flash drive.

Natalie took her bag off her back when she arrived at the tree. She rummaged through it, looking up every other second to ensure they hadn't caught up to her yet. She felt her fingers find the flash drive before she gripped it in her hand and pulled it out of her bag. She went behind the tree, using it as a shield to hide her from the direction in which she came. She found a nook in the tree, large enough to fit something in there but small enough to be unnoticeable.

Natalie heard the men approaching, their feet

crunching the leaves with every step. It was now or never. She put the drive in the nook of the tree and spun around to rest her back on the trunk. Gripping her gun, she waited for them to get to her. It was inevitable that she would end up here, running away from predators. She just hadn't expected Carter to be a part of that group.

The footsteps became apparent, now sounding right behind the tree. Natalie heard the panting breaths and knew she was about to be taken.

"Come on out, love," the taller man's voice said, "We just want to take you back. I promise we won't bite."

His words were slimy, bringing a sour taste to Natalie's mouth. She forced herself to choke down her disgust. She wasn't getting out of this. She knew she would be taken and subjected to God only knows what. Taking a deep breath, praying that she would find a way out and find a way back to this tree, Natalie straightened and came out from behind the tree, her arms raised, and she took in the faces of the men. They looked at her with hunger and triumph.

"Take me away, boys."

# Chapter 25

She had another attack. As soon as she was thrown in a van, she felt the world around her closing in. Her lungs tightened as she attempted to suck in a breath to no avail. She gripped her chest, tears streaming down her face as she fought to calm herself. She was lost in her mind, focused on managing her breathing or trying to suppress the panic. She lay on the cargo van's cold floor, hyperventilating until she lost consciousness.

When she came to, she was still in the van. She didn't have her bags with her anymore, sure that the agents had taken them from her. She sat and prayed that she would be rescued from this dark abyss of despair. The air was stale, the metal interior of the vehicle sending sharp spikes of cold through Natalie's body.

She didn't know how long they had been driving for, her blackout taking away her sense of time. She hadn't known if she had been out for five minutes or five hours. She felt the van slow down until it came to a stop. She heard voices outside, laughter filling her senses. It brought a sick feeling to Natalie's stomach, sure of what they could possibly be laughing about. They had a kidnapped girl in the back of a van and were aiding a government agency in kidnapping others.

The doors to the van opened, and the brightness of the day crept past the people standing at the entrance. Natalie attempted to shield the sun from her vision, putting her hand up to block it. She couldn't distinguish who stood outside, squinting to make the figures appear clearer. It wasn't until they spoke that Natalie realized in horror who had come for her.

"Hello, Miss Walsh," Agent Jannis said, his tone a cruel amusement. "You are a hard woman to capture. You let my men run around like chickens with their heads cut off as you did your best to evade them." He paused, waiting for Natalie to say something in response.

"What do you want from me?" Her voice was raspy from the trauma she had just suffered.

"You know exactly what I want, Natalie. You see, I was going to let you go once I got those files you stole. Now that I have those files, I have all the power to do just that." He paused, looking down at her with his mouth curved up in a sinister smile.

"However, you have been bad, haven't you? You went as far as to threaten your own boyfriend," he laughed. "Had I known how violent you could be, I would have never agreed to let you go." He leaned closer into the van, his hands gripping the open doors. "I like a feisty woman."

Natalie bared her teeth at him, her gut recoiling at his words. She knew this man was sick, and everything he was saying to her now was solidifying that. It made sense to her now why the two men who had captured her got jobs working with the CIA.

Jannis stepped back from the door, letting Bennet through. Natalie shuffled herself to the back of the van. She knew there was no getting away from them, but she wouldn't go down without a fight. She screamed as Bennet grabbed hold of her, digging his nails into her arm as he pulled. Natalie thrashed her arms and kicked her legs, doing all she could to escape his grasp. It was a fight she knew she would lose, but she had to make it clear to them that she would keep on fighting no matter what.

Bennet finally got her out of the van and threw her on the floor. His face was hot with anger at the inconvenience of her fighting. There was no way Natalie could get out of this situation. He swung his leg, landing a kick on her stomach. Natalie let out a pathetic whimper and folded in on herself on the muddy ground.

Bennet was about to land another kick before Jannis stopped him. "That's enough! We can have fun with her later. Let's get her inside."

Bennet nodded and picked up Natalie off the ground like she was nothing more than a rag doll. He gripped her arm, letting her walk on her own, leading her towards a warehouse. Natalie tried to look around at her surroundings, ignoring the pain of being kicked. It was an area secluded in trees. Natalie knew they couldn't have been driving too long if it was still morning and they didn't seem to leave the forest.

She walked into the warehouse, color draining from her face as she took in the building around her. This had to be the black site where the experiments were taking place. Her mouth went dry as her eyes adjusted to the bright light of the building, and she took in the sight around her. The warehouse had hundreds of rooms separated by glass walls. Each room had a steel door for an entrance. The glass allowed for a clear view of everything going on in the rooms, bringing a sick feeling to Natalie's stomach.

The agent continued to lead her deeper into the warehouse until they came to a room towards the back of the building. This particular room had steel walls, blocking her view from whatever was inside. For some reason, that made Natalie feel worse than being placed in a glass room. At least in those rooms, witnesses could see everything that happened. In the steel room, she would be all alone with no one to witness the atrocities that would likely be done to her.

Bennet opened the door to the room, shoving Natalie in. He entered, followed by Agent Jannis. Natalie put her back to the wall farthest from where they stood, staring daggers at them. Her lip was curled in a snarl, making her look like a feral animal.

The agents stood side by side, smug expressions painted on their faces.

"Don't worry, Natalie," Jannis said begrudgingly, "We won't touch you. We have this unfortunate deal with Mr. Bailey promising no harm to you as long as he gives us what we want."

"He's not my boyfriend," Natalie cut in, her voice laced with anger.

Her words brought a smile to Jannis' face. "Well, if that's true, we'd hate to give you away against your will. We'll have to talk with Mr. Bailey to see how he wants to proceed since your behavior is unacceptable right now."

They motioned to leave the room, causing Natalies inside to tighten. She didn't want to be left alone in this room.

"Wait," Natalie said urgently. "Where is Elijah?" She didn't know why, but she was curious about where he was hiding. Natalie knew in her bones that he was responsible for her capture.

Jannis let a cruel smile spread across his face as he turned back towards her. He stepped towards her, coming so close that her back was flat against the wall. He reached up and cupped her face in his hand, making her cheeks hurt as they pressed hard against her teeth.

"Don't worry about him, dear. Agent Walker is exactly where he needs to be." That was all they said before exiting the room, leaving Natalie in the cold darkness without even a chair to give her feet a break.

She ran towards the door as it closed, trying to pry it open before it locked, but she was unsuccessful. Cursing at herself, Natalie banged on the door with her fists, hoping someone would hear her and let her out. It was wishful thinking, knowing the people they were experimenting on probably behaved the same and had no one care to answer their pleas for help.

Natalie gave up, slumping to the floor. She didn't allow herself to cry or to panic. She just sat there, a shell of herself, as she blocked out everything that was happening. She knew she would have to fight to get out of there. It wouldn't be easy, but she would find a way. For now, she just wanted to disappear from it all. She was mentally and physically exhausted from this entire situation, and, for a moment, she wanted to waste away into nothingness.

***

Natalie didn't know how much time had passed when Jannis returned to the room. She was still lying down in a pathetic heap on the floor. She sat up, shuffling her body further into the room to avoid the agent.

Her eyes widened as she watched Carter walking in behind him. The light from outside was the only thing that allowed her to see the evil grins the two men had on their faces. Natalie flinched as they entered, Jannis shutting the door behind them.

"Hey Nat," Carter started, his voice deceptively calm. "I'm sorry they treated you this way." His eyes traveled around the room and back to her, his face contorted in disgust. "Just come with me, and we can get you home."

Natalie didn't say anything. She just stared at Carter, her disbelief written all over her face.

"I told you she was being rude," Jannis started. "Can't even bother to respond when a man speaks to her. Quite embarrassing for you that you allow her to act like this."

He spoke about Natalie like she was nothing more than an animal. His tone was dehumanizing, and it made Natalie sick to her stomach.

"She wasn't always like this," Carter said, cutting through her thoughts. "She used to be easier to manage. It was that Walker who changed her." He spoke with pure hatred.

It gave Natalie a sense of satisfaction that Carter still felt jealous of Elijah. She was betrayed by both of them, but she reveled in the idea that Carter finally knew he would never be what Elijah was to her.

"Don't worry about Walker. He will be dealt with."

The words rang in Natalie's mind. *Dealt with*? Was he not working for them?

"What are you guys talking about," Natalie cut in, her confusion evident in her tone.

"Oh, that's right. You are still under the impression

that your dear Elijah betrayed you," Jannis said with a chuckle. "Stupid girl, he was telling you the truth. He stole from us, just like you did, and he's been hiding ever since. Thanks to you and this kind gentleman," he motioned to Carter, who was standing with a wicked grin, "we found him, and he will be punished for treason."

Natalie's face drained of all color. He was telling the truth, and she foolishly left his side. She refused to think she could trust him after he had kept everything from her, but she was wrong. Her feelings raged, sobs erupting for her. She couldn't contain her guilt and sadness at the thought of Elijah's face when he realized she left.

"Shut her up," Jannis said, his voice filled with rage.

Natalie looked at him, tears still streaming down her face. She began screaming, allowing the anger and despair to consume her.

Carter rushed forward and grabbed her by the throat. She refused to meet his eyes, feeling his anger. He pushed her body up against the wall and slapped her. Natalie, stunned by what he had just done, finally looked into his eyes. Any goodness that was there was gone, his eyes black. His grip on her throat tightened as he reveled in Natalie's shock.

Natalie's lip quivered as she looked at this man she thought she knew. He was nothing but a stranger now.

"W-why are you doing this," Natalie asked in a whisper. Her voice shuddered with every word.

"Because," Carter said. "All I have ever done was to protect you. How do you repay me? By cheating on me. After all your self-righteousness, you sleep with someone you've only known for a week." He talks through his teeth, disgusted.

Natalie's face turns stone cold. She knew this would be

something he would throw in her face when he found out. It was precisely the man who Carter was. He used her actions and mistakes against her to maintain power over her. She wasn't going to let it happen again.

"I did sleep with him," she started, Carter maintaining his grip on her throat. "I'm not going to apologize for it. He is a better man than you will ever be, Carter." Elijah would always be twice the man Carter was.

"You know what they do here, don't you," Carter said, his voice low.

He leaned into Natalie's ear and whispered, "They torture and kill people. They sell people, too. They wanted to sell you, but I didn't let them."

He moved back to look Natalie in the eyes again. "I don't think you understand how lucky you are."

"Why don't you show her," Jannis said, cutting into their conversation from across the room.

Natalie looked back and forth from the Carter to the Agent, her stony expression softening with fear that started to spread within her.

Carter's eyes looked up and down Natalie's face and body as he began to unbutton his pants with his free hand. "You aren't going to scream for him anymore, Nat," Carter whispered. "You're only going to scream for me."

Those were the last words Natalie heard before she was totally and completely violated over and over again.

# Chapter 26

The room around her was small, the air-conditioning unit being the only noise she could hear. She tried multiple times to listen for any other noise than the whirring of the AC. She placed her ear on the door, straining herself as she fought to hear any different sound. It was a poor attempt. She couldn't escape the noise that existed as a constant reminder of where she was.

It was the sound that she heard when she was being used by Carter and by the agents who helped themselves to her body afterward. It was the sound she heard while lying in a pile of tears and humiliation. Natalie lay down on the cold floor, her hands covering her ears, and she felt her sanity slipping away with every second. She tried humming a song, willing to do anything to drown out the noise, but it still bled through her fingers and scratched at her eardrums.

Natalie had lost track of how long she had been kept

in this room. They put her here after Carter's first attack on her. He had made it a scheduled occurrence to return and shatter her very being every few hours. He wanted to ingrain it into her mind that she had no power over her own life and that he would always be in control. It was working.

She tried her best to keep her thoughts positive but was failing. Whenever she tried imagining her life with Elijah or seeing her mom again, she was met with a darkness that crept in and destroyed any trace of light.

When Natalie thought of her mom, all she could remember was how she had broken Nancy's heart to chase the secrets and lies of the government. That train of thought led to her thinking about how her actions had left her here to be a piece of meat for any of the agents to take a bite out of.

She tried thinking about Elijah and how happy they were by the waterfall but was immediately covered in guilt at leaving him. Her decisions about him brought her here, in a dark room with nothing but fear surrounding her.

Natalie was about to start screaming, her mind growing tired of the endless buzzing of the AC, when she heard something. It was different from the sound that had been depriving her senses of anything peaceful. The noise came from outside the room. She sat up, her ears perking as they listened intently, waiting for the noise to sound again.

She heard it again, the sound of a muffled scream before a silent thud. It was just outside the door of her prison. Natalie quickly got to her feet and backed away further into the room. She waited, hearing whatever was making the thudding noise get closer and closer to the door. Natalie flinched when the door was hit, making a loud banging noise now. She didn't have any way of defending herself, her gun having been left by the tree.

The banging stopped. Natalie froze when the next thing she heard was the door lock clicking. She waited, fighting the urge to rush forward and swing the door open to make a run for it, knowing she would never make it past whoever was on the other side.

The light from outside started to stream in as the door opened. It creaked, the sound making Natalie's skin prickle as goosebumps spread across her skin.

She searched through all the possibilities she could come up with of who was about to enter this pit of darkness. Her first thought was that it was Carter wanting another piece of her. She had no more fight in her to stop him, but Natalie felt a surge of hope when the footsteps she heard didn't sound like Carter's.

She didn't let her body shake as she stood firm, her feet planted in a fighting stance. She was too stubborn to let whatever was to happen without making them regret it. Still, fear battled the courage within her. After everything she had endured, she prayed determination would outshine her trauma.

The door was open enough to reveal a tall figure as it entered the room. Natalie's breath caught. She couldn't believe who she was seeing.

"Elijah," she whispered.

The figure stepped further in, letting out a soft chuckle. "No, not Elijah. I'm much better looking than him."

Natalie didn't recognize the voice, but she cringed at the humor. As the man crept further into the room, Natalie was finally able to make out his features. He was gorgeous and almost as tall as Elijah, only lacking a couple of inches. He had dark, textured hair cut short and beautiful brown skin complemented by his hazel eyes. Every inch of him was chiseled to perfection. God did good when sculpting this man. His shirt strained to contain his muscles. Natalie compared him to Elijah, knowing that not even his size compared to the man standing before her.

As Natalie scanned him up and down. She noticed he had a gun holstered at his hip. Her mind snapped to attention as she tried to sink further into the wall.

The man looked at her, his eyes lacking the evil Natalie expected to see. Instead, she saw sorrow and sadness in his eyes.

Disarmed by his expression, she asked, "Who are you?"

He blinked before his eyes softened again. He sucked in a breath before answering. "My name is Malek Foster. I'm here to help you, Natalie."

She froze. Millions of questions ran through her mind as this man spoke. How had he known her name? Why was he there to help her? How did he even find her? She looked at him with confusion and distrust.

Seeing the questions running through her mind, Malek broke the silence. "Natalie-" he was cut off.

"Stop." She said, her voice almost breathless. "How do you know my name?"

"Just let me explain," he said, his arms coming out in front of him in surrender. "Elijah sent me."

Natalie stiffened at his words. Questions erupted through her mind at his words. Elijah sent him? Despite knowing she could now trust Elijah, Natalie still didn't feel like she could trust this man.

Seeing that she wouldn't respond, Malek said, "I can explain everything, I promise. We need to get out of here first."

Natalie didn't move.

"Come on, Nat," he said, noticing how Natalie cringed at the nickname. Still, he continued, "Those men aren't going to be unconscious for long. Let's get you out of here, and I'll tell you everything.

Malek's voice was a stark contrast to Elijah's. His voice was velvety and smooth. There was no rasp in his voice. He was clear with every word, and he had the kind of voice that made you want to listen to every word he spoke.

Natalie nodded in response and allowed Malek to lead her out of the room. He didn't bother touching her, not wanting to make her more uncomfortable than he could sense she was. He simply let her walk out, and he followed close behind her.

Natalie's eyes widened as she entered the central area of the warehouse. It looked the same as it had before, but now there were bodies everywhere. Malek had done this. The thuds she heard were actually bodies as they fell to the ground, unconscious. Natalie thought back to what Elijah had told her about himself. He had once been in the military before he was recruited for the CIA. If Elijah sent Malek, they must have known each other from that period of their lives. Malek was built like a man in the military, and she didn't dare to doubt that he could incapacitate a room full of CIA agents.

Malek stepped in front of her, taking the lead.

"Wait," Natalie said, her voice hushed but urgent. "I want to see something."

She turned towards a wall of filing cabinets and

motioned to open them. Malek stepped before her, stopping her from what she was about to do.

"What are you doing?" His tone urgent.

"I just want to see if I can find any more information," Natalie responded, and she pushed past him and opened up the first drawer. She sifted through the files and looked for anything she didn't already have. Not seeing anything new, she moved on to the next drawer.

Malek cursed, "Nat, look, I know you want to play detective, but we don't have time to review all these files. From what I know, you have more than enough information on these guys. Let's go." He tugged on Natalie's arm this time.

She glared at him, looking from where his hand touched her to his face. His eyes widened before he took his hand away, putting them up in a show of surrender. Natalie simply nodded and turned to follow him out. She knew it would be foolish to stay longer than they needed to.

Malek rolled his eyes and walked away. He led Natalie out of the entrance from which she had been dragged. Natalie spots the vehicle before Malek approaches it.

"Is that your car," she asked, her voice soft.

"Yes," he said, "Isn't she gorgeous?"

Natalie suppressed the smile that threatened to form on her lips. The car was anything but beautiful. It was an old Jeep Wrangler that had scratches all over it. The only things nice about it were the tires that looked like they had been recently purchased.

Natalie didn't comment about the car's aesthetic as she approached it. Malek hopped in with no care in the world. Natalie paused just outside, debating if she should get in or make a run for it,

"Before you try to run," Malek said, as if reading her thoughts, "ask yourself, do you know where you are? Do you know how to get back to where you need to be? If you do, by all means, go. I held up my end of the deal. I got you out. Now Elijah owes me a boy's night." Malek put the keys in the ignition and started up the car. Natalie paused only for a moment. He was right. She didn't know where she was or how to return to the swimming hole. She needed to go back there to retrieve her gun and flash drive from the tree.

Wasting no more time, Natalie got in the car and buckled herself in.

Malek turned on the music as if this was a normal situation and like he didn't just take down an entire unit of CIA agents. He bobbed his head to the tune, and he drove away. Natalie stared at the warehouse through the rearview mirror as it disappeared in the distance.

# Chapter 27

Malek only drove for three hours before Natalie began recognizing the woods around her. Realizing how close she was to the swimming hole, her heart fluttered with hope.

Somehow, her mind drifted to Carter. The hope that sparked dimmed to an ember as she thought of the things he had done to her. The things he had allowed other agents to do to her. She had been at their mercy and was left alone for hours before the attacks started again. Any control she once had over herself was taken from her.

Natalie had prayed for rescue, feeling her faith dwindle with every moment. Just as she was ready to give up, to believe that she was alone in the world with no one looking after her, Malek showed up and took her out of that place.

She thought about Elijah and where he was right now. Why hadn't Malek saved him too? Natalie would get her answers when they were back at the oasis.

As he drove deeper into the forest, Malek veered between trees with his jeep. Natalie now understood why it was so beat up. He drove until the trees became too thick to go through. They hiked the rest of the way, only having to walk an hour before finally arriving. As soon as Natalie heard the muted crashing of the waterfall, she knew she was safe.

She went into the clearing, seeing how trashed it had become. Elijah was gone. She didn't know where he had been taken, but she could tell by the scene that he didn't go down easily.

Natalie approached the water, sinking to her knees as she stared at the water. It looked so peaceful, and Natalie wanted to laugh at the irony. Her experience has been anything but peaceful. It has only been heartbreaking and soul shattering.

She felt Malek approach her, dropping down to sit beside her. She wasn't going to start the conversation, so she remained quiet, taking in the sound of the water.

"Elijah told me how to find you," he started, not wasting any time. "He had this radio that he kept in his bag. Whenever he needed anything, he would contact me, and I would do all I could to help him. This time, he mentioned you and that I needed to get over here as soon as possible to find you." He spoke with a velvety calm, his voice soothing to Natalie—nothing like Elijah's low rasp.

"How did you two meet?" Natalie asked softly. She was genuinely curious about the man who had saved her.

"We met in the Navy," he said, smiling as if remembering the experience. "We went through basic training together and were stationed in the same unit. Pretty soon, we became Navy SEALS. I was at the top of the class in firearms and combat. Elijah was right behind me in those areas, but he didn't have the natural skill that I have." Malek smirked with a playful arrogance.

When Natalie didn't look amused, he continued. "Elijah was favored for his technological skills. When he wasn't in the field with me, he sat at a computer and guided me through the mission. I can't count how many times he's saved my life."

"So, if you were both Navy Seals, how did you end up working for the CIA?" Natalie asked, understanding why Elijah seemed so skilled with his gun. According to Malek, he was highly trained and one of the best out there. Their careers must have been made if they were both so skilled.

As far as Natalie knew, becoming a Navy SEAL was one of the most challenging things in the entire military. They had highly trained soldiers, and only the best made it through the training. There were still no women in the Navy SEALS. The physical strain the training put on the body and mind was too great. She remembered her father talking about how difficult it was to join their ranks. Her father was a marine, but he always admired the willpower that those who became Navy SEALS carried.

"We were recruited," Malek continued, interrupting Natalie's thoughts. "The CIA first went to Eli. Everyone coveted his technological skills, but the CIA came with the best offer. His marksmanship didn't hurt either. Everything about him was what the CIA needed for their special activities department. After they hired him, he gave them my name. They recruited me soon after, and we've worked together ever since. At least, until those sketchy agents took him for their cybersecurity team."

"Wait," Natalie started, "how did Agents Bennet and Jannis find out about him?"

"Everyone knew about him," Malek said in a dark tone, such a contrast to the playful demeanor he's been presenting. "Elijah could hack into anywhere. He knows how to get past any firewall cipher or encryption. Those skills also give him the knowledge to know what security measures work best for keeping information secret. He set up new security measures in our unit. When other departments in the CIA caught wind, they all tried to poach him. None were successful until those two agents requested him. We were about to head out to take down a national security threat in Russia when Agent Jannis showed up with transfer papers. It messed up our entire mission to lose him, but they took him anyway. We kept in touch as often as possible, but he changed. Don't get me wrong, he's always been a standoffish prick. He doesn't trust easily. But something about this new place made him different." Malek's tone turned somber, but he continued, "I tried asking him about what he was doing and why he was acting so different, but he never told me.

"I looked around for information myself, but there was nothing about this research unit in our system. It was like they didn't exist. Even Eli's information had disappeared. There was no sign he had worked for any other unit in the CIA or that he was in the Navy. They erased my best friend. My brother. About two weeks into his new assignment, he radioed me and told me he was leaving the CIA. He didn't give me any details.  He just said that he had to go and that he'll reach out when it's safe." Malek tensed with every word he said but kept talking, needing to get every piece of information out.

"I heard from him twice since he left. Once, to tell me he was safe and not to worry about him. He said that if he needed me, he would reach out. The second time was three days ago when he told me about this girl named Natalie who needed my help."

Natalie nodded at the new information. She knew all about Elijah running. He had told her as much as Agent Jannis had. One thing still prodded at Natalie's mind.

"If he took the information, why didn't he expose them?"

Natalie asked this in frustration, turning her gaze away from the water to look at Malek. She felt panic building in her core, confusion fueling her anxiety.

"I don't know," he replied softly.

Malek noticed immediately that her mind was starting to attack her. Elijah had permitted him to be completely transparent with her, so that's what he did. He didn't hold a single piece of information back. Seeing what it was doing to her sent a wave of guilt through his body. The last thing he wanted was for her to have a panic attack.

Unsure of what to do, Malek wrapped an arm around Natalie, and she stiffened. He pulled back a moment, looking at her in question. She leaned into him to let him know his touch was okay. He tucked her body close to his. He held her and ran his hands up and down her back. Surprised, Natalie looked at him.

Malek returned her gaze and asked gently, "Are you okay?"

Natalie didn't respond, frozen by his touch despite giving him her silent permission.

"I'm not sure what to do in this situation, but you looked like you could use a hug." He gave her one last squeeze before letting her go. "My wife has anxiety, but she's never had an all out attack. Whenever I notice her getting overwhelmed, I just hug her. Sorry if that made you uncomfortable."

Natalie's head tilted. "You have a wife?" She welcomed this change of topic. It was a good distraction from her emotions at the moment.

"Yeah," he said through a smile. It was evident by the look on his face that he loved his wife deeply. "We met in high school, and I married her after my first tour with the Navy. Elijah was actually my best man."

"Why are you here with me and not with her?" A valid question, Natalie thought. If this man was clearly in love with his wife based on the look on his face as he spoke about her, why did he bother coming at Elijah's beck and call?

"Elijah is my brother. Esme, my wife, knows that. She loves Elijah just as much as I do. I can promise you that if I hadn't come, she would have. But I don't think I can survive our two daughters alone. That woman is a force to be reckoned with, and I'm too weak to say no."

Natalie smiled at that. Based on how his body was built, Natalie had difficulty seeing Malek as a softy. Children can make even the burliest and most dangerous men drop to their knees. Especially daughters. Natalie knew that all too well, remembering how she could get anything she wanted out of her dad. The bond between a daughter and a father is fierce.

Malek continued, "Elijah had been there for me when I needed him most. This is the least I can do."

Natalie studied him for a moment. Everything about this man was trustworthy. He was very genuine, and it was apparent how much he cared about Elijah. Natalie didn't know if she wanted to open her heart to trust again after everything she had just gone through, but Malek was breaking down those walls. Everything about his demeanor and how he spoke about his family softened

Natalie's heart. She knew the love of God was in this place by how Malek communicated.

She shouldn't have left Elijah. She should have listened to him. Instead, she didn't. When she heard the truth from the agents, she knew she was wrong for leaving. Now, hearing how Malek spoke of him, her guilt only grew. She left him. She left him to get taken by the agents.

Malek watched patiently as Natalie processed everything she had heard. It didn't look like another attack was threatening, but he stayed prepared just in case. He knew that the reality of what she did would hit her. She left him. She left his best friend to be taken by the CIA. Malek wasn't mad at her. He understood why she did it. Still, he waited for that fact to hit her before suggesting a plan to get him back.

Natalie finally met Malek's eyes, tears brimming. "They took him," she spoke in a whisper. "I let them take him. We have to get him back!" She stood, the urgency flooding her senses.

"I know," Malek said kindly, standing with her. "We will, and I have a plan on how to do it. I did some research before I got to you. I know where they are holding him."

"Tell me now," Natalie said, her voice rising. "Is he not at the black site? We need to get him back." She needed to tell him how sorry she was. How much she regretted not listening to him.

"He isn't at the black site they took you to. There's a second one. We will save Elijah, but I know him. He would kill me if I let you starve."

Natalie looked at him, confused. "We can eat later. He needs me!"

Malek didn't give in. "We can eat now, and we will get Elijah before they move. Besides, I think it would be good for him if he sat there thinking about what he did. Keeping secrets from the woman you love is never the right move to make, believe me."

"He doesn't love me," Natalie shot out before she could stop herself. He didn't love her, right? He had never told her so. He had threatened to marry her, but he never outwardly said it.

"Oh, yes, he does," Malek said playfully. "You're the woman of that sad man's dreams. It was about time, too, that he found someone he liked enough to invite to his waterfall. He's never even invited me here, the jerk." Malek looked around the oasis, feigning jealousy on his face.

Natalie didn't say anything. She knew it was true, as hard it was to admit. She knew it because she loved him too. She knew she loved him when his secret destroyed her.

"Anyways," Malek said, pulling her away from her thoughts. "I'm going to go get some grub. You stay put, and I'll be back soon. Sound good?"

Natalie nodded in answer. Malek grabbed his bag and took out his wallet. He gave her a quick nod before leaving her alone by the water.

# Chapter 28

Natalie took it upon herself to find her flash drive in Malek's absence. After Malek left to find food, she figured she would take that as her opportunity to find her things. Natalie knew where to go, but she had to retrace her steps. She wandered the woods, trying her best to find the tree where she hid all the secrets of the CIA. The forest was warmer today than the day she had been taken. She should have known that day wouldn't end well when summer's weather was gloomy and dark.

Natalie was close to giving up when she noticed tracks. She scanned them, kneeling to get a better look at them. Once she saw them, she knew they were her own from the night she ran. Sending up a prayer of thanks, she followed them in a run. She hadn't realized how far she ran to hide the flash drive that night due to the adrenaline coursing through her veins. Now, she was winded by all the running.

As soon as Natalie spotted the tree, she let out a laugh

of relief. She approached the tree and made her way to the nook where the flash drive still lay. She grabbed it, and her eyes welled in tears. She still had a chance to expose them and save Elijah. She looked around the area for her gun, spotting it several trees over. She picked it up and secured it in her belt. Remembering Malek's mention of a plan, she began her trek back to the swimming hole.

She recognized the forest well enough now that she got back quickly. She spotted Malek as she arrived, realizing how long she was gone for. He turned to her and sighed in relief.

"Nat, what the heck," he said, irritated. "Where did you go? I thought I was going to have to save you again. It would have been very inconvenient and rude on your part because I'd have to skip breakfast." Malek's hands rested on his hips as he looked up toward the sky, looking for why Natalie had caused him stress.

Natalie just showed him the flash drive.

He stopped, looking at it. "What is that?"

"It's all the files and documents from the CIA," she smirked.

"Uh huh, and where did you get that? I thought they took all your stuff."

"I copied the files onto a flash drive while preparing to release the documents to the public. I hid it before they captured me."

A smile now formed on Malek's face. "You are a clever girl. I like you."

Natalie chuckled as she slid the drive into her pockets. She scanned the area where Malek had laid out all the food he had obtained. She saw that he had returned with sandwiches and snacks from a convenience store. Natalie grabbed a sandwich and ate, not realizing how hungry she was until that first bite. She hadn't eaten since before she was taken, since that last meal Elijah made for her. Her heart ached at the thought of him.

"So," she started, "What's this plan of yours?"

Malek looked at her, his mouth filled with a bite of sandwich, before giving her a mischievous smirk.

*** 

The rest of the day was spent preparing. Malek had a laptop that he allowed Natalie to plug in the flash drive and ensure it still had everything she needed. Thankfully, the drive wasn't corrupted, and she was able to copy them onto his laptop.

Malek's plan seemed simple enough, though Natalie wasn't sure if they would successfully pull it off. According to him, Elijah was being kept in another warehouse similar to the one Natalie had been in. It was about one hundred miles away from the town library, in the opposite direction from where Natalie had been taken. The agents didn't think putting them in the exact location would be wise.

The fact that there was a second larger black site made Natalie nauseous. Their experiments had to be bigger than she could have imagined if they needed two locations to operate.

Natalie's posture straightened as she wondered how deep their research indeed ran. She thought about how much larger this second location was, comparing it to where she had been held captive. Natalie had noted how empty the warehouse was when she walked in. They must have transported the victims away from her.

"You ready to go," Malek asked, slinging a pack over his shoulders.

Natalie nodded, grasping the flash drive in her hand.

"We have to move fast," Malek said, "I don't know how many people will be at the library and if it will be swarmed with agents. We need to run as soon as you send the files and schedule your mass statement."

Natalie knew the plan well. She was going to go back to the library, just like she had initially wanted to. She prepared herself for the job as Malek drove. She kept checking for her firearm in her belt, anxiety threatening to consume her. The feel of her gun helped steady her mind.

They arrived at the library, and Natalie was shocked at how quickly they could make it by car. She was thankful for not having to walk another 6 hours on foot. Malek pulled the car up to the library.

"Okay, Nat," he said, unbuckling his seatbelt, "I'm going to make sure the coast is clear. Wait here."

Natalie nodded and watched Malek walk away from the car and enter the library. She looked at her surroundings, paranoid that an agent would pop out of nowhere and take her back. She did her best to steady her breathing, taking deep breaths as she scanned the streets of the town,

She saw Malek exit the, giving her a subtle nod before she left the car and walked towards the library.

"You got this," he said as they passed each other.

His words of encouragement were all she needed as she entered the library, sat at the same computer she had been at before, and got to work.

***

Malek waited in the car as Natalie was in the library executing her part of the plan. He was in awe of this woman who had so much strength and courage. He saw why Elijah had fallen for her. As he waited, he stayed on high alert, making sure no surprises would come up that would compromise Natalie.

He knew Elijah would not be happy that he brought Natalie to the library. She was left exposed, and they would have difficulty getting out if she was caught. Still, he knew it was the only way to make this a success. Malek would deal with Elijah's wrath if it meant those animals at the CIA got what was coming to them.

The longer Malek waited, the more anxious he grew. He knew what Natalie was doing wouldn't be easy, and he felt like agents could show up at any moment. His hands rested on the steering wheel, his thumbs tapping on it in an attempt to relieve his panic.

He was about to run in there to ensure she was okay when Natalie walked out of the library with a look of success on her face. Malek pumped his fist in victory. She walked quickly to the car, getting in and fumbling with her seat belt.

"We need to go," she said, urgency in her voice.

Malek reversed out of the parking spot and drove off towards the black site.

Natalie sat in the seat, triumph written all over her face. She did it. Now, she had to fight her way into the warehouse and save the man she loved. The thought of this next task brought daunting feelings to Natalie, knowing this part would be a lot more complicated.

Natalie scanned the car she sat in as they drove until her eyes fell on Malek. He was staring ahead, singing along to Hotel California by the Eagles. He looked as if he wasn't about to infiltrate a secret CIA black site.

Natalie thought about how Elijah would interact with him, knowing how broody he was. Elijah's personality was quite the contrast to Malek's.

Natalie leaned forward and turned down the volume, earning an offended look from Malek before he returned his gaze to the road.

"I know you didn't just touch my radio," he said, shaking his head.

"I had a question," Natalie said, blatantly ignoring his annoyance. "Can you tell me anything about Elijah?"

Malek snapped his head towards her, confused by her out-of-the-blue question.

"It's just," Natalie continued, "I really don't know anything about him other than he used to be in the military and then worked for the CIA. I know how caring he can be, but anything about his past or where he comes from is a mystery to me." Natalie's shoulders sagged as she looked down at her hands.

"I don't know if you noticed, but he's one broody prick," Malek began, his hands loosely gripping the steering wheel. "He's always been that way, as far as I know. I tried getting him to laugh while in basic training, but that just earned me a black eye."

"He hit you," Natalie asked, her eyes wide.

Malek laughed. "Yeah, not the last time that happened either. I always managed to get myself beat up by Elijah," he said with a smile. "Don't worry though. I gave him his fair share of black eyes and busted lips. Anyway, he's a good guy at his core. You're right, he's caring, and he's the most loyal man I've ever met. That's part of why I was so concerned when he went awol." Malek paused.

Natalie looked at him, waiting for him to continue. His playful demeanor turned sad.

"Elijah lost his parents when he was a kid," Malek said, his voice low. "They were murdered in a home invasion. He never told me many details, but it messed him up. He ended up living with his aunt and uncle. They had a daughter who he grew up with. He was the most protective older brother to her."

Natalie smiled at that.

"He loved that little girl so much. Elijah used to go hunting with his uncle a lot and always brought her along. He taught her how to shoot and how to fish."

Natalie noticed Malek's voice growing sad with each word.

"She ended up developing depression when she was in high school. Elijah was fresh out of basic training and on track to join the SEALS. He was in the middle of firing practice when he got the call. She committed suicide. He knew she struggled and would do his best to make her feel better when he was home, but I guess she didn't know how to cope without him."

Natalie's eyes welled with tears. That is how Elijah knew how to calm her anxiety. That is why he worried so much about ensuring Natalie felt comfortable after her attack.

Malek cleared his throat before continuing. "That man has been through the wringer. That is why he's so broody. He has a hard time letting people in because he refuses to get hurt again. Me and Esme are the exception. We forced our way in and refused to leave."

Natalie felt her lip pull up into a smile. "I'm glad he has you two," she said.

"He has you now, too," Malek said. "And I promise, he won't leave you in the dark about anything again. I won't let him."

"Thank you for telling me all of that."

"No worries, Nat," he said. "Now, if you appeased your curiosity, I'm going to turn my music back on.

Malek leaned forward and turned the volume up, Queen playing full blast through the speakers. Natalie smiled and looked out the window. After everything Malek told her, she felt like she could understand Elijah more than ever. She knew that as soon as she found him, she would choose him always and never make him feel like he would lose another person he loved.

*** 

Malek made it to the warehouse in an hour and a half, driving 70 the entire way. They didn't speak since Malek blasted 70's rock, his lucky number apparently, and belted to each song. Natalie wanted to be annoyed, but she appreciated how the music kept her from drowning in her thoughts.

Malek approached the warehouse, turning off his car lights and parking far enough away to avoid being spotted. The sun had set, and there was only the glow of the moonlight and the warehouse lights to provide visibility.

Natalie's suspicions from earlier were confirmed as she looked at the warehouse. It was much larger than where she was being held. She pulled her gun out of her belt, checking that it was fully loaded, before looking towards Malek.

He looked at her in awe. "That was hot," he said.

Natalie raised her eyebrows at him, "What? You've never seen a girl with a loaded gun before," she asked playfully.

"Of course I have," he said incredulously. "My wife tends to walk around our house with a loaded shotgun strapped to her back, and I think it's the sexiest thing in the world."

Natalie let out a chuckle. "So all women with guns are

hot to you?"

Malke nodded. "Yeah, it's an obsession of mine. Elijah is lucky to have landed you."

"I don't think Elijah would appreciate you flirting with me."

Malek roared in laughter. "Well, let's rescue my friend to test that theory."

Malek exited the car, leaving Natalie shaking her head. She sucked in a deep breath, looking in the direction of the warehouse. This could either be a success, or it could go very wrong. Having a little faith, Natalie hopped out of the car and followed Malek as he strode towards the warehouse.

# Chapter 29

The chill of the Northern California night surrounded Natalie as she walked beside Malek toward the warehouse. They left the car behind, hoping it wouldn't be found so they could have a getaway car if they got out of this alive.

A few agents stood guard at the warehouse entrance, holding rifles as they paced back and forth. Malek had his gun, a military-grade rifle that was almost the size of Natalie.

"I'm gonna take them out," he whispered. " Stay here."

Natalie nodded, her pistol held at the ready, as Malek stalked off into the darkness. Natalie kept herself low while waiting for Malek to pop up, but he never did. She searched the area she saw him walk off toward but couldn't see any sign of him. When she looked back at the agents, they were on the ground. Natalie's eyebrows rose, and she stood there in shock. Malek crept out of the darkness, now standing over the motionless bodies.

Natalie paused for a moment, unsure of what just happened, before she met him at the door. She looked at him, eyebrows raised, saying, "That, I was not expecting."

Malek only grinned as he leaned down, patting down one of the agents. He searched his pockets and rolled over his lifeless body until he found the keycard to the warehouse. Malek gripped it in his hands and brushed past Natalie. She stepped aside, letting him get to the door. Before she scanned the card, he looked back at her.

"Are you ready for this," he asked.

"Let's do it," Natalie said, her grip tightening on her weapon.

Malek smirked before turning and unlocking the door to the warehouse. He opened the door, peeking his head inside, before motioning for Natalie to follow him. As she stepped into the warehouse, she saw everything. It was worse than where she was held. This warehouse had the same glass rooms and the medical chairs, but there were more rooms here. There were endless rows of rooms that contained the kidnapped people who were strapped to the chairs, unconscious.

Natalie stood there, her vision blurring with the tears she tried to fight. Malek suddenly pushed her to the side behind a filing cabinet, taking hold of her shoulders and staring into her eyes. Natalie looked at him, confused.

"I know it's hard to look at," he said, sorrow in his tone, "but we need to stay focused. We need to find Elijah."

Malek's eyes bore into her own, and she nodded reluctantly. She knew what she was getting herself into. She'd seen the files. She knew what they would find here. Taking a deep breath, Natalie scanned the room before bringing her eyes back to Malek.

"What's the plan," she asked.

"We're going to split up. You take the west end, and I'll take the east end. Look in every room for Elijah. Be ready for anything. If the wrong person catches you, you will die. We'll meet back in the middle, hopefully, one of us with Elijah." He spoke in a hushed tone.

"Okay, got it."

"Stay safe, Nat."

Malek gave her one last smile before he turned away from her. He crouched down, walking as stealthily as possible to avoid unwanted eyes. Natalie was shocked that no one had noticed them walk in, but from what she saw, they were too focused on their computers to look up.

Natalie scanned her surroundings before stepping out from the coverage of the filing cabinet and making her way to the first hallway of rooms.

Cement walls surrounded the first few rooms she looked into. She had to open the doors to peek inside. Each time, she feared she would be met with an unfriendly face. Fortunately, the rooms were empty. She walked in a low crouch identical to how she saw Malek walking as she moved up and down the hallways, peering through the glass walls in each room. She had not been able to find Elijah yet.

Natalie was rounding another corner, heading to the next hallway, when she ran into someone. Stepping back, Natalie looked in horror at who stood before her.

"Well, well, well. Couldn't stay away, could you," Agent Bennet asked.

Natalie wanted to scream, but her voice escaped her. She turned to run, but she was met by the two men who had taken her. They gave her those slimy grins before grabbing her arms. They took her gun away from her, handing it to the agent.

Not again. Natalie couldn't be taken again. Not when she was supposed to save Elijah. She began to fight their grips, but it was no use.

"Take her to the interrogation room," Bennet said, his eyes on the gun they had taken from her. "Agent Jannis will want a word with her."

Natalie screamed as they hauled her away. They dragged her to one of the cement rooms she had initially searched. She hoped Malek heard her screams before they were muted by the shutting door.

The men threw Natalie into a chair. She pushed back on the floor, sliding away from them. When they approached her, she evaded them by moving below their reach. She didn't get far until they grabbed her from behind. Natalie swung her head back, hearing a crunch before one of the men started to yell.

She was thrown to the ground. Natalie turned to see the damage she had delivered, smirking at the blood that trailed down the shorter man's face from the broken nose she gave him. His face was pink with anger as he reached for her. Natalie attempted to fight him off, but his anger fueled his strength. He placed her back in the chair, slapping her before handcuffing her to the table.

"Wait here, you whore," the shorter one said before both men walked out of the room.

Natalie's mind was reeling. She had come so close to finding Elijah and getting out of there. She still had to make sure her plan from back at the library worked. She knew what the risks were in coming here. Still, she had hoped she could get in and out without getting caught. She wondered if this was how their lives would be—coming so close to an escape only to have the rug swept from underneath their feet, never able to make any progress.

She thought about Malek, hoping that he was still out there looking. She hoped that he would be successful in saving Elijah. She figured this would be worth it as long as they got out. She wanted Elijah to be safe, his safety mattering more than hers. She wanted Malek to make it out and return home to his children. If her plan worked, she would be saved soon, and the agents would be exposed. If it didn't work, maybe Malek and Elijah would fight for her. Regardless of what happened, she just wanted them to be safe.

Natalie sat at the table, unable to move. She wanted to stand and to pace. Sitting there, unable to do anything, was messing with her nerves. She didn't know how long they would make her wait. Based on how it was the last time she was captured, they would resort to sensory overload to drive her mad. The room's brightness was already giving her a headache, and the room was eerily quiet. It starkly contrasted with the noise of an AC unit in a pitch-black room. She didn't know which one she hated more.

The entire situation triggered memories from when she was held captive before. Images of hands invading her body flashed through her mind. Sweat began to bead on her forehead as she tried with all her power to suppress her fears, but it was useless. She couldn't stop the panic that flooded every cell in her body, knowing there was a chance that she was going to be assaulted again.

After what seemed like an eternity, she heard the door knob move. Her attention snapped to the door, her terror moving through her veins as she waited to see what nightmare would haunt her now.

Natalie's blood began to boil as she watched Carter walk into the room, trailed by Agent Jannis and Agent Bennet.

As Natalie looked at Carter, disgust in her eyes, as she saw the look of smug satisfaction in his eyes. He knew what he did to her at the other warehouse location. He knew how badly he wounded her and was glad that she cowered in fear at the sight of him. He was glad he still had a sense of power over her, even if he got it in an unspeakable way.

Carter walked toward her, his stony indifference towards her painted across his face. He leaned on the table, placing both his hands on the cool metal as he towered over Natalie. Behind him stood Jannis and Bennet, their arms crossed with looks of amusement. Natalie looked back and forth at them, waiting for one of them to make the first move. She refused to break under their stares. She wouldn't utter a word until she knew what they wanted from her.

It was Jannis who spoke first. "Did you enjoy your little vacation, Miss Walsh," he asked cooly. "We weren't happy when we saw what had been done to our agents. You left quite the mess."

Natalie looked at the agent, her eyes filled with hate. "They got what was coming to them, in my opinion," she said, mustering up any ounce of arrogance she could find. "But I'm not the one responsible for that." She smirked as she finished her sentence.

"Don't make this difficult, Nat," Carter said, his words laced with annoyance. "Listen to the Agent, and then we can go home."

Natalie scoffed. How could Carter still think she would

leave here with him? He was delusional. Still, Natalie listened. She straightened in her chair, pulling on the cuffs that held her, before settling back down. She trained her gaze on the chains that bound her to the table.

The two agents stepped to the table and sat in the two chairs opposite her. Carter walked to the side of the table, towering over her from the right. Natalie could feel their stares. She felt how their eyes grazed over her. It made her want to recoil into herself as she remembered what each and every one of them had done to her. She still refused to look at them.

Agent Bennet placed a bag on the table that Natalie hadn't noticed before. She took a quick glance at it and saw that it was her bag. She gave them the bag, saying it had everything they wanted. It was a lie, and they knew.

Agent Jannis looked at Natalie with a cruel satisfaction. He knew she realized the truth: they found nothing on her laptop. Any piece of information that was supposed to be on it was gone. That is why they had brought her in here. They wanted to know what she did with all the files. Jannis knew that she wouldn't have deleted them. She was too bright for that. She hid them somewhere, and he wanted to know where.

"Tell me, Natalie. Do you take us as fools?" Jannis started, his voice cold. "Because it feels to me that you do. I can assure you, I am no fool."

Natalie didn't respond.

"We know you hid the files somewhere. Tell us where they are." Jannis continued.

Silence.

Bennet slammed his fist on the table. Natalie flinched, her eyes flying to the agent. Pure rage was all over his face. Natalie felt fear growing in her stomach. Bennet always seemed like the good cop to Jannis' bad cop, but now he looked like he was worse. Like there was a darkness, he kept hidden for occasions like this—a wolf in sheep's clothing.

"Where are the files?" Bennet asked, speaking through his teeth.

"I don't know what you're talking about," Natalie said. "When you stole my laptop from me, they were on there. Whatever happened to them afterward is not my fault," she said knowingly. She failed at disguising the fear in her voice.

"Liar!" Bennet said, his voice rising. "Tell us where they are, or else."

Natalie almost smiled at his words. Or else? It was such a cliche thing to say in this situation. Jannis saw the amusement in her eyes.

His sneer contorting into a menacing smile, he said, "Natalie, you're going to tell us where the files are," he paused. "Or we will kill your mom."

Shock slammed into her like a truck, the air around there threatening to choke her. Natalie moved her gaze from Bennet to Jannis, any amusement in her eyes now gone. Now, she looked at them with pure hatred. She didn't bother saying anything. She didn't believe them. Still, she knew they would show their hand if she held out a little longer.

Jannis then looked back towards Carter and nodded as if giving him an unspoken order. Carter walked to the wall behind him, pressing in a hidden panel that revealed a row of buttons. He pressed a green button, and to Natalie's right, the wall lifted to reveal a window that led to another room.

Color drained from Natalie's face as she took in the

sight before her. It was her mom, strapped to a chair, unconscious.

# Chapter 30

Nancy Walsh sat in the medical chair with straps on her arms and legs. She resembled a dead fish with the way she lay there motionless. There were researchers in the room around her. One held a clipboard, likely noting how Nancy would react to their tests. Another researcher stood to the side, filling syringes with liquid from various vials.

Natalie pulled on her restraints, fighting to get to her mom. She blinked back the tears that threatened to fall as she looked back towards the agents. They looked amused at her horror.

She then trained her eyes on Carter. He stood there, a blank expression on his face.

"How could you?" Natalie said, her voice cracking.

"How could I?" Carter said, taking a small step forward. "How could you, Nat? You left and started shacking up with that guy. You betrayed me all for what? A guy who validated your feelings? I made you stronger,

Nat. I could have been the one to help you. Instead, you left me. I had no choice but to help these agents. I'm doing all this for you."

Natalie looked at him, completely stunned. "You're insane," she whispered.

Jannis cut in. "Listen, Natalie. We just want what you took from us, what you stole. We don't care about any petty arguments you have with Mr. Bailey. Just tell us where the files are."

Natalie slowly moved her gaze from Carter to Jannis. "I'm not telling you a thing until you let my mom go." She spoke softly but firmly.

"If we did that, we'd have no leverage. Tell us where you put the files, and we'll let her go." Jannis looked at her with what looked like compassion.

Natalie almost bought it until Carter stepped forward.

Piercing eyes never leaving her, he said, "Let me talk to her. Alone. I can get the information you need."

Natalie's stomach clenched.

Jannis and Bennet gave each other a quick look before Jannis sighed and stood.

"You can talk to her, but we aren't leaving this room," Jannis said with a look of annoyance toward Carter.

"Fine," he replied.

Bennet and Jannis moved to stand at the entrance of the room. Carter moved one of the chairs out of the way before centering the other one directly in front of Natalie. He paced back and forth behind the chair as if deciding what he was about to say. He seemed like he was at war with himself, and it made Natalie uneasy.

Carter knew what he was about to do. He was trying to muster up the courage to do it. Finally, after multiple grunts of annoyance from the agents, he stopped pacing.

He pulled out a chair from the table, and he sat.

Sitting across from Natalie, he scanned her face and thought about how to formulate his words. He had to be careful with how he spoke to her to avoid her shutting him out further than she already had. Carter knew he needed to appeal to Natalie's better nature. The fact that her mom had been captured and was now strapped to a medical chair was not a good start.

Carter had to atone for that. He had to atone for everything he had done to her and how he violated her in the worst possible way in a fit of anger. He had felt sick about it, but he knew there was no other way to get Natalie to listen to him. Carter had to make her see that he hadn't wanted any of it. He had done it to save her. Carter wanted nothing more than to make sure Natalie returned home to him. To safety.

Natalie didn't spare a single glance at Carter. She didn't care about a single thing he had to say. She just stared at her mom. Her sweet mom was now suffering. All because Natalie wanted to fight for the lives of innocents. Wasn't her mother innocent, too? How could she have chosen the lives of strangers over her mom's life? All Natalie could think of was a verse she had once read. *Whoever is kind to the poor lends to the LORD, and he will reward them for what they have done, Proverbs 19:17.* But what reward was this? Her mom's life hung in the balance all because she wanted to save strangers. It made no sense to Natalie. Tears falling from her eyes, she lifted a silent prayer. It was a simple prayer. One that she felt deep in her core. *Help.*

"Nat, look at me," Carter said, interrupting her thoughts. "You need to listen to me."

Natalie looked at Carter but said nothing. She just

stared daggers at him until he spoke again.

"You need to tell them about the files," he said, sounding sincere. "I promise they won't hurt your mom if you give them what they want. Please."

"How could you?" It was all she could say.

"Babe," he breathed, "I did it for you. Everything I have done has been for you."

Silence.

"Please, Nat. You have to believe me. I never wanted you or your mom to get hurt. I didn't even know they took her." A lie. "As soon as I found out, I tried to get them to release her. I just want all of us to go home. I want things to go back to how they were."

"I don't," Natalie said, her tone sorrowful.

Carter looked hurt, but he continued. "Baby, I love you. I want to protect you. Please. Please give them the files. I can't lose you or your mom." His voice broke as he finished.

Natalie's head tilted to the side, assessing him. He was on the brink of tears as if everything he said was true. He hadn't known the agents would take her mom. He didn't know what he was risking. He thought he was helping. He wanted to make sure she was safe. He didn't know Elijah, which explains the hostility towards him. He just wanted to help, right?

Natalie looked into his eyes, hoping to find the sincerity in his gaze. Instead, she found nothing but pure evil. She saw the eyes that ate away at her soul with every moment of torture he had put her through. He looked at her with empty eyes, only seeking what he wanted from her. It was then that Natalie indeed saw Carter for what he was. Carter never loved her, and he never loved her mom. He just wanted power and control and her submission. Carter had forced it out of her before. Everything he was saying right now was a trick to get her to fall for him all over again.

Natalie straightened in her chair, narrowing her eyes at Carter. "You're lying."

She spoke only two words, but they were enough for Carter to lose it. He slammed his fists on the table. Natalie didn't give him the satisfaction of flinching. She just looked at him in disgust.

"You know the things they do here, Natalie," he was screaming now. "I was trying to avoid that. I was trying to protect you. But you won't listen. It's like you want to be their slave. I was offering you freedom."

"Life with you has been its own kind of slavery," Natalie said, emotionless.

Carter laughed. It was the most terrible noise Natalie had ever heard. "You think you were a slave to me? No, Nat. Slavery was what happened back at the other warehouse. I let them do that to you so you could learn. You needed to know what was in store for you if you didn't listen to me. It seems you need another reminder."

Carter stood up and came around the table. He took Natalie's chin in one hand and stroked her hair with the other.

In a deep voice, Carter said, "I will give you the reminder you need. Then, I will let Alan and Bruce remind you, too." So those were their names. "Then the agents and anyone else who will have you until you learn that life with me is better than anything else you can find."

Natalie's face drained of all color just before Carter wrapped a hand around her throat. Lifting her by her neck, he spun her around and slammed her face onto the cold metal table. Her arms were still cuffed to the table, and they strained with the forced movement. She let out a cry of pain that was drowned out by the sound of Carter loosening his belt.

Natalie did all she could to fight back. She kicked behind her, hoping to land a foot anywhere on Carter, but she failed. She tried her hardest to free her hands, but it was impossible. Carter pressed down on her back, pinning her down with the strength of his arms. Natalie was helpless as she lay face down on the table. She turned her head towards the agents, looking for any help they would be willing to offer. She was met with stares of smug approval. Tears started streaming down Natalie's face. She closed her eyes, knowing there was nothing to be done.

Carter unfastened his belt and lowered his pants. He scanned Natalie up and down, taking in every curve as she lay before him. He ran his hand up her back, sending chills throughout her body.

"I'm going to make you wish you never ran away and found that man. I'm going to make you forget how he made you feel because I can make you feel better," he said as he leaned down to whisper in her ear.

Natalie sobbed, unable to contain herself. She wouldn't be able to stop what was about to happen. She had no way of fighting back. He had her pinned, and he was stronger than her. Instead, Natalie kept praying her simple but powerful prayer. *Help.*

"Don't cry, baby," Carter continued, his one hand now working to lower her pants. "You're going to love this. Then maybe you'll talk."

Natalie remained silent, her tears still falling. She closed her eyes hard, trying to make her mind go elsewhere. She could only think of Elijah. Of the way, he had saved her. The way he had opened her eyes to the truth. Elijah was the man who helped her with her anxiety. He was the one person who didn't make her feel like her emotions were a burden. He encouraged her to be open and honest with her feelings without fear. He helped her see the toxicity that Carter had brought to her life. He even accepted her intimate boundaries without question. He never made her feel bad or guilty. He refused to accept her apologies because she never had anything to apologize for. It was at this moment she knew that God had led her to Elijah. He took her away from this controlling and toxic person and led her to someone who helped set her free.

Natalie let peace fill her mind, body, and soul. She cast out the darkness and accepted only light. Tears still fell from her face, but they were tears of grace. They are tears that said no matter what happened, she wasn't alone in her suffering. She never was.

Just as Carter began to lower her pants, the door burst open.

# Chapter 31

Malek quickly moved up and down the hallways as he looked for his best friend. As he rounded another corner in the large warehouse, he heard her scream. It sounded far away, but the warehouse walls echoed it, playing her terror over and over in his head. It became all he could hear as waves of fear and anger rushed through him like a tsunami. It stopped him dead in his tracks as he thought about what to do. He had two options. He could give up looking for Elijah and rush to save Natalie. If Elijah knew Malek had abandoned her, he would kill him. His second option was to ignore her screams and continue searching for Elijah. Once he found his friend, he could channel their rage to wreak havoc on this warehouse and look for Natalie.

He went with option two, making a silent promise to Natalie that he and Elijah would tear this place apart until they found her.

Malek let go of all his restraint then. He didn't make it

a secret that he was there. He opened fire on anyone who got in his way. With every room he passed, agents came out and demanded his surrender. Malek only gave them an answering smirk before killing them where they stood. He left a trail of bodies behind him, not stopping until he came across the room that held Elijah.

As soon as he saw his friend, he sighed in relief. Elijah was handcuffed to a table, the space around him trashed. Two agents were standing in the room with him, keeping guard. Malek smiled, opening the door to the glass room and walking inside, knowing these agents would not survive the storm that was coming for them.

***

Elijah had been sitting in this room for three days. There were guards on a constant rotation to keep watch over him. He didn't know what they had planned for him, but he knew he had to figure out a way out soon.

He trashed the room, trying at every opportunity to fight his way out. They had interrogated him for days, trying to get him to reveal where Natalie's files were. He had refused to comply, promising the death of each of them.

It was when they revealed they had captured Natalie that Elijah stopped fighting. They promised to make her death long and painful if he even attempted to escape. They threatened her life if he even thought about attempting an escape. He hoped Malek had gotten to her in time.

The two agents that were with him were armed to the teeth. One stood with his back to the entrance, gun pointed directly at Elijah. The other agent stood to the left of the room, his gun lowered in his hands, hanging by the strap around his neck. Elijah had never seen these agents before, knowing they never assigned the same agents to guard him twice. This pair looked brand new to the agency. They weren't about to talk to a prisoner. If anything, they would do all they could to impress their superiors. This meant Elijah was in a very compromising position. The slightest movement from him could spook the agents, so he had to tread carefully.

Elijah turned slowly to the agent, who had his gun lowered. The man's grip tightened on the weapon, but he kept it lowered. Elijah looked him in the eye and offered him a friendly smile.

"How long have you been in the agency?" Elijah asked, attempting to show some decorum.

"Shut up," the agent responded, his voice deep and aggressive. He moved his gun up slightly, warning Elijah what would happen if he didn't comply.

Elijah didn't listen. "I've been with the CIA for about three years now. But after they brought me to this department, I left. Wanna know why?"

"I said shut up, Walker," the agent said, finally pointing his gun directly at Elijah.

Elijah took a peek over his shoulders, seeing that the other agent had moved away from the door and had come closer to where he stood. Elijah slowly put his hands up, his movement constricted by the cuffs he had on.

"I don't want any trouble, guys. I just need you to understand something. They're kidnapping and selling people into trafficking." Elijah saw no reason to hold back. "I'm here to put a stop to that."

"Do you not know how to listen?" It was the agent behind him now. "Keep your mouth shut, or well, glue it shut."

Elijah ignored him, keeping his eyes focused on the agent before him. His face had drained of color when Elijah revealed the truth about the CIA. This was a good thing. It meant that only some people here knew about the experiments. It allowed room for Elijah to inflict doubt in the minds of those not deemed trustworthy by Bennet and Jannis.

Elijah was in the military. He knew that a squad performed as well as its weakest link. Everyone needed to be on the same page and know where their weaknesses were in order to have a successful mission. If there was no trust and some people were withholding information, everything would fall apart. The fact that Bennet and Jannis forgot that simple rule regarding their leadership made Elijah smile.

"You believe me, don't you," Elijah asked the agents standing before him.

The agent didn't say anything.

"Don't listen to him, Cody. This guy is insane," said the agent behind him.

Elijah's brow rose. "They haven't told you everything," he continued. "Jannis and Bennet can't trust just anyone, and it seems you didn't make the cut." He was still speaking to the agent in front of him.

Cody's muscles tightened.

"Shut up, Walker!" Said the agent in the back. "Cody, he's just trying to get in your head. Ignore him."

"I don't think you were deemed trustworthy enough, but your friend was," Elijah said. "Cody, is it? Don't you ever wonder if there's something they aren't telling you?"

"That's it, Walker. You're done."

That's when the door burst open, and Malek walked in. He wasted no time in killing both agents before looking at his brother, a look of playful arrogance on his face.

Elijah snapped his head up, his eyes filled with a deadly promise. They softened as soon as they saw who had entered the door, his head moving behind his friend in hopes of seeing Natalie.

She wasn't there. Elijah's face fell at the absence of Natalie. He trained his gaze on his friend, eyes searching for an explanation.

"Where is she?" His voice was low.

Malek only smiled, leaning on one leg and swinging his gun up to rest on his shoulder. "No, 'it's nice to see you' or 'thank you, my bestest friend, for saving my life'?"

Elijah advanced on Malek, paying no mind to the weight of the table he was still cuffed to. He landed a kick in the center of his friend's chest, eyes wide with anger. The force of the kick pushed Malek back, his body slamming against the wall.

Elijah was in Malek's face as he yelled, "Where is she?"

Malek's gaze darkened, his time for fun now over. "I heard her scream while she was looking for you." Elijah's spice straightened, but Malek continued, "They took her."

Elijah didn't rage. He didn't yell at his friend. He just closed his eyes, allowing the rage that filled him to become his very being. When he opened his eyes, Malek saw nothing more than the slaughter he was about to commit.

"Take these cuffs off me," said Elijah.

Malek wasted no time as she fired his gun at the spot where the cuffs met, snapping them in half. He handed Elijah a gun he had strapped to his back.

Elijah checked that it was loaded before looking at his friend, "Let's go."

They exited the room and unleashed the monsters that lived within.

Malek knew where Natalie had begun her search, so he led Elijah there. No one was left alive behind them as they plowed through everyone who tried to stop them. As individuals, they were deadly. They were impossible to defeat. Their skills alone were why other agencies were so interested in them. Their skills combined are why they had worked together from the beginning. They were unmatched in strength and marksmanship. They both knew with confidence they would find Natalie and leave a graveyard in their wake.

It was a mistake for Natalie to be taken to the first room she had searched. That made it all the easier for Elijah and Malek to find her. As soon as they burst open the door, they saw what Carter was about to do to her. In the blink of an eye, they opened fire on everyone in the room.

The first thing Elijah saw was Carter, his body towering over Natalie as he attempted to lower her pants. The second thing he saw was Natalie's crying face. Rage pulsed through Elijah. It was more rage than he had ever felt before. He knew that Natalie would undergo serious interrogation and torture, but this? Carter was about to rape her.

Elijah fired off his weapon. He hit Bennet almost immediately, but Jannis evaded every bullet. Carter stood frozen, hands still on Natalie and his face red with anger.

Right when Natalie Heard the door open, her crying ceased. She looked around the room to see who was there, who had come to save her.

She gave up her opportunity to find her savior as she felt Carter's hold loosen. Not sparing another second, she kicked her feet back, landing a hit to his groin. She heard his grunt of pain, lifting her body to find who had come to save her.

Gunshots were going off, and her attention was kept on finding their source, knowing she would discover who she was looking for. Natalie looked at the entrance, and her eyes met the people she sought. Elijah and Malek. They had found her. They were shooting their way into the room.

Elijah's eyes motioned to meet Natalie's, and she felt a rush of relief and happiness. He had come to save her from a nightmare. Natalie turned back to Carter, a newfound motivation to fight. He looked at her with fear in his eyes. She smiled, knowing his fear was for the courage and strength he had never seen before. Natalie's attention was stolen as a hand brushed her arm. Turning her head, she saw Elijah.

"Hey cheeks, happy to see me," he asked with the rasp she loved so much.

Natalie let out a relieved laugh and nodded rapidly, tears streaming down her face. "You came for me," she said breathlessly.

"Cheeks, you know I only come for you," he said with a wink.

Natalie's cheeks reddened, causing Elijah to smile. He motioned her to stand back before he shot her handcuffs off the same way Malek had done his. Once she was free, she planted a kiss on Elijah.

Pulling away, she started, "I'm so sor-"

He cut her off. "Later, Natty. We need to get out of here now."

She forgot where she was for a second and what had just happened to her. She nodded, and Elijah began to lead her out of the room. Malek had been covering them, only stopping to reload his gun. He had managed to take down Jannis with a shot to the side before he pulled the table over to him to use it as a shield.

"About time, you two. My trigger finger is getting tired," Malek said, wiggling his finger as if to show them.

"Let's go, Malek," Elijah said with a rasp that Natalie missed.

Malek chuckled, following Elijah and Natalie out of the room, his gun still trained on the agents and Carter.

# Chapter 32

The moment Elijah opened the door, they were met with bullets. He acted as a human shield to Natalie as he unloaded on the agents ahead. As soon as the agents took cover and ceased fire, Elijah pulled Natalie away.

"Go to the cabinets," Natalie yelled towards him. "We'll have cover there."

She recalled this from when she and Malek first entered the warehouse. Following orders, Elijah made his way to the cabinets as Malek watched their six, weapon raised. If any agent came out to fire at them, Malek was there to fire back. He managed to take down four agents that dared peek out.

As soon as they were secure behind the filing cabinets, Natalie rushed forward to hug Elijah. Malek kept guard. Natalie let go of Elijah and turned to hug Malek, too. She foolishly believed they would leave her there and she would never see them again.

Natalie turned back to Elijah. "How did you escape?"

She asked, her voice a whisper.

"Self-hatred and anger," he said with a smirk.

"Actually," Malek started, turning his head towards them, "you can direct your thanks to yours truly. Eli wouldn't know how to save himself if the answers were written on his big forehead."

Elijah let out a grunt of disapproval, but Natalie chuckled.

"I wish we got there sooner, Cheeks," His eyes were grim. "I'm sorry I didn't get to you before-" his voice broke.

Natalie knew what he was thinking. "Stop, Elijah. Don't feel guilty. What Carter did… what he was about to do… you stopped it. That's what matters. You saved me." She reached up and cupped his face in her hands.

"So did I, Nat," Malek said from behind her.

Natalie rolled her eyes, but couldn't help the smirk that formed on her face.

Elijah reached forward and brushed her hair behind her ear. He then brought her face to him and kissed her. He wasn't gentle with it. He kissed her passionately and longingly. Their mouths clashed in a wave of ecstasy. Natalie let a soft moan escape her lips, the passion of the kiss overtaking her senses. Elijah brought his hand around her waist and pulled her close to him, holding her there and not wanting to let go.

Their moment was short-lived. "We need to get out of here," Malek said, interrupting them. "Maybe wait until we've escaped to take each other's clothes off."

Elijah broke the kiss and shot Malek an annoyed look.

"Wait," Natalie said. "We can't leave yet!"

Elijah looked at her, his eyebrows furrowing as he waited for her to elaborate.

"They have my mom," she said, her voice turning sorrowful.

Immediately after she finished speaking, gunfire began to come their way as agents surrounded them. Malek cursed at her words and pulled back behind the cabinets. He gave Natalie a look of compassion before checking his ammo. Seeing that he needed to reload, he pulled a fresh magazine from his pocket.

"I have a little more fight in me," he said. "I can't pass up a chance to meet the woman who brought you into the world. What do you say, Elijah?"

Elijah's face morphed into a deadly mask as he went to Malek's side. He looked around the cabinets, having to snap his head back as another gunshot fired.

"We're not leaving until we save your mom," said Elijah.

Malek pulled out a pistol from his belt and handed it back to Natalie. Elijah saw the exchange and nodded in approval. A mask of strength and violence came over Natalie's face as if forgetting everything that had just happened to her. This, she was comfortable with. Guns were her peace. They cleared her mind and allowed her to forget about the anxiety and panic. Nothing was in her mind now other than survival. She had to get her mom. They had to get out of here. They had to survive.

Elijah looked at her, his eyes filled with a wicked carnality. His knees grew weak at the sight of the strength and courage she radiated. Seeing her with a gun wasn't bad either. They would make it out of this. He would get her out, and once he did, he would marry this woman he had come to love so much.

Still smiling, he said, "You ready?"

She shot him a shameless smirk. "Absolutely."

"You got yourself a bombshell, Eli," Malek said. "Please keep her."

A ghost of a smile flashed across Elijah's face before it was replaced by lethal rage. The three of them came out from behind the cabinets, weapons raised, and opened fire.

Bullets began flying when Natalie and Elijah came from behind the cabinets. The three of them fired off their rounds, more for cover than to kill. They didn't want any more innocent lives getting destroyed. The only people they wanted to see at the end of their barrels were Agents Jannis, Agent Bennet, and Carter.

Elijah was angry that he didn't get to end their lives when he got Natalie out of the interrogation room, but he knew the time would come to give them what they deserved. He would provide Natalie with the first punches, allowing her to take the revenge she deserved. After, he would make them wish they never existed. He would inflict so much suffering on them that everything they did to their victims would seem like child's play.

The gunfire coming from them was enough to push some of the agents back. Jannis was among the group of agents firing at them, making Elijah hot with anger. He wanted to rush forward and kill him where he stood. Still, he refused to leave Natalie's side. Elijah would get him soon. For now, he just had to get Natalie to her mom.

Natalie took cover behind a corner. Malek had a limited supply of extra ammo, so they had to be smart about their shooting. They were taking turns firing off rounds, gaining room to move forward. Natalie's main priority was to get to her mom. She needed to locate her mother so she could get her out of the warehouse and to safety.

"You can end this now, Miss Walsh!" Jannis yelled over the sounds of guns. His voice was strained, likely due to the bullet wound Malek gifted him with.

"Just surrender, and we can work something out," Jannis continued.

His voice was enough to silence the gunfire as Natalie came face to face with the man she hated the most.

# Chapter 33

It took everything in Natalie not to kill Jannis where he stood. She needed him alive to tell her where her mom was, so she controlled herself for now.

Jannis continued to speak, his arrogance shining through with every word. "By all means, keep shooting. You'll run out of ammo soon enough. Then, my men will grab you, and I can finish what Carter couldn't." He held the side where Malek had shot him, pain mixing into the anger on his face.

Natalie paled, nausea curling in her stomach at his words. She knew it was a fear tactic, but she knew his words rang true. She had already experienced that promise once. Her hands shook as the memories began to fill her mind.

Elijah reached over, putting his hand on Natalie's shoulder. Natalie jumped at the touch, putting her arms out to brace for an attack. She hit Elijah in the chest, her eyes blurring from tears. He managed to grab hold of her hands, and when she couldn't hit him anymore, she opened her eyes. Natalie immediately calmed when she saw Elijah, realizing he would never let them hurt her again.

Elijah's heart shattered at the fear written on Natalie's face. He would have Jannis's head for the vile things he had said to Natalie. He knew this reaction meant they had done something to her when they captured her. Before he could think about that, he had to ensure Natalie didn't slip into another panic attack. He had to keep her head on straight.

Malek kept his gun trained on the agents, prepared for any misstep they made. At Jannis' words, he had the urge to murder every person in this room until there was nothing left but corpses. He had grown fond of Natalie in the couple of days he had come to know her.

Elijah motioned his head, signaling Natalie to start shooting. He knew how shooting a gun was calming to her. He knew that she was able to clear her mind as soon as her finger touched the trigger. He also enjoyed watching her in action, so it was a win-win. Taking a moment to admire her, he scanned her body and reveled at the violence this beautiful woman could inflict.

Elijah took back the firing position when he saw that Natalie had cast out all the negative thoughts from her mind. Her eyes were clear and determined. He had to make sure he could clear a way for her to get closer to her mom. Bullets were flying back and forth. Natalie was scanning the area to see if there was anywhere ahead she could take cover behind.

"There's a big tank of something in the middle of the room!" Elijah yelled, voice barely audible over the gunshots. "It should give you a good vantage point and help you see where your mom is. I'll cover you. Go, Now!"

Natalie nodded her head in confirmation before taking off. She ran as fast as she could in a low crouch, avoiding the bullets flying above her head. Elijah and Malek were doing an excellent job at returning the fire, advancing a few more feet with each round. Natalie made it to the tank, wondering about the substance that sat in it. It was likely chemicals that were used for the experiments.

Shaking away the thoughts, she peered around the tank. She looked toward the room where she saw her mother being held before, but she wasn't there. They couldn't have taken Nancy far and most likely hid her away somewhere in the warehouse. Natalie looked around the room again for any sign of where they could have taken her. As her eyes darted around, sweat beaded on her forehead, and her eyebrows furrowed. Worry swirled inside of Natalie as she failed to find any trace of where her mother was being held.

It wasn't long before Elijah and Malek joined her, both gasping for breath. Elijah slammed his back against the tank, his chest heaving from his exertion.

"I'm all out of shells, Mal," he said, panting. "You got any for me?"

Malek shook his head, his hands on his hips as he looked toward the ceiling and gasped for air. Natalie looked towards Elijah before handing him her gun.

"My mom isn't there," she said, voice shaky.

Bullets were still flying as Elijah turned his body towards her and cupped her face in his hands.

"Listen to me. We will find her. I promise you." He spoke with a low rasp that made Natalie's knees weak. She nodded quickly, taking a deep breath to recenter her mind. He took her gun and checked how many bullets were left.

Natalie didn't think it was going to be easy to get her mom. Nothing about this had been easy. She needed to recenter her mind and remember who she was and where she came from.

Natalie scanned the room again, this time looking around the other side of the tank. She noticed the door to one of the glass rooms was open, but the lights were off. The lights from the warehouse were casting a glare that made it impossible to see what was inside. The hair on her arms lifted, and her heart began to pound. That's where her mom had to be. She knew it.

"Eli," she said, waving her hand to get his attention. "That room," she said, pointing, "I think she's in there."

Elijah looked over her shoulder towards the room. He furrowed his eyebrows before looking back at her.

"Are you sure?" He asked.

"Positive," Natalie said with confidence.

Elijah smiled. "Perfect. Let's go."

Natalie returned his smile before looking back towards the room. This time, when she looked, the lights were on. She was able to see everything now. She was able to see the man who stood just outside the door.

Carter held her unconscious mom in his arms, holding a needle in her arm as he stared daggers toward where Natalie stood.

Her eyes widened as the color drained from her face. Elijah and Malek stood behind her, staring at the nightmare they could sense was about to unfold before them.

After staring for what seemed like hours, Elijah noticed the gunshots stopped. He hadn't seen when the bullets ceased fire or the reason why. They were surrounded by an eerie silence, filled only by their heavy breaths.

"Come on out now, Natalie," Carter yelled through the room, breaking the silence. "I promise you, I won't hurt your mom if you just come out."

Elijah gripped Natalie's arm. "I'm not going to tell you not to go," he whispered, "I just want you to know that I've got your back. You go, I go."

He let go of her arm. Natalie straightened, making her decision. If she walked out, it could be a trap. If she stayed, her mom would die. It wasn't a hard decision to make, especially knowing of the two giants that stood right behind her, ready to do whatever was necessary to keep her safe.

"I don't have all day, babe," Carter said. "You have ten seconds to come here, or I inject your mom with whatever chemicals Agent Bennet was gracious enough to mix together for me."

"You dated that chump," Malek asked under his breath. "How did you not want to rip out his vocal cords?"

Elijah elbowed Malek in the gut at his comments. "Shut up," he said.

Malek only smirked before securing his weapon in a shooting position.

Natalie stepped out into the clearing towards Carter, not taking another second to think. Elijah followed close behind her, his gun raised and ready to fire on anybody who tried to get too close. Malek went around to the other side. The agents that were there before were now gone. He wondered where they had gone, but he would figure it out once they secured Natalie's mom.

Carter watched as they slowly walked closer, face turning red as he saw how closely Elijah kept to Natalie. It made him angry to see that Natalie would let another man be close to her. She was his. He would take her back and away from this brute who thought he had a claim to Natalie.

"Well done, Mr. Bailey," Agent Jannis said, stepping out in front of the other agents who had been firing at Elijah and Natalie. He had managed to patch up his gunshot in the middle of all the chaos. They had all moved forward to focus their aim on Natalie as she approached Carter and her Mom.

"Well done, indeed. You are welcome to take Miss Walsh out of here, along with her mother, as soon as you can get the information from her." Jannis' mouth curved into a sickening smile.

Natalie looked from Jannis to Carter. "Let my mom go, Carter." There was no fear in her voice. No softness. She was livid.

"Now, now. Calm down, baby." Carter said in a condescending tone. "We just have to tell the agents where the files are, and then you can have your mom. And I can take you both home."

"You're sick, Bailey," Elijah interrupted. "Natalie will never go with you, and you know it," Elijah said, annoyance laced in every word.

"Shut up, Walker!" Carter said, driving the needle deeper into Nancy's arm. "Natalie, come here!"

"Carter, just stop," Natalie pleaded. "I don't love you! I want you to let my mom go! Please!"

She stepped forward, looking around the room for a clock. It was 2 pm. Natalie's stomach flipped with anticipation. She stood frozen for a moment as if waiting for something. When nothing happened, she looked back towards Carter and her mom.

"Just come back with me, Nat. We can get through this." Carter was on the verge of tears again. "I will kill her to get you back. You're all that matters, anyway. I will kill everyone who gets in my way. Please."

Natalie would have pitied him if it hadn't been for his words. How he could say such things in a voice that begged for her love was beyond her understanding. She just looked at him with disgust.

"I'll never go back to you," Natalie said with a finality that made Carter straighten, understanding that she was done with him.

He moved to pull out the needle before alarms started blaring throughout the warehouse. The agents began to scurry like rats, looking for the cause of the warnings.

"It's a security breach!" A far-off agent yelled.

Jannis and Bennet came into view, their eyes red and their bodies stiff.

"What did you do?" Jannis asked, his voice gravelly.

Natalie turned to look at Elijah. She offered him a soft smile. Then she looked at Carter. Then Bennet. Then Jannis. To each of them, she shot a wicked smile.

"It's over," she said, relief in every word.

"Nat, what did you do?" Elijah asked from behind her.

She didn't turn around. She just stared at Jannis when she said, "I can tell you where the files are now."

# Chapter 34

Natalie orchestrated the files and documents she had obtained to be sent out to every individual in the United States. It wasn't an easy task, but she knew it was the only way to ensure people knew about what the government had been doing.

Natalie managed to get into the National Emergency Alert system using the holes in the CIA mainframe. It helped that Malek had given her his credentials to access the servers from the inside. Once she managed to find FEMA's firewalls, she hacked away at their security codings. Their encryptions weren't as extensive as the CIA, so she had no issue getting access. Natalie created a National Alert containing all the information she had gathered. She scheduled the alert to be sent out to each and every device with a cellular connection. The data would spread across every inch of the US, leaving no one ignorant of the wickedness of the CIA.

Once that was set up, she emailed news agencies

directly using an alias email so the information couldn't be tracked to her. It was also a scheduled email that gave the organizations an outline of everything they would find in the files.

Using Malek's credentials, she hacked through the CIA's systems to provide him with access to Agent Jannis' unit. She set up a mass email that sent every single file, including any additional ones that had been added since her hack in the library, to every government organization and higher-up individual. As soon as that was done, she got out of there.

***

Malek came out of the coverage he had taken as the agents hurried around and looked for the source of the breach. He fought past a few agents who attempted to disarm him, leaving them lifeless on the floor. He raised his gun and set his sights on Jannis and Bennet. He had a sinister smile on his face, ready to shoot at the slightest movement.

He had known everything Natalie had planned, having helped her formulate the plan himself. Seeing the looks on everyone's faces as they attempted to figure out what she meant by *she'll tell them where the files are now* was priceless. He couldn't wait to see their faces when she finally revealed what she had done. The information would be out in the world by now, and this warehouse would be surrounded by every government and news agency in the United States.

***

The warehouse felt as though all the fresh air was sucked out. Everyone who surrounded Natalie stilled, too stunned to move or speak. Elijah stood behind her, utterly shocked at the words she just said. Carter stood frozen in the doorway, still holding a needle in Nancy's arm. The agents were stunned, their mouths hanging open.

"What do you mean you'll tell us," Jannis asked, his tone still shocked.

The rest of the warehouse was in an uproar. The alarms were blaring, signaling a data breach. Personnel were running amok, trying to shut off the alarms and find the source of the breach. There was shouting and agents typing frantically on computers as they attempted to circulate the data breach and prevent anything from being stolen. Natalie knew they wouldn't be successful. Everything was out, and they could not stop it or get their files back.

"Natty, don't tell them anything," Elijah whispered from behind Natalie.

Why the alarms blaring gave Natalie a change of heart about the location of the files, Elijah didn't know. She didn't even have the chance to tell him where they were. He was as oblivious as the agents. Still, he'd rather remain ignorant than have her give up everything they have worked so hard for.

Natalie didn't even look at Elijah when saying, "It's over. I had a copy of all my files on a flash drive, and I released them." She glanced at Carter, who stiffened at her words.

Continuing, she said, "I left the flash drive in a tree right before you let those monsters take me. After I got it back, a dear friend of mine took me to the library, where I was able to send every single file and document to anyone in the US with a phone number using the National Emergency Alert System. I also ensured every news organization received a copy of the files to have all they needed to make it breaking news."

Natalie had a triumphant smile on her face, knowing she had won. She had exposed them. She had Malek to thank for that. She glanced in his direction and saw a look of pure satisfaction on his face. The shocked faces of the agents were a pleasure he was glad to witness.

Jannis and Bennet stood frozen, their faces falling as the truth hit them like a truck. They were done. Their illegal experimentation was done. The human trafficking would become the most extensive internal investigation. There was no way they would get themselves out of this. Natalie enjoyed seeing the looks on their faces as their entire worlds came crumbling down.

Jannis moved first, finally breaking out of the shock that consumed him, replacing it with white hot rage. He lunged towards Natalie. Elijah didn't let him get within an inch of her before he tackled the agent to the ground. They were in an all out brawl on the floor, Natalie and Carter only staring as the scene unfolded.

Bennet attempted to join the fight, but Malek was on him instantly. Malek slammed the butt of his gun into the agent's face, causing him to fall back. Elijah had managed to pin Jannis to the ground, landing repeated punches to his face, turning him into a bloody pulp. Jannis was left unconscious when Elijah stood and moved to help Malek subdue Bennet. Elijah shoved Malek aside as he unloaded his punches on Bennet as well.

Elijah beat Bennet just as he beat Jannis. He didn't pull a single punch, leaving both of them looking almost unrecognizable as they lay there, their faces bruised and bloody. He made sure to leave them alive. If Natalie wanted to enact some revenge on them, he would make sure she got the chance. As much as he wanted to end their lives himself, he would leave it up to Natalie. For now, he left them unconscious on the floor. Elijah peered around at the other agents in the warehouse, ready should any of them decide to help out Jannis and Bennet. He was shocked to find the warehouse empty. All who were left were him, Malek, Natalie, and Carter.

Carter stood there, Nancy still unconscious in his arms, barely able to process what had just unfolded before him. As he heard Natalie explain what had happened, he understood. She was about to walk out of her with Elijah. She was about to force him to let go of her mom. He wouldn't have it. He wouldn't be the loser here, even if he knew in his gut that there was no way he would bring down Elijah. He was deranged enough to have a fool's hope.

"Congratulations, Natalie!" He yelled, his voice sounding crazed. "You win! You exposed everyone like you said you would. Now you're coming with me!"

"You're out of your mind, Bailey!" Elijah said, now stepping in front of Natalie like a shield.

Carter let out an unhinged laugh. "You haven't seen what I can be like when I'm out of my mind." He finished his sentence in a low voice.

Carter looked down at Nancy, almost looking sorry for what he was about to do. But he couldn't survive without Natalie. As quickly as he could, he emptied the syringe into Nancy's arm and dropped her to the floor. He left the empty needle in her arm, stepped over Nancy's unmoving body, and barreled toward Natalie.

Natalie couldn't move. She just stared at her mom, silent tears falling from her eyes. She had no idea what they had done to her mom that made her go unconscious. After what Carter had just done, Natalie knew her mom wouldn't wake up. She would never get to look into her mom's eyes ever again. She wouldn't get to return to her home in Portland and tell her mom everything.

Everything that Nancy would miss out on began running through Natalie's mind. She wouldn't know what it would be like to see Natalie graduate college. She wouldn't experience her wedding. She wouldn't become a grandmother. She was gone, and it was Carter's fault.

Natalie was so broken and shattered that she hadn't noticed when Elijah and Malek lunged for Carter.

It was a fool's move for Carter to run towards Natalie, with Elijah as her shield. With Malek there alongside him, there was no chance of surviving. Carter had a false sense of strength if he thought he could fight past the two warriors. It made Elijah smile, reveling in the fact that he was finally going to be able to get his hands on Carter.

Elijah stopped Carter's movement with little effort, landing a left hook to his jaw. Carter recoiled, actually shocked at the blow. Elijah didn't stop. He kept coming on Carter, landing blow after blow to the stomach and face. Malek moved behind Carter, holding his motionless body upright as Elijah used him as a punching bag.

Elijah wouldn't kill Carter. That was Natalie's kill, and he refused to take it. But he would make him suffer for the pain he had caused Natalie. Elijah threw Carter to the ground, causing him to fall on his shoulder. It must have dislocated because Carter gripped his arm as he screamed in pain. Elijah then took his gun out and shot Carter once in the thigh. He was careful not to pierce his femoral artery, ensuring a slow but painful death.

Carter writhed on the floor, the pain from his shoulder and leg becoming too much. Elijah turned to Natalie, watching in emotional distress as she crawled towards her mom's lifeless body. Natalie had brought her mother in her lap and was sobbing, apologizing for everything that led up to her death. Elijah approached her, kneeling beside her and wrapping an arm around her.

Malek watched the scene in horror, still keeping his guns trained on Carter and the agents in case they would try to get up. His heart broke for his new friend as she sobbed over her mother.

"Natty, I am so sorry," Elijah said, trying his best to keep his voice from cracking.

Natalie just sobbed.

"Please, baby, tell me what you want from me. How can I make this better?"

Elijah wanted to take her pain. He wanted to make it so she wouldn't be so heartbroken. He knew that was impossible. He knew she would feel her mother's death the same way, if not worse, than how she felt her father's death. Elijah knew all too well how it felt to lose both parents. Still, he couldn't imagine what it must be like for her to lose both parents in such devastating ways.

Natalie looked up at him, tears streaming down her face. She looked from Elijah to Carter, who was still writhing on the floor. She wanted to make him suffer. She wanted to make him pay for the pain he had caused her. Make him pay for the years she wasted thinking their love was real.

As Natalie looked at Carter, she felt her anger festering into an evil side of her that only wanted destruction. Natalie had to close her eyes. She sent up a prayer, asking the Lord for guidance. She didn't want to act in anger. She knew that revenge was well within reason after all Carter had taken from her. She knew she could end him painfully and enjoy every second of it. Still, she didn't jump at the opportunity. Instead, she looked at Elijah and found the comfort she needed in his eyes.

"He killed my mom," she said, her voice breaking. "He took years from my life and made me into this victim that I know I'm not. He took away my autonomy and freedom. You, Elijah, helped me find it again. Somehow, Jesus led me to you and used you to be my beacon of hope and freedom. I know that I am safe with you. I know I don't need to rely on anyone for strength. I don't want revenge. I don't need it. The best revenge I can give is to live happily with you, so that's what I want to do."

Natalie had tears streaming down her face as she finished speaking. She bowed her head back down, allowing herself to wallow in her grief for a bit longer.

Elijah understood what she wanted. He knew that she was strong and she would be able to move on. He felt foolish thinking she would want revenge. He knew her well enough that she wasn't the kind of person to seek revenge against those who wronged her. She was a spirit of forgiveness and a new life. She brought light to every place he walked.

Elijah would never again forget who Natalie was at her core. She was a fighter. She was strong, stronger than he ever was. She was strong enough to forgive Carter, but he wasn't.

Elijah kissed Natalie on her forehead before rising to his feet. He went into the glass room where Carter had originally held Nancy. He found a vial of chemicals that he assumed was what was used to kill Nancy. He found an empty syringe and filled it with the chemicals. He walked over to Carter, lifted him to a sitting position, and stared lethally into his eyes.

Malek moved to stand by Natlaie, offering her a hand

in comfort as Elijah enacted his judgment.

"She is the strongest woman I know if she can forgive you," Elijah said, death lacing his every word. "Unfortunately for you, I don't have a similar penitence."

Carter's eyes were wide, and his lip quivered, but he didn't speak.

Elijah continued, "You're going to die at my hands. I could let you bleed out. You'll lose consciousness with only the pain of your shoulder and the bullet wound. Or, I can inject you with whatever this chemical is and let you suffer the fate of so many other people. I've heard it's painful, and the death will be gruesome. I want to thank you for avoiding such a sight when you killed Nancy. Still, the pain that you caused to the one person I love most in this world is unacceptable, and I don't feel like sparing you from the death you deserve."

Carter screamed out as Elijah slid the needle into his arm. Elijah held his gaze as he slowly injected the chemicals into Carter's bloodstream. The reaction was almost instantaneous as Carter began to writhe in pain, screaming and begging for the pain to end. Elijah looked at him with no pity. He felt no remorse as he watched Carter's life drain from his body until he was a motionless corpse on the floor.

Natalie looked at Elijah, horror all over her face. "Why?" She started. "Why would you do that? I told you I didn't want revenge!" She was in pain. She had seen so much death in one day that she didn't know if she could take anymore, even if it were Carter.

Elijah just walked over to her and lifted her to her feet. "You may have the strength to forgive those who harm you. You may have it in your heart to turn the other cheek when people cause you pain." He spoke with such authority that Natalie couldn't look away from his eyes. "I don't have the strength to do the same. I will always repay others for the harm they inflict on you. From now until my last breath, I will make sure those who cause you any amount of pain will burn until they are ash in the wind."

Natalie closed her eyes, knowing that he spoke the truth. She would try to change his mind later. She would try to make him see that revenge isn't the answer. She would teach him how to forgive. In her heart, she knew she would be with him long enough to show him a better way to live. Later. She would think about that later.

Right now, they needed to get out of here. She opened her eyes and cupped his cheek in her hand. She gave him a soft peck on the lips before stepping away from him.

"We need to go," her voice gravelly from crying. "Can you pick up my mom?" She couldn't leave her here. She couldn't just abandon the body of the woman who had showered her with love all these years of her life. Natalie didn't know where she would take her mother's body, but she refused to part from it.

Elijah nodded. "Of course, cheeks, But first, I need to make sure these two scumbags can't go anywhere. They need to be here when the feds show up."

Elijah walked over to the two agents, who remained unconscious on the floor. He reached into their pants, looking for handcuffs. Locating them in the back pockets of the agents, he cuffed them to a pipe that was on one of the large tanks. Once he was done, he walked over to Nancy. Suddenly, he felt a hand on his arm. He looked over and saw Malek standing there.

"I'll do it," Malek said, his voice low. "Go be with Nat."

Elijah nodded and walked off to be with Natalie.

Malek lifted Nancy's lifeless body in Malek's arms and followed them out of the warehouse.

# Chapter 35

Lights of oncoming cars flew by like fireflies in the night sky. The roar of the car's old engine was the only noise in the silent cabin. No one spoke. No one talked about what happened back at the warehouse. How they had managed to escape just before herds of FBI vehicles and police cars flooded the scene was beyond them. They didn't speak as they blended in with the rest of the traffic, watching as news vans from hundreds of different stations followed the law enforcement vehicles close by, wanting to be the first to break the story before the competing news agencies.

Malek drove his jeep while Elijah sat in the passenger's seat. She had left the warehouse and sat on a curb, Elijah following suit. Malek had gently set her mother beside her, vanishing for a few minutes before returning with his jeep. He quickly but carefully placed her mom in the back of the car before holding the door open for Natalie to get in. After he ensured she was safely buckled, he got in the driver's seat and began the trip back to the forest. They had been lucky that no government vehicles made it to the warehouse until after Malek made it on the highway. The freeway heading towards the site was free of any cars, law enforcement having cleared it so the different agencies and news stations could make it there quickly.

The other agents scurrying around had received the same texts and emails as the rest of the world. When the ignorant agents saw what they had been aiding in, they fled in disgust, wanting to get away from the atrocities. As for the agents who knew very well what was happening, they ran purely out of self-preservation.

Once law enforcement arrived at the scene, they would find bloodied up agents handcuffed to a pipe and a dead man who had been injected with poison. Because of the nature of the experiments, Elijah deemed it best to make sure Jannis' fingerprints were all over the syringe he had used to kill Carter. He did that when Malek had gone to find a car. He had to make sure Jannis and Bennet were proven criminals and that they would face the consequences of their crimes. He knew the files detailed everything about them and what they had done, but this physical evidence would be the extra nail in their coffins.

Elijah didn't speak to Natalie, knowing she was dealing with a war in her mind. As he sat in the passenger's seat, he reached back and rested his hand on her thigh as a reminder that he was there. She appreciated this, placing her hand on his and smiling before returning her gaze toward the window. She watched the cars go by, unable to celebrate the success of bringing down the CIA because of one detail. Her mom. Her mom had died. After everything she had done to ensure her mom remained safe, she still died, and it tore Natalie in half. On the inside, she was screaming and vomiting her guts up. But on the outside, it was as if she was an empty shell, unable to utter a noise as she suffered in silence.

Malek drove and drove until they reached the outskirts of the Plumas County town. Natalie knew where he was headed without him having to say it. The waterfall. The little swimming hole that had become her safe haven after days on the run and fending for herself.

She didn't know how long they would drive, but she kept her eyes open. She didn't want to risk sleep. She wasn't ready for the nightmares that awaited her in her mind, so she stayed awake the entire drive. She began to recognize the small buildings that made up the familiar town. It felt like a lifetime ago when she first came here. She was a different person then. She had changed so much since leaving Portland. It struck her that her life would never be the same once she found her way back home.

Home. She probably didn't even have a home anymore. She didn't want to go back to her mom's house. The memories that those walls held were too great for her to face. She didn't even know if she wanted to go back to college. Her entire life goal was to work for the government, and she just spent the past couple of weeks working to dismantle the credibility of one of its most essential agencies.

No, she didn't know what to do now that the files were out in the world. All she could think of was getting back to that waterfall. Once she was there, she would figure it out.

Malek drove the car as deep into the forest as he

could. He would have left it in town, but he couldn't risk walking around with a corpse on his shoulder. He couldn't do that to Natalie. So he drove until the trees were so thick that the car refused to move. They were close to the waterfall now.

Malek exited the car and carefully took Natalie's mom out of the trunk, carrying her body toward the swimming hole. Elijah helped Natalie out of the car, and she walked alongside him, saying nothing as she wallowed in her despair. They remained silent as they finally walked through the thickening of the trees and into the small paradise the Lord had gifted them in the middle of the forest.

Natalie decided she would bury her mom here so she would forever live in the place she knew as her sanctuary.

"I'll start digging," Malek said softly.

He set Nancy's body by the water. Malek walked back out to his car to his supplies. He picked up a shovel and found a patch of soft soil near the tree line by the water. He started digging.

Elijah helped Natalie sit by her mother before finding a second shovel in Malek's car, joining his friend in his digging efforts.

Natalie just watched, heavy sobs escaping her, as the two most important people in her life dug a grave for her mother.

***

Natalie slept in the tent Malek had erected for a couple of hours. By the time they had returned to the swimming hole, it was already the early hours of the evening. The sun was beginning to set. Malek told Natalie to take the tent, and he and Elijah would sleep outside. Elijah bristled at this, arguing that Malek had no say in who slept where. He ended up conceding because he was going to have Natalie sleep in the tent anyway. It was fun for Natalie to see them interacting. Malek was the sunshine to Elijah's grumpy. Their banter helped Natalie forget for a moment that she had lost her mom.

When she woke up, the sun was shining through the trees. She heard light chatter outside of the tent, accompanied by the cracking of a fire. She slept in her clothes despite her reluctance to stay in them. They smelled of body odor and chemicals. They brought terrible reminders that she didn't want to think about. She ruffled through the bags that were there, surprised to see her clothes. Malek or Elijah must have found her clothing somewhere in the forest and brought them back here. She let herself smile at their kindness and changed into a pair of shorts and a loose T-shirt. She put her shoes back on before stepping out of the tent.

Immediately when she walked out, her eyes shot toward her mom's burial site. Her eyes welled with tears as she saw that a cross was erected, marking where her mom lay. She looked towards the men, and they, too, had tears lining their eyes.

Elijah spoke, "We carved the cross after you fell asleep. We wanted to make sure that your mom was comfortable where we buried her." His words were gentle, a caress to Natalie's ear. She walked over to him and sat in his lap, kissing him deeply on his soft lips.

Malek cleared his throat, causing Natalie to break free from the kiss.

"What, do you want a kiss too?" She asked, an attempt at playful humor.

Malek smiled at her effort. "As tempted as I am by your offer, my wife wouldn't appreciate that," he said playfully.

Elijah just grunted before squeezing Natalie into a tight hug. "I made you breakfast," he said, his voice low and raspy. "I figured you should eat before we tell you the news."

Natalie stiffened under his touch. She looked between the men, her questions remaining unspoken.

"Jannis and Bennet got arrested," Elijah revealed. Natalie gasped softly, as she didn't believe it was possible. She knew there was no way of them getting out of paying for their crimes, but it still seemed almost too good to be true.

"All the homeless people that survived were rescued and sent to rehab facilities to heal from the torture they had to endure," Malek continued. "The only people left to save are those lost in sex trafficking. Luckily, the documents you so graciously stole highlighted the names of everyone who paid money for "product," and they are being investigated as we speak."

Natalie let out a laugh of relief. It wasn't until this moment that she felt the weight of what she had done. She exposed illegal experimentation and saved innocent lives. It hadn't seemed like much when she was at the warehouse. Knowing that the world knew everything, that the homeless people were safe now, that those sold into trafficking were being diligently searched for, and that Jannis and Bennet were paying for their crimes made her heart swell with pride. She actually did it, and these two men helped her. The three of them did the impossible and took down the CIA organization.

"You're pretty awesome if I do say so myself," Malek said with a large grin.

"She is, isn't she," Elijah whispered in agreement,

looking longingly at Natalie.

"You guys are gross," Malek said. "I will take that as my cue to let my wife know I'll be home soon. You two have fun *canoodling*." He stood and walked past the trees until he was out of earshot.

Natalie just giggled before looking back at Elijah. Her face fell when she saw the look on his face. "What's wrong?"

"Nothing," he said, "I'm just sad I have to take you back to Portland."

"Oh," Natalie said. "Right."

Silence filled the space between them for a moment.

"I don't have to go back to Portland, you know," Natalie said softly.

Elijah smiled. "Oh, I'm well aware. I actually plan on taking you away from there. But we have to go back to get everything in order with your mom's house and all her belongings."

Natalie understood the sadness in his face. He knew how painful it would be for Natlaie to return to her mother's house. He no longer wanted her to suffer, but she had to endure for just a little bit longer. Her heart filled with love as she leaned forward and kissed him. She let her lips brush across his until he opened for her. Their tongues danced passionately as their mouths clashed over and over again.

Natalie slowed the kiss to soft pecks before saying, "Thank you."

"For what, cheeks?" He asked playfully.

Natalie just smiled. "For seeing my strength and deciding to protect me anyway. For backing off when I needed to brave the storm alone. You've helped me as I took my freedom back, and I love you for it."

"My pleasure, love."

They spent the rest of the day sitting out by the water. Natalie sat by her mom's grave for a bit, soaking up the little time she had left to be near her. While she sat with her mom, Malek shared with Elijah everything about how he and Natalie formulated their plan to release the files and rescue him. Elijah then shared with Malek everything that he had to endure when he was taken. It was primarily threats to kill Natalie and threats of beatings.

Natalie hadn't yet felt comfortable to share what she had gone through in the days before Malek found her in the dark room. She would tell Elijah eventually, but she needed to find healing on her own. Once she knew she could talk about her experience without having flashbacks, she would tell Elijah everything.

In the evening, the three gathered all their belongings and went into town. They bought a few snacks at the store Natalie had purchased food from when she first walked here. The same girl was at the checkout counter, still scrolling her life away. Natalie wondered if this girl cared enough to look at the National Alert.

After buying food for the road, they returned to the car and started the drive back to Portland.

# Chapter 36

Natalie decided to catch up on sleep for the first part of the drive. Elijah held her as she slept, Malek deciding he would drive before Elijah could get in the driver's seat.

"You need to be with her," Malek had said. "She's going to need you next to her. You know I'm right."

Of course, Elijah knew his best friend was right. Still, he hated being told what to do by Malek. Fortunately for his meddlesome friend, he was going to sit with Natalie anyway. He wanted to hold her while she slept. He wanted to be there for her if her nightmares became too much. He wanted to be by her side, never parting from it.

"So, what are you going to do after this?" Malek asked, eyes meeting Elijah's in the rearview mirror momentarily before returning to the road.

Elijah glanced down at Natalie's sleeping face for a moment. She looked so beautiful and at peace. He wanted to see that on her face every time he looked at her. He would stop at nothing to make sure she never wanted for anything.

"I'm going to get her out of Portland, for starters," Elijah said. "She didn't even want to go back, not when there's nothing for her to return to other than broken memories."

"I meant about work, man," Malek said, his tone a playful annoyance. "Geez, not everything is about a woman."

Elijah actually chuckled before saying, "Well, you weren't specific, so I was going to give you the play-by-play." He thought for a second. "I don't know what I'll be doing after this. I might put in for an early retirement if I can. I want to be here for Natalie whenever she needs me. Working a government job won't really give me the flexibility for that."

Malek nodded. "Retirement shouldn't be a problem. Your genius of a girlfriend erased your name from any documents she found."

Elijah's face snapped to Malek's, confusion written all over his face.

"What do you mean?"

"I mean what I said. She ensured your name wouldn't be traced to anything relating to Jannis and Bennet. Any record of you leaving our unit in special activities is gone. She even went as far as to forge a document saying you were on sabbatical for a couple of months." Malek spoke in awe, clearly expressing how impressed he was with Natalie.

Elijah remained quiet in the back seat. Natalie never failed to amaze him. She really was the most intelligent person he had come to know, even more intelligent than him. He hadn't even thought about covering his tracks. He was only concerned with ensuring

Natalie would make it out okay. It comforted him that not only was he looking out for her, but she was looking out for him.

"You gonna say anything," Malek asked, interrupting Elijah's train of thought, "or are you just going to sit there looking like you just won the lottery?"

Elijah rolled his eyes. "Anything I have to say right now isn't meant for you."

Malek just nodded, a smirk formed on his lips.

They fell into silence. Malek decided to turn on the radio, making this drive seem like a fun road trip. He drove until he arrived at Klamath Falls. He went through the little town before pulling up to a little diner. He put the car in park just as Natalie woke up.

She sat up and looked around, trying to grasp her surroundings. She saw Elijah, who was still holding onto her. He gave her a questioning look as if to ask if she was okay. She gave him a tender smile before her eyes moved to Malek. He was watching her from the mirror. She smiled at him, too.

"Finally, you're awake," Malek teased. "I'm starving, but Elijah didn't want to eat until you woke up. You almost made me die of starvation."

Natalie chuckled, but it was Elijah who spoke. "We just got to the diner. He had just finished parking when you woke up." He brushed her hair behind her ear as he spoke. Then he moved his hand to her arm and softly moved his thumb back and forth, causing her skin to erupt in goosebumps. Natalie looked into the sea of Elijah's eyes, longing for a kiss.

"Dude, you're no fun!" Malek remarked. "Let me guilt trip her in peace."

Natalie turned her gaze to him. "Come on. Let's go get

something to eat before little Malek throws a tantrum," she said jokingly.

Malek roared with laughter before opening his door and exiting the vehicle. He then opened Natalie's door, helping her out. Elijah let himself out, and all three of them walked into the diner.

Natalie swore she could have jumped for joy when she walked into the diner. She hurried up to the counter before Evangeline turned and saw her.

"Well, if it isn't little miss mysterious!" Evangeline said, her face lighting up with happiness. "I was wondering when you would turn up around here again. You left last time without even saying goodbye."

Natalie nodded, unable to contain the smile on her face. "I know, I'm sorry. I had an emergency and had to make a run for it."

The irony in her words was lost on Evangeline as she just said, "Well, I'm glad you decided to come back and give me a visit!"

Evangeline's eyes moved to the two men standing behind Natalie. She recognized Elijah instantly. Her eyes darkened as she looked between Elijah and Malek. Turning back to Natalie, she said severely, "Do you need me to call the police?"

Malek broke out into laughter before saying, "I don't think that will be necessary. You can just think of us as her sexy bodyguards."

Natalie rolled her eyes and said, "No, you don't have to call the police. They're helping me get back home."

Evangeline nodded. "Okay, whatever you say, girl." She looked at Elijah. "But if that one causes me any trouble, I'm stabbing him with a chef's knife." She swore with a seriousness that made Natalie scared to laugh.

"I'll make sure he won't cause trouble."

"Alrighty, hun. Well, you guys can take a seat anywhere you like. I'll be by soon to take your orders."

"Thank you, Evie," Natalie said, smiling.

She turned and followed Elijah and Malek to a booth. They sat and looked over menus before Evangeline came by to take their orders.

They ate a good breakfast, chatting away like their lives were completely normal. Natalie ordered a large milkshake in remembrance of her dad. Just like when she was younger, she couldn't finish it. Elijah did the honors, making Natlaie's heart swell with love as he helped her finish the milkshake.

After they ate, they hit the road again. Natalie was sure to say goodbye to Evangeline, promising her that she would visit again. After a big hug, Natalie walked out and got back into the car with Elijah and Malek.

Elijah drove this time, Natalie sitting in the passenger seat.

"No fair that Elijah got a cuddle partner while sitting back here," Malek said, sounding serious. "I wish I had someone here to keep me company."

"Don't worry," Elijah started, "I'm sure your wife will give you all the cuddles when you get back home."

Malek laughed, "Probably not. As much as that woman likes cuddles, she takes more enjoyment in my suffering."

They all laughed before Natalie turned up the music. They listened to music and sang along to songs as Elijah drove the rest of the way to Portland. Natalie wasn't sure what was going to happen. She knew she would have to sell her mom's house. Living there was not an option. After that, all she knew was that she never wanted to go back. It was too painful. As for college and her career, she guessed she would have to figure that out another day.

Natalie looked around at Elijah and then spotted Malek in the rearview mirror. She realized it was here, with these people, that she felt the most secure. She didn't want to continue life without them being a part of it. Whatever she decided about college and work, she knew these two men would be there for her, giving her the support she needed. It was around them that the pain of losing her mom was dulled, still there but more bearable. No matter where she ended up, she took comfort in knowing she would have Elijah by her side.

Natalie smiled at the thought of her future with Elijah as she took his hand. She looked out her window, watching the trees as they passed by as the secrets they kept were left in the past, and all she could think about was the excitement of her unknown future.

# Epilogue

The house was quiet other than the pattering rain on the roof in the early hours of the morning. The clouds covered the sun, making the world gloomy and dark. The chill of the morning had crept inside, making Natalie throw on one of Elijah's hoodies. She looked outside the window, finding comfort in the rain. She didn't know how much she would miss the smell of the rain after leaving the Pacific Northwest. It wasn't until mornings like this that she truly remembered how much she loved it. The idea of staying inside cuddled up to the man she loved as they read together, was a dream come true.

As she got out of bed, she noticed Elijah wasn't lying beside her. She wandered around the house, looking for him silently. She knew that he had to be outside working if he wasn't in the house. She didn't understand why he insisted on working even when the weather was like this. All she wanted was to relax and have a peaceful day with her husband. But of course, he had to get work done, rain or shine.

Natalie walked to the front door, stepping out into the crisp morning air. The rain became louder, a roar that filled her senses. She stood underneath the covered porch, scanning the fields, looking for him. She walked around to the side of the house, thankful for the wraparound porch Elijah had built for her, and searched for him until she found him. He was in the shed, lying down on a creeper and working on his truck.

"Eli!" Natalie yelled for him, almost inaudible in the rain.

Elijah still heard her, though, drawn to her voice like a moth to a flame. He came out from underneath the truck and sat up, his eyes immediately finding hers. For a moment, they just stared at each other. Elijah scanned her body up and down, drinking in every ounce of her being from where he sat in the barn. How he managed to marry this woman, he still didn't know. He knew he didn't deserve her, but he tried. He tried every day to be worthy of her.

He started going to church for her. At first, it was to appease her. He was never interested in going to church, not understanding how, if God existed, He could let such terrible things happen. Then, he became undone by the grace of God, learning the truth about who God is. Knowing that despite the evil in the world, He is good, and His love can bring healing to those with the hardest of hearts.

Elijah gave his life to Jesus a month before they got married. He got baptized two weeks later. He had entered into their marriage as a new man. One who had been redeemed. He thanked God every day for helping him find Natalie.

Elijah knew that she thought he had saved her, but honestly, it was the other way around. She saved him and showed him a better way to live. All the violence in his past, the killing, had been a significant weight to live with. Still, he knew his Father in heaven redeemed him. The grace of God washed away his sins.

"Come inside," Natalie yelled from the porch. "I'll put on a pot of coffee!"

"I'll be right in, cheeks!" Elijah watched as she walked inside, the light of his life. He smiled, standing up to start putting his tools away.

Natalie walked into the kitchen and started boiling water. She felt Elijah's stare on her even as she stood alone in the kitchen.

Natalie had transferred schools. She couldn't stand the idea of going to Boston College anymore, but she still wanted to finish her degree. She transferred to West Virginia State University and finished off her education, graduating with a bachelor's degree in technological forensics and criminal justice.

Through connections with Malek, she got a job with Homeland Security. Now, she worked her dream job. She investigates human trafficking cases and fights to save people from a life of slavery. She also began working with Inspector General Criminal Investigators. After everything she went through five years ago, she developed a taste for fighting against corruption in the government. When she isn't saving people from trafficking, she's investigating CIA corruption and ensuring nothing like what happened with Agents Bennet and Janis ever happened again.

They ended up getting life sentences for crimes against humanity. Now, they were taking up space at Guantanamo Bay. Every person who had been used in the experiments was found and taken care of. It angered Natalie that they weren't given any attention until there was a spotlight on them, but she was grateful they weren't left to figure it out themselves again. Those who were sold in sex trafficking still had yet to be found. Natalie had dedicated much of her time to Homeland Security to look for them. Though it was likely she never would, she couldn't give up hope of finding them.

She married Elijah a month before she graduated, wanting to graduate with his last name on her diploma. It was the only thing she could think of that would thank him for everything he had done for her. She told him everything that had happened to her in those days after she left him in the forest. She told him about the sexual assault she had to endure and how it nearly destroyed her. It was hard to share, but it gave her a sense of authority. Those cruel acts held no power over her anymore.

At her graduation, Malek had brought his wife and kids. She finally got to meet the feisty  Esme, who lived up to the reputation Malek had given her. She was definitely feisty when it came to Elijah and Malek, but she was nothing but pleasant when interacting with Natalie.

After her graduation, Elijah retired from the CIA. He continued working there, ensuring he brought in an income to help pay for Natalie's college and ensure she didn't have to worry about anything. She had money she inherited from her parents, but he refused to let her spend it on school. Once she finished school, he bought a piece of land in Summersville, West Virginia. He now cared for the land and made money as a farmer and mechanic. Natalie loved her new home. The land was big enough that they had seclusion when they wanted it but small enough that she could visit her next-door neighbors, Malek and Esme, whenever she wanted.

Natalie's attention went to the screaming kettle. She removed it from the fire, setting it down on the counter. As she was grabbing mugs from the cupboard, Elijah walked in. He walked up to her, pulling her into a hug from behind. She giggled as he leaned in and landed kisses along her neck and up to her cheek. Spinning her around, he pulled her in for a real kiss. It was deep and full of love and affection.

Elijah's hands roamed her body, feeling every curve of her waist under his sweatshirt. He leaned over and picked her up, never breaking their kiss. Natalie wrapped her legs around Elijah, her hands gripping his hair as they kissed. He placed her on the counter and pulled out of the kiss. His eyes roamed her face as if reading the words from his favorite story. His hand reached down and took her hand.

He brought her hand to his lips and planted a gentle kiss before leaving her on the counter to finish the coffee. Natalie sat there watching him move, admiring the way he mixed the coffee grounds with the water. She watched his muscles flex with every movement as he poured the concoction into the two different mugs. She would never get over the fact that he was hers. That she was blessed to be able to look at him, to hold him, to touch him. He was hers, and she was his. After everything, she felt blessed to be able to look at her life and be content.

He handed her her cup of coffee, and she sipped it, blissful that this was her life now.

# ACKNOWLEDGMENT

First and foremost, thank God. This story isn't something that I came up with on my own. It isn't something my mind put together and said, "Ta-da!" This book was inspired by a dream I had when I was sixteen. I have always known that all of my meaningful dreams were gifts from God. Just like Joseph in Genesis, I know my dreams have meaning. The dream started the story. My God-given interest in law enforcement, psychology, and justice for human trafficking victims fueled the story, turning it into what it is today.

Therefore, whether you eat or drink, or whatever you do, do all to the glory of God. (1 Corinthians 10:31).

I want to thank my husband. Before him, I never took this book seriously. It was just something that I worked on when I was bored. After him, I was given the motivation to write it, finish it, and put it out into the world for people to read. He has been my number one cheerleader. There is no way that this book exists without him.

I want to thank my family, both my blood relatives and my in-laws. Their support is more than I could have ever hoped for. Where I expected laughs and judgment, I was given love and words of encouragement. Their support gave me the confidence and willingness to share my book and know that I can always go to them in times of need.

I thank my baby sister, Becky. She designed my book

cover and helped me create all my promotional materials. There is no beautiful book without her. I attempted to create my own cover and knew within seconds that I couldn't do it. My sister was the first person to pop into my head, and she did not disappoint. She is a senior in high school, and her skill with art is something that I have always envied. I remember her drawing all the different Disney characters when she was maybe six or seven years old. They were always perfect. I feel privileged to have her design as my book cover.

I want to thank my bookish friend Shelbie for all her help in writing this book. She was brutal, and I did a lot of rewriting because of her, but I am so grateful for her help.

I thank the entirety of the Bookstagram community. I have made over 3.6k friends on that platform, and I am overwhelmed with gratitude for their continuous support. This book would likely be sitting on Amazon with zero orders and reviews if it wasn't for the ARC readers who took a chance on my book. I owe any success I get for this book to the bookish accounts that help promote my book and encourage me to keep going. You are all so amazing.

# About The Author

G. N. Darland is a 23-year-old stay-at-home mom living in Dallas, TX. She lives with her husband, Ben, her son, Caleb, and their cat, Cheeto. She has a bachelor's degree in Psychology and Criminal Justice from Washington State University (#GoCougs!).

G. N. Darland spends her free time reading books from various genres. Her favorites are fantasy/romance and mystery/thriller. She is active in the Bookstagram community, where she has amassed over 3.7k followers by reading and reviewing books.